CW00661866

Fritz
and
Kurt

Fritz and Kurt

JEREMY DRONFIELD

illustrated by David Ziggy Greene

PUFFIN

PUFFIN BOOKS

UK | USA | Canada | Ireland | Australia
India | New Zealand | South Africa

Puffin Books is part of the Penguin Random House group of companies
whose addresses can be found at global.penguinrandomhouse.com.

www.penguin.co.uk
www.puffin.co.uk
www.ladybird.co.uk

First published 2023

001

Text copyright © Jeremy Dronfield, 2023
Illustrations copyright © David Ziggy Greene, 2023

The moral right of the author and illustrator has been asserted

Set in 10.75/17pt Sabon LT Std
Typeset by Jouve (UK), Milton Keynes
Printed and bound in Great Britain by Clays Ltd, Elcograf S.p.A.

The authorized representative in the EEA is Penguin Random House Ireland,
Morrison Chambers, 32 Nassau Street, Dublin D02 YH68

A CIP catalogue record for this book is available from the British Library

ISBN: 978–0–241–56574–2

All correspondence to:
Puffin Books,
Penguin Random House Children's
One Embassy Gardens, 8 Viaduct Gardens, London SW11 7BW

This book is dedicated to the memory of

Gustav
Tini
Edith
Herta
Fritz
Kurt

and all victims and survivors of Nazi persecutions.

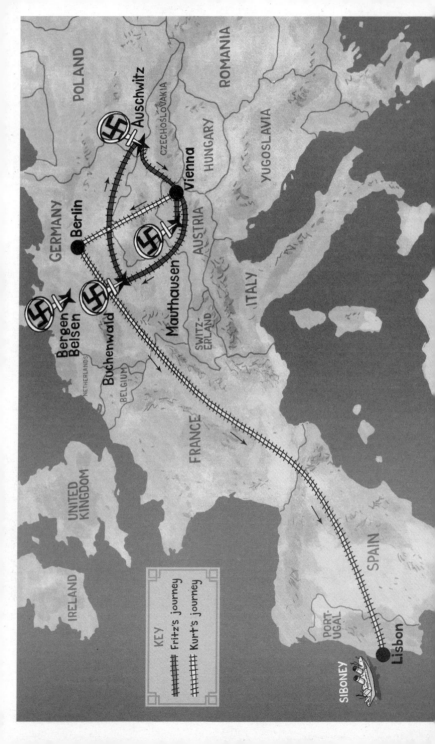

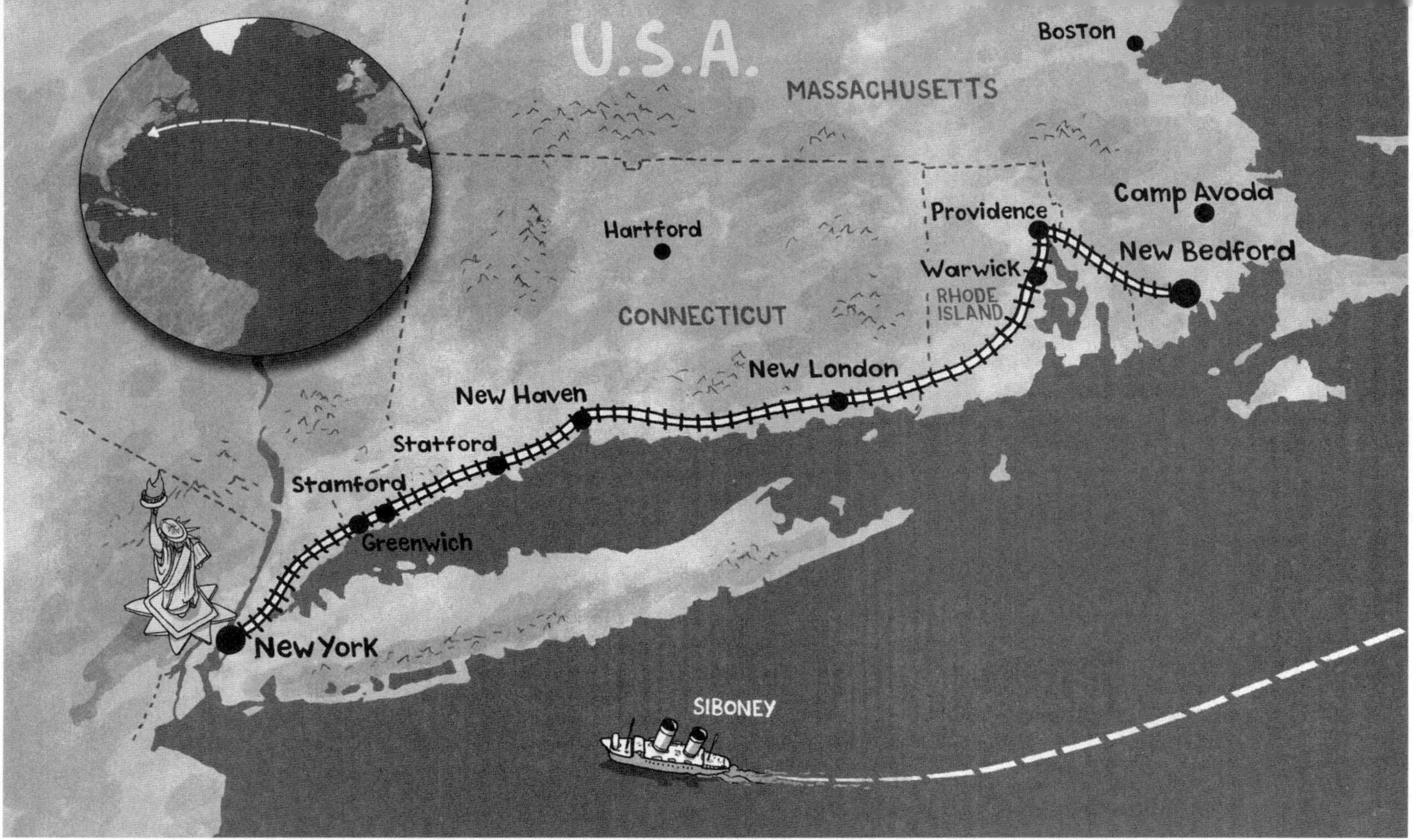
U.S.A.
MASSACHUSETTS
Boston
Camp Avoda
Providence
Hartford
New Bedford
Warwick
RHODE ISLAND
CONNECTICUT
New London
New Haven
Statford
Stamford
Greenwich
New York
SIBONEY

Contents

CONTENTS

Introduction

The story that you're about to read in this book is true. I feel I have to say that more than once because sometimes you might wonder if it's an invented tale. So many shocking and astonishing things happen to the people in it that you'd be forgiven for thinking none of it could be real.

I knew one of the people who lived through it. Kurt Kleinmann was eight years old at the time the story begins. When they were kids, Kurt and his brother Fritz saw things that would make your hair stand on end and your skin crawl. Kurt's mother had to send him halfway round the world, all on his own, so that he would be safe. Fritz was older and wasn't so lucky. He was sent to a terrifying camp where people were killed every day.

Some members of Kurt's family – including Fritz and their father – wrote about the things that happened to them in diaries and books. Other people who lived through the same times also wrote about what went on. And there are official records too. I've studied them all and can promise you that this story is true, even if you think it sometimes seems unbelievable. I often wish it wasn't true, because it contains so many horrible things that should never be allowed to happen. But it also has bravery in it, and love, and the goodness of people.

It took place during the Holocaust, a terrible time which happened in Germany and elsewhere in Europe between the years 1933 and 1945. It began when a man called Adolf Hitler became the Chancellor (prime minister) of Germany. Hitler was leader of the Nazi Party. The Nazis emerged just after the First World War, which ended in 1918. Germany and its ally Austria had lost the war, leaving Germany in a terrible mess, with awful poverty and unemployment. Hitler and his Nazis blamed Jewish people for all of it – for the defeat as well as for the mess that came after. The Nazis were fanatical racists – they despised everyone who was different from them, and they disliked Jewish people especially.

Mistrust and hatred of Jews is called antisemitism. Although it has been around for hundreds of years, Adolf Hitler and his Nazi followers took antisemitism to a whole new level. In Hitler's mind, Jews were the cause of everything that was wrong in Germany, including losing the war. He believed that Jewish people had enormous influence in world politics and business, and that they used their power for evil purposes. This was completely false, as well as being horrible and unfair. Jewish Germans and Austrians had fought bravely in the war, and Germany's defeat was no more their fault than anyone else's. But it was simple to blame Jews, so that's what the Nazis did.

By 1933, so many Germans supported the Nazis and shared their ideas that Hitler managed to get into power. Even though the Nazi Party hadn't won the general election, they'd got more seats in the German parliament than any of the other parties. Hitler did a deal with powerful people in business and politics, and they let him become Chancellor. The powerful people thought they could control Hitler and make sure the Nazis did no harm. They were wrong. The Nazi Party quickly took over everything, from schools to the police and the armed forces. They got rid of elections and banned all other political parties. Adolf Hitler was now known as the *Führer*, which means simply 'leader'. Nobody in Germany was allowed to disobey him or even criticise him.

Right away the Nazis started bullying Jews, taking away their jobs and businesses, excluding their children from school, and trying to make all Jewish people leave Germany. The Nazis sent people they didn't like to prison camps called *Konzentrationslager* (German for *concentration camps*). At first they imprisoned their political opponents and people who protested or resisted the Nazis' power, but eventually they began sending Jews to the camps too, just for being Jewish.

Hitler invaded several other countries – including Germany's former ally Austria, as well as Czechoslovakia and Poland – and in 1939 the Second World War began. The war made it impossible for Jews to leave Europe. There wasn't enough room in the concentration camps to hold the millions of European Jews, so the Nazis decided that to get rid of Jewish people once and for all they must kill them. This monstrous act was called the Holocaust – an ancient word which means *total burning*. The Nazis themselves didn't name it that. They called it 'the Final Solution to the Jewish Question'. Nowadays, when we talk of the Holocaust, we usually mean the whole Nazi mistreatment of Jews, from 1933 to the 'Final Solution'.

The Holocaust only stopped when the countries fighting against Nazi Germany – including Britain, the United States and the Soviet Union (Russia's empire) – finally won the war in 1945. By that time, six million Jews had been murdered, along with millions of other people who were also hated and feared by the Nazis, including Romani travellers, Poles and Russians, as well as gay and transgender people, and people with disabilities.

My friend Kurt lived through some of that before he

escaped. His brother Fritz lived through all of it. They were children when it began, and it changed them forever. Their story is told in the pages you're about to read. It begins in 1938, the year when Hitler decided to invade Austria, where Fritz and Kurt lived.

This story is true. It really happened to real people in the real world.

It was a very long time ago. Your grandmothers and grandfathers hadn't even been born yet, and *their* mothers and fathers were still children. Maybe the same age as you are now. The year was 1938. The world was a scary place in those days, full of dangers and threats: wars, angry people, lots of things changing in ways nobody could predict. Parents worried about how they could keep their children safe in such a world.

The story I'm going to tell you is about a family who had more reason to worry than most. Their surname was Kleinmann. The parents were Gustav and his wife Tini, and they had four children – two girls and two boys, Edith and Herta, Fritz and Kurt. They lived together in Vienna, a beautiful old city in the country of Austria.

CHAPTER ONE

Say Yes!

'Head it!'
Fritz leapt in the air, stretching for the football his friend Leo had kicked. It flew over his head, hit a lamppost and rolled into the road. He ran to fetch it, as a cart pulled by a huge shaggy horse came thundering along.

'Get out the way!' yelled the driver, and Fritz leapt back. There was a clatter of hooves and iron wheels, then it had passed by.

The horse had trodden on the ball and squashed it flat. It wasn't a proper football, just a bundle of rags rolled up and tied tightly. The local kids were mostly poor and couldn't afford a real leather football. Fritz squeezed and rolled the bundle until it was round again, then kicked it back to Leo.

Fritz Kleinmann and Leo Meth lived round the corner

from each other. Fritz had lots of friends – a great big gang of them – but Leo was one he would remember forever.

The boys were playing in the open space of the marketplace, which was called the Karmeliter market, across the street from Fritz's apartment. It was after school, and the stalls had closed down for the day. The farmers had packed up their unsold produce and clopped off along the street on their carts.

Fritz and the other kids ran among the empty stalls, kicking the ball back and forth. Only Mrs Capek, the fruit seller, was still there. She never packed up until it got dark. In summer she gave the kids corn cobs. Most of the boys and girls around here were poor and would take all the free food they could get. They sometimes got bits of sausage from the butcher, stale bread rolls from the baker and – the best of all – whipped-cream cakes and pink wafers from the confectioner in Tabor Street. The cakes in Vienna were the best in the world.

Leo kicked the ball high again. Two other friends went for it, but this time Fritz stopped it with his head, and as the ball dropped to his feet, he started dribbling it along the cobbled square. He was about to give it a mighty kick, which would have sent the ball right over Mrs Capek's stall, when he spotted a policeman heading their way. They could get into trouble if he caught them playing. Ball games weren't allowed in the market, even though it was the only open space near their homes.

The stern-looking policeman glanced in the boys' direction. Quick as a flash, Fritz tapped the ball under the stall, and Mrs Capek dropped a box over it. She put her finger to her lips. *Shhh.* The policeman walked by, staring suspiciously at the boys, who all tried to look innocent. Then he was gone.

As Fritz was retrieving the ball and thanking Mrs Capek, they heard the piercing sound of horns in the distance. *Ta-raa! Ta-raa!*

The fire engine was going out on a call!

Fritz and Leo had the same thought at the same time. They started running towards the sound before their friends had even realised what was happening. They raced to the end of the line of stalls and turned into Leopold Lane.

'Fritz! Wait for me! Fritz!'

Looking back, Fritz saw his little brother, Kurt, come running through the market, waving his arms. He stood no chance of catching them up – Fritz and his friends were fourteen, and Kurt was just eight years old. He had a gang his own age, and they often tagged along with the older boys for safety.

Fritz waited, itching with impatience. By the time Kurt caught up, Leo and the others were almost out of sight.

'Mum says you're to come home,' said Kurt. 'It's dinner.'

Fritz wasn't ready yet. He wanted to go and see the fire engine. He stood at the edge of the road, trying to make up his mind whether to cross it and follow his friends, or turn back with Kurt. The road was busy with vans, lorries and the horse-drawn carts of the coal sellers and breweries.

Then he noticed their neighbour, Mr Loewy, trying to cross from the other side. He'd been a soldier in the First World War and had lost his eyesight. He stood at the kerb, listening to the thunder of traffic and tapping his walking stick on the ground.

Fritz dodged across quickly and took Mr Loewy's hand. 'It's Fritz,' he said. 'I'll help you.'

'Gustav's boy?' said the old man. 'How's your father?'

'He's fine, thank you, Mr Loewy. Here's a gap! Hurry now.'

Fritz guided him across. Mr Loewy thanked him and went on his way, his stick tap-tapping on the paving stones.

When Fritz came back, Kurt was staring at the pavement. 'What's that stuff?' he said, pointing.

Fritz looked down and saw that someone had written words all over the ground – on the pavement, on the road, even on the walls – in white paint. The same slogans over and over again.

SAY YES!

YES FOR AUSTRIA!

YES FOR FREEDOM!

Fritz knew what it meant. It was part of the reason their mum had been so worried lately about them being outdoors when it was getting dark. The slogans were about the big vote that was happening in a few days.

'It's to do with Hitler,' said Fritz. 'We're showing him who's boss.'

Kurt knew that name. Hitler. Although he didn't really understand who Hitler was, Kurt knew he was dangerous. A chill went through him.

Fritz understood that of all the dangers in the world, Adolf Hitler was the worst. The country of Austria – where Fritz and Kurt lived – was next door to Germany, which was ruled by people who called themselves 'Nazis'. Adolf Hitler was their leader.

The Nazis were driven by anger and determination to control everything and everyone. Hitler and his junior leaders dressed like soldiers; they loved war and hated everyone who was not like themselves. That meant foreigners, people of colour, traveller folk, gay people, anyone who had different beliefs about how society should work, anyone the Nazis thought was not a 'true German'. Because the Nazis were in charge of the government in Germany, *they* got to decide what 'not being a true German' meant, and it was basically anyone the Nazis didn't like. It didn't make any sense, but the Nazis believed it. They wanted Germany to be great and powerful, and they wanted it to be the way they imagined it had been in the old days. Even modern artists who painted in new and different styles were called 'degenerate' and their artworks were banned.

Most of all, the Nazis hated Jewish people. Jews have been in the world for thousands of years. Their religion has some similarities with the Christian faith, but their beliefs about God are different from Christian beliefs, and they have their own traditions and special holy days. Many people distrust anyone who is different from themselves. The Nazis were especially suspicious of difference, believing that anyone who was not a 'true German' (according to their idea of what that meant) was a danger to the whole of German society. And when it came to Jewish people, the Nazis believed – without any justification at all – that they were the cause of virtually everything that was wrong with the world.

Adolf Hitler wasn't satisfied with only ruling Germany. He wanted Austria too. Austrians speak German, the two countries have a lot in common, and Hitler was born in Austria, so he thought the country should be his too. He'd demanded that it be given to Germany, but Austria's leader, Mr Schuschnigg, wouldn't give it up. There was going to be a big vote next Sunday to prove that Austrian people wanted to stay free. That's what the slogans on the pavement were about – *Yes for Austria! Yes for freedom!* Hitler was extremely angry about the whole thing. So angry that he might even send his armies to conquer Austria.

There were hundreds of Jewish families in the neighbourhoods around the Karmeliter market. Fritz and Kurt and their family, the Kleinmanns, were among them. To those Jewish people, the idea of the Nazis coming there was terrifying.

What was even more scary was that some people in Vienna *liked* the Nazis, and wanted Hitler to come.

Fritz and Kurt turned to head home.

'Hey, Fritz!' It was Leo and another friend, Hans. Leo was carrying a sweet pastry filled with whipped cream. Both boys had cream smeared around their mouths. 'Anker's bakery were giving away cakes!' said Leo. 'I saved this one for you. We lost the fire engine, though.'

The pastry was past its best and a bit squashed, but it was still delicious. Fritz broke it across the middle and shared it with Kurt as the four of them walked home.

Fritz asked, 'Do you think Hitler will come?'

'To Vienna?' said Leo. 'Dunno.' Leo was Jewish too. A lot of their friends were.

'I think he will,' said Hans. 'That's what he's like.'

Hans, who was part Jewish, knew what he was talking about. His family had moved to Vienna from Germany a few years ago after his father got in trouble for speaking out against the Nazis. Hans's father was a barber, and all the men in the neighbourhood who sat in his chair to get their hair cut heard about the terrible things he'd seen happening to Jewish people in Berlin.

'Yes, Hitler will come here,' said Hans again, licking cream off his fingers.

'Not today, though!' said Leo, giving Fritz a cheerful nudge.

Leo was right. Today had been a good day. Fritz took Kurt's hand, which was sticky with icing sugar. They crossed Island Street to the apartment building where they lived. Hans and Leo ran off through the market towards their own homes.

'*Will* Hitler come?' asked Kurt anxiously. To him, Fritz was a hero, older and wiser. Kurt would trust his brother over anyone.

Fritz didn't answer straight away. In truth, he just didn't know. He didn't like to think about it. 'Maybe,' he said. 'Maybe not.' He ruffled Kurt's hair, getting a smear of cream in it. 'Like Leo said, it won't happen today! Now let's clean up a bit. Mum'll be mad if she knows we've had cakes before dinner.'

CHAPTER TWO

Shabbos

As Fritz came out of school the next afternoon, something peculiar happened.

He was a student at the trade school, where boys went to learn skills like plumbing and carpentry (girls didn't get to do things like that in those days). Fritz was learning to be an upholsterer, which means making the soft coverings for chairs and sofas. His father was an upholsterer, and Fritz wanted to be like him.

Today was Friday, and Fritz's head was full of plans for the weekend. As he came through the doors, a blizzard of fluttering white was falling from the sky, whirling in the street among the noisy traffic and settling in the trees. Fritz quickly realised it wasn't snow, it was paper!

He looked up and saw a plane flying over, dropping

hundreds and hundreds of leaflets, which were flitting and scattering across the roads and rooftops.

Picking one up, Fritz found the same message as the slogans painted all over the pavements near his home: 'PEOPLE OF AUSTRIA!' it read, and then went on about freedom, and not letting Germany boss Austria around. It ended: 'Vote YES for Austria!' and was signed 'Schuschnigg' (the name of the Austrian prime minister).

Only two days to go until the grown-ups would all go and vote. Most people in Vienna supported Mr Schuschnigg, but some were Nazi supporters who wanted Hitler to take over and make Austria part of Germany.

With a roar of engines, a long convoy of army trucks filled with soldiers went thundering by. Fritz guessed they were heading for the border to guard it against the Germans. He felt a little shiver of fear. The idea of Hitler coming to Austria was starting to seem a little bit more real.

It was a long walk home through the city centre and across the Danube Canal. When Fritz reached the Karmeliter market, the stalls were getting ready to close. There wouldn't be any football today. Fritz had other plans this evening.

His mum came out of the market with bulging shopping bags. She spotted him and called out, 'Fritz, help me with these.'

Taking the heaviest bag, Fritz could smell flour, fresh

bread and cabbage. Mum looked worried. Her mouth was set tight, and there were frown lines around her dark, pretty eyes. She often looked like that these days. She worried about everything, and Fritz worried about her.

The market and Island Street were littered with the 'People of Austria' leaflets. As Fritz and his mum waited to cross the street, a convoy of lorries came along, filled with the boys and girls of the Austrian Youth (which was like scouts and guides combined). They were singing the national anthem, and some of them were shouting, 'Say yes!' and, 'Vote yes for Austria!' and tossing out more leaflets.

People cheered the parade, waving their hats as they joined in with the singing and shouted, 'Hooray for Austria!'

Mum smiled, and the frown lines faded. But Fritz noticed that some people weren't cheering. A little group of older boys and men standing on the corner scowled angrily and muttered to each other. *Nazis*, Fritz thought as he crossed the road. The Austrian Nazi Party was banned by law, but it had lots of secret members.

Fritz ran up the two flights of stairs to their apartment, Mum trailing behind and telling him to slow down. When Fritz went in, he found Kurt already home (his primary school was only a couple of streets away), sitting at the piano with their big sister Edith. She was teaching him to play a chirpy little tune called 'Cuckoo'.

It was a tiny apartment, with just two rooms – a kitchen and a bedroom. (They had very little money and couldn't afford anything bigger.) The kitchen was also their living room, and they all shared the bedroom. They had three beds and a sofa for the six of them. There were Mum and Papa, whose names were Tini and Gustav. (The kids called their father 'Papa', which somehow suited him better than 'Dad'.) Kurt, being the youngest, slept in Mum's bed, and Fritz shared with Papa. Then there were their sisters: Edith, who was eighteen, slept in her own small bed, and Herta, who was fifteen, slept on the sofa. They all shared a bathroom and toilet with the families in the other apartments on the same floor. It was very crowded, and just as well that they were friendly with the neighbours.

Mum caught up with Fritz, and they put the bulging shopping bags on the battered old kitchen table. 'Now run down and tell your papa dinner will be in an hour.' Fritz ran to the door, and she called after him, 'And remind him it's Shabbos!'

'OK!'

Shabbos is a holy time of the week for Jewish people, as Sunday is for Christians.* Shabbos starts when the sun goes down on Friday and lasts until sunset on Saturday.

---

* Some call it *Shabbos* and some say *Shabbat*. Both words mean the same thing – sabbath. *Shabbat* comes from Hebrew (the Jewish language) and *Shabbos* is Yiddish (a mixture of Hebrew and German).

15

For many Jews, it is a time for prayer and is marked by lighting special candles. Those who are very strict about their traditions won't do any work on Shabbos, or even anything that's *like* work, such as driving a car. Fritz's family weren't strict at all. For them, it was simply a time to be together, and to eat a traditional Shabbos dinner.

Papa had his workshop on the ground floor of the apartment building, with a sign by the door that read:

GUSTAV KLEINMANN, MASTER UPHOLSTERER
Modern Furniture – All Repair Work Accepted

When Fritz went in, he found Papa hard at work on the covers for an armchair.

The chair stood ready on the floor, all bare wood and horsehair padding and springs. Papa was preparing it while his assistant, Mitzi Steindl, sewed the covering. The sewing machine whirred, stitching the thick feather-pattern material. Papa couldn't really afford an assistant, but Mitzi's husband didn't have a job, so Papa gave her work to help her pay their rent. That was the kind of man Gustav Kleinmann was – always ready to help out a friend or neighbour.

'Hi, Fritz,' said Mitzi with a smile. 'Good day at school?'

'Hi, Mrs Steindl. Yes, thanks.'

'You'll be taking over this shop soon!' Mitzi

pressed the footswitch, and the sewing machine went *VVVRRRRRRRR*.

'Papa, Mum says dinner in an hour,' said Fritz. 'And she says –'

'I know, I know. It's Shabbos. Come on, Fritz lad, help me with this. Show me what they've been teaching you at that school.'

Mitzi finished stitching, and together Fritz and Papa fitted the cover to the chair. Fritz watched his father closely as he worked, admiring his skill.

Papa was a quiet man. He never yelled at the kids, and had a smile for everyone and didn't seem to worry much. He had fought against Russia in the First World War, before Fritz was born. He didn't seem like a soldier at all, but he had the medals to prove it. The younger men all admired him, and Fritz was proud to be his son.

Fritz held the fabric in place while Papa hammered in the special nails to fix it. He worked quickly, the little hammer darting with a *tap-a-tap-tap*.

By the time they'd got the fabric done, said goodnight to Mitzi, and returned upstairs to the apartment, the kitchen was busy with dinner-making. Kurt was standing on a chair at the table, helping Mum cook. Edith was reading, and Herta – kind-hearted Herta, in Fritz's and Kurt's eyes the beauty of the family – was sewing the hem of a dress. Music was playing softly on the radio.

Kurt loved Shabbos evening. He enjoyed helping

Mum with her cooking. Sometimes they made a delicious dish called Wiener Schnitzel. Mum would tenderise the meat pieces until they were soft as velvet, then Kurt would dip them in egg, then flour, then breadcrumbs, and Mum would fry them. Tonight, though, it was chicken noodle soup. Kurt's job was to roll the noodle dough until it was thin as a pancake, then Mum sliced it into ribbons and put it in the frying pan.

Papa took off his boots and settled into his armchair, unfolding the *Vienna Daily News* and disappearing behind it. He muttered about the lack of real news in its pages. He'd heard rumours of fighting on the German–Austrian

border, and of Nazi protests in some towns in Austria. People were saying that if the Nazis rose up here in Vienna, the police would side with them. There was nothing about any of this in the newspaper.

When dinner was ready, the family gathered round the table. It was a happy occasion, and Kurt would always remember these meals. But he ate quickly, because the other reason he loved Shabbos came *after* dinner, when he went to sing in the City Temple choir.

'Don't gobble your soup!' Mum said. 'You'll get stomach ache.'

'Sorry,' he said, and tried to eat slower.

'It's OK, Kurty, we won't be late,' said Fritz. It was Fritz's job to go with him on choir nights, to keep him safe in the streets.

Within seconds, Kurt was spooning up his soup as fast as ever. Papa chuckled. 'You can't correct a *Spitzbub*,' he said, and winked at Kurt. 'Right?' They were always calling Kurt a *Spitzbub* – a German word that means *rascal*.

Kurt finished the last of his soup and dropped his spoon in the bowl with a clatter. Mum tutted, but Papa just smiled.

By the time Fritz finished his dinner, Kurt was already in his coat and shoes and standing at the door, bursting with impatience. 'I'm going to Mr and Mrs Neuberger's,' he said. 'I forgot their lights. Back in a minute!'

He hurried across the hall and knocked on the door of number 15. It was opened by an elderly gentleman with a long grey beard and glasses. 'You're a little late, young man,' he said, peering down at Kurt.

'Sorry, Mr Neuberger. Just on my way to choir.'

It was dark in the apartment. Mr Neuberger and his wife were Orthodox Jews. They were *very* strict about their traditions, which didn't even allow them to do things like switch on the lights during Shabbos. It was Kurt's task to do it for them.

'Thank you, lad,' said the smiling Mrs Neuberger, who didn't think Kurt was a *Spitzbub* at all.

'You're welcome!'

When the Neubergers' rooms were all lit up, Kurt went back out to the hall, where he saw Fritz coming out of their apartment and pulling on his jacket, an end of bread in his mouth.

Fritz mumbled through the bread, 'Cfome om them.' He slammed the front door behind him and together they hurried down the stairs.

It was dark, but there were lots of people about. Vienna was a lively city in the evening, with brightly lit cafes, bars and restaurants. It got brighter and livelier as the boys crossed the Danube Canal bridge into the city centre.

They were heading for the City Temple, one of the most important synagogues* in Vienna. Kurt was proud

---

* A synagogue (sometimes called a shul or a temple) is a Jewish place of worship, like a church is for Christians or a mosque for Muslims.

to be a member of its choir. He loved the singing and the chanting, and was fond of the pocket money and chocolate bars the choirboys got as a reward. In the summer they had choir holidays to the countryside. (Not to the seaside, because Austria doesn't have a coast. Kurt had never seen the sea except in pictures.)

'Hi! What took you so long?' said Leo, who was waiting for Fritz at the corner by the bridge.

Fritz nudged Kurt. 'You know your way from here, right?'

'Sure,' said Kurt. 'It's just round the corner.'

'Me and Leo are off to play pool. See you later.'

There was a club near the City Temple where Fritz usually went while Kurt was at the service. Fritz was really too young to go there, but Kurt never told on him to their parents. Kurt walked on alone along the cobbled lane leading to the synagogue.

It was busy there tonight. The City Temple was a beautiful place – a round chamber with white pillars, trimmed with gold, holding up balconies. Kurt, up in the high balcony where the choir sang, looked down at the packed benches. It was so crowded that people were standing shoulder to shoulder in the aisles. The Jews of Vienna were fearful of Hitler's threats, and many had come to pray and find comfort. The beautiful music reassured Kurt, and the familiar chanting during the service lulled him.

At the end, the synagogue's scholar,* Dr Lehmann, gave a rousing speech. He praised Austria's leader, Mr Schuschnigg, for standing up to Hitler, and ended with the familiar rallying call: 'We say yes! Yes for Austria!' Everything was going to be all right, Kurt thought. Austrians would vote *YES* and they'd all stay free. Hitler wouldn't be able to come.

After the service, Kurt was surprised to find Fritz and Leo waiting for him outside the synagogue. Often Kurt had to wait for his brother, who sometimes got so wrapped up in his pool game that he forgot the time. Fritz and Leo looked anxious, and Kurt's heart instantly started to beat faster.

'Come on, quick!' said Fritz. He took Kurt's hand and started hurrying along the lane.

Kurt had to trot to keep up. 'What's going on?' he said. 'You're hurting my hand!'

'We've got to get home fast,' said Leo.

'Why? What's happening?'

'Never mind,' said Fritz. 'Just hurry.'

It was bad enough when parents said things like that and wouldn't explain. It was worse coming from his big brother. 'I don't understand! Fritz, tell me.'

---

* A synagogue scholar (or 'scholar in residence') is an expert on Jewish religion, history and culture, and helps everyone to understand them. The priest who leads the services in a synagogue is called a rabbi (pronounced *rab-eye*).

Now that they were in the wide main street, they could hear the sound of people cheering and chanting, like a football crowd in the distance. It was getting louder and nearer.

'It's the Nazis,' said Fritz.

It took Kurt a few seconds to find his voice. 'Hitler's here?'

'No,' said Fritz. 'Austrian Nazis. Hundreds of them!'

'Thousands!' said Leo.

'It was on the radio in the club,' said Fritz. 'Mr Schuschnigg has given up. Hitler threatened him, and he's given up! They've cancelled the vote.'

Looking back, the boys saw the yellow glow of flaming torches flickering in the darkness of the city centre, getting closer. 'Down with the Jews!' the crowd roared as they marched along. They yelled out Hitler's name – 'Hail Hitler! Hail victory!' In German it was a phrase that all the world would come to fear – *Heil Hitler! Sieg heil!* 'One people, one empire, one leader!' they roared. 'Today we have Austria, tomorrow the world! Death to the Jews!'

Just as the rumours had warned, men from the Vienna police were marching alongside the Nazis and their supporters!

Fritz grabbed Kurt's hand again and broke into a run.

All three boys sprinted to the bridge, the cheering of the mob echoing through the streets behind them. They reached the Karmeliter market, where Leo turned and ran off home. Fritz and Kurt hurtled across Island Street and launched themselves up the stairs, their shoes clattering on the stone steps. The apartment door was open, and their parents were standing there.

Mum grabbed Kurt and hugged him. 'Thank goodness you're safe!' she said.

'It's Nazis, Papa,' said Fritz, gasping for breath. 'They got together in a mob in Saint Stephen's Square. They're marching this way!'

Papa shepherded them all inside and closed the door. Edith and Herta were sitting at the table, looking scared. The radio was playing sad music. Papa switched it off.

Fritz described again what had happened in the city centre. 'Did you hear the news on the radio?'

Papa nodded. 'Yes, we heard.'

'What does it mean?' asked Kurt.

'It means the Germans are coming,' said Mum. 'Hitler will invade us.'

Papa shushed her and said to Kurt, 'I don't know. Maybe they won't come.'

'Of course they will,' said Mum crossly. 'We have to be prepared, Gustav. Listen!'

They could hear the crowd now, close by, in the marketplace. Thousands of Jewish people lived in this part of the city, and the crowd was looking for them, yelling hateful, angry things.

Papa went to Herta and Edith, putting his arms round them as if to shield them from harm. Mum hugged Kurt tight. He could hear her breathing, and when he peeped, he saw her eyes were shut tight.

Fritz stood by the door, listening. He was scared, but if any Nazi tried to get in, he was ready. He'd fight them, even if they were twice his size.

After a while, the chanting of the mob got fainter. When Fritz and Papa peeped out of the window, they saw that the people with flaming torches were starting to wander back the way they had come. It looked as if the Nazis of Vienna had tired themselves out and were going home.

Fritz wondered what would happen when the *real* Nazis came – Hitler's Nazis. Would *they* just shout and make noise and then go home again?

'What if they come back?' asked Herta.

'They won't,' said Papa. 'Not tonight.'

Kurt looked at Mum, but she didn't say anything. She was pale and seemed more worried than he had ever seen her before. But she took a big breath and smiled. 'Don't be afraid,' she said. 'I'll always keep you safe, my little Kurt. I'll keep all my children safe.'

Papa smiled and said, 'We'll be OK. We're a family, we're strong. Whatever happens, we'll get through it.'

CHAPTER THREE

The Monster

Aeroplanes flew through the skies of Fritz's dreams that night. Their engines droned and their propellers whirled through clouds made of millions of shreds of paper. In the streets below, flames crackled. Angry people shook their fists and yelled. They hated Fritz and wanted to hurt him. The noise of the planes grew louder and louder, until it began to drown out the mob.

Fritz woke suddenly, his heart racing. He was in his bed, safe. His family were there, and everything was peaceful. He could hear their breathing and the quiet snoring of his papa beside him in the big bed. Their familiar shapes beneath the quilts and blankets comforted him. Only Mum was missing; he could hear her preparing breakfast in the next room.

But Fritz could still hear the drone of the aeroplanes from his dream. Was he still asleep?

Papa woke up. He noticed the noise too. He went to the window, but there was nothing to see. Putting on his trousers and shoes, Papa left the apartment. Fritz got dressed quickly and followed. The noise was getting louder.

In the market square, the Saturday traders were setting up their stalls. As the noise grew, they all stopped what they were doing and looked up at the sky.

There were planes – dozens of them, German bombers, flying so low over the city that you could see the black and white crosses on their wings. The rumble and roar was so loud it rattled the windows, and Fritz could feel it through his feet.

The planes' bomb doors started opening. Everyone on the ground stood frozen in terror . . . but no bombs fell. Instead, there came leaflets. It was just like the day before, but much bigger – a real snowstorm of paper falling and fluttering over the whole city.

As the leaflets settled on the cobblestones around his feet, Fritz saw the message printed on them. At the top was the Nazi eagle, and then these words, which chilled Fritz's heart:

NAZI GERMANY GREETS HER NAZI AUSTRIA AND THE
NEW NAZI GOVERNMENT. JOINED IN A FAITHFUL,
UNBREAKABLE BOND!
HEIL HITLER!

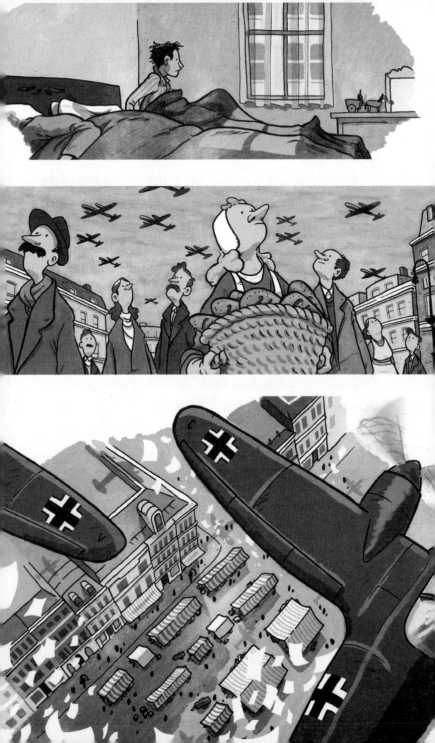

The leaflets settled on the pavements, covering the painted 'Say Yes!' slogans and mixing with the leaflets still lying there, discarded and trampled, from the day before. Austria's freedom had ended. The Germans were already here.

Fritz and his father didn't know it yet, but some of the planes were heading for Vienna airport, carrying soldiers. As the morning went on, news and rumours rattled through the city. *Germany's invading us*, people said. *Thousands and thousands of soldiers filling the roads, marching, riding in lorries. Cannons and tanks and troops, all heading for Vienna.* For Jewish people in the city, it was terrifying.

But worse still was the news that many people in the Austrian towns near the border were *welcoming* the Germans. They cheered and threw flowers at the soldiers marching through. The Austrian army didn't fight at all. In one town, Austrian soldiers greeted the Germans with a parade.

But one rumour was more frightening than any of the others for Jewish people. The news ran from person to person in terrified whispers: *Hitler himself is coming to Vienna.*

Only one day had passed since everyone had been so hopeful about the forthcoming vote. It was Saturday now, still Shabbos, and Kurt was supposed to go to the City Temple again to sing in the service. But by now it was far too dangerous for Jewish people to go outside. Anyone who risked it soon wished that they hadn't.

All through Vienna, the local Nazis were going wild with excitement – especially at the news that Hitler was coming in person. And when Nazis got excited, people were likely to get hurt. They didn't have to hide that they were members of the Austrian Nazi Party any more, and started wearing red armbands with the Nazi swastika symbol on them. Most of the men wore uniforms with boots, caps and leather belts. People called them 'Brownshirts' after the colour of their uniforms, but the proper name of their group was the Storm Division, and the men were called stormtroopers. They worshipped Hitler as their leader and hero.

Hitler had in fact been born in Austria, in a little town in the hills. He had lived in Vienna as a poor outcast before moving to Germany. Now that he had risen to become the leader of Germany, he was returning to his homeland in triumph. On this first day of the invasion, he was said to be in the town of Linz, only two hours away.

The Kleinmann family stayed indoors all that day. Planes flew over constantly, shaking the walls and rattling the windows. To the Jews of Vienna, it felt as if the end of the world was coming.

That night, knowing that Hitler would be here soon, the stormtroopers got so excited that they began attacking Jewish people. They went to shops owned by Jewish

people and forced their way in, stealing and smashing things and beating up the owners. Some people's houses were robbed too.

Hitler didn't come that day. All weekend, German troops poured through Austria. The roads were filled with their tanks and big guns, and trains loaded with supplies were on every railway line. When the trains reached Vienna, armoured vehicles rolled off them and drove through the streets. Tens of thousands of soldiers poured into the city.

Some of them were regiments of Hitler's own stormtroopers, called the SS, who joined in the attacks against Jewish people. The Brownshirts were bad, but the SS were a nightmare. They wore grey uniforms like the other German soldiers, they carried military weapons, and their hats had silver badges in the shape of a skull and crossbones. The SS were violent and cruel and showed no mercy.

At night, huge searchlights lit up the clouds over the city, in case other countries sent planes to interfere with the invasion. But none appeared. All the world's governments had decided to let it happen. As far as Britain, France and America were concerned, the Jews in Austria were on their own.

But still there was no sign of Hitler himself.

While all this went on outside, Fritz, Kurt and their family waited. What would happen next? Mum was afraid, although she tried not to show it. Papa wasn't scared. It would take more than a lot of noise and threats to frighten Gustav Kleinmann; he was brave, and he always believed that things would work out for the best. He'd served in a war – a real shooting war, much worse than this.

'They'll leave us alone,' he said. 'They'll go after the rich folk, the bankers and big business owners, not working-class people like us. The Nazis are always saying they'll show Jews how to work. Well, I've worked all my life. I know what work is.'

Mum didn't share Papa's way of thinking. Fritz could tell how scared she was. He'd heard from his friend Hans about the terrible things the Nazis were doing to people in Berlin, Germany's capital city. Fritz thought Mum was right to worry.

As the weekend dragged on, Fritz felt frustrated at being cooped up in the apartment. By Monday morning, he was dying to know what was really going on out there. He and Kurt should be in school today, and Herta and Edith should have been going to work.

At last, Fritz couldn't stand it any longer. When Mum was busy cooking and Papa was out of the room, he went quietly to the door, opened it and slipped out, closing it softly behind him. He hurried down the stairs, through the lobby, and then ventured warily out into the street.

A car went racing by, its horn blaring. A teenage

Brownshirt was at the wheel. Another car went tearing along, also driven by a young stormtrooper yelling furiously at people to get out of his way. All over the city, the Nazis were taking Jewish people's cars off them for their own use.

Island Street was bustling with pedestrians, but as he walked along, Fritz didn't see any of the Jewish people he knew. They were wise to stay indoors. Most of the shops in this district were owned by Jews, and lots of them had been vandalised.

Fritz hoped he wouldn't be noticed. On every street corner German soldiers were standing guard. Nearly all the adults he passed were wearing either swastika armbands or swastika badges on their lapels. Taxis drove past with swastika flags fluttering. And all the people looked happy, as if they were having the time of their lives. Fritz couldn't understand how they could be like this, when families like his were huddled indoors, frightened half to death.

Nobody took any notice of Fritz as he walked along. When he reached the city centre, it was even busier. Soldiers were everywhere. Huge, long Nazi flags hung from the buildings. By the central post office, a group of boys with hammers were smashing a statue of one of Austria's former prime ministers. Open-top trucks drove through the streets, filled with young stormtroopers, their arms outstretched in the Nazi salute. The crowds cheered them, just as they had cheered the trucks carrying the Austrian Youth a few days earlier.

Everywhere Fritz went, people were talking excitedly about Hitler. After all the waiting, he was coming today! Everyone called him 'the Leader' – *Führer* in German. People were chanting, '*One people, one empire, one Leader!*' He would be here at any moment!

Fritz crossed the city centre, past the City Temple and St Stephen's Cathedral, following the route he would usually have walked to school. The crowd grew thicker, and soon he was being swept along on a tide. Men and women, young and old, mothers and fathers, children, teenagers, policemen, people in posh clothes and shabby ones, all heading in the same direction.

Soon Fritz found himself at the Ring, the great tree-lined avenue that circled the centre of Vienna; a grand, beautiful place of parks and palaces. The crowds were so dense that Fritz could only weave and elbow his way through. Surrounded by grown-ups, he couldn't see a thing. The shouting was ear-splitting, thousands of people all thundering out: 'ONE PEOPLE! ONE EMPIRE! ONE LEADER!' over and over and over again.

At last Fritz made it to the edge of the crowd at the side of the road. It was lined with police in strange uniforms. They had been brought from Germany in case the Viennese people caused any trouble. Fritz was surrounded by kids about Kurt's age, waving Nazi flags on sticks. He was the only Jewish person there.

Then it happened. The event that everyone had been waiting for, and that the Jews of Vienna had been dreading.

Adolf Hitler himself appeared.

The police and soldiers stood to attention as a fleet of thirteen gleaming Mercedes limousines drove along the wide street. They all had open tops, and in them were grim-looking officers of the Gestapo – the Nazi special security police. They watched the crowds for any sign of trouble, like dogs staring at a suspicious noise. In the middle of the procession was a car bigger than all the others, glossy grey and black, with six wheels and a huge, long bonnet. Beside the driver, standing upright, dressed in a brown uniform, stood the monster himself.

Fritz knew that face. Everybody did. It was in newspapers and news films around the world. The hard, staring eyes, the little black moustache, the scowling mouth. The crowd went wild, cheering and waving swastika flags. 'HEIL! HEIL! HEIL!' Adolf Hitler glared back at them and gave his Nazi salute. (The crowd didn't know it, but Hitler was in a furious mood. His invasion hadn't gone as well as he'd planned. Tanks and vehicles had broken down all over Austria, slowing down the advance.)

The car swept by, and in a moment, Hitler was out of sight.

Then there came a long procession of German soldiers in their best parade uniforms. Amidst the cheering, Fritz heard angry shouts. There was jostling in the crowd, and from somewhere near where he was standing, some people yelled out 'Austria!' and began throwing stones at the soldiers.

There weren't many of them – just a few brave men and women who were loyal to Austria. For a few astonishing seconds, stones rained down on the German invaders. Fritz's heart rejoiced at the sight. Then the police waded into the crowds with their batons, and the stone-throwers fled.

In the days and weeks to come, that was the only resistance to the Nazis that Fritz would see from the people of Vienna. Many gave their loyalty to Nazi Germany gladly, and the rest kept their heads down.

When Fritz got home, he was too sad and upset to care whether he was in trouble for sneaking out. He told Kurt what had happened.

'Some people threw stones at the soldiers,' he said. 'But by tomorrow there'll be nobody left who doesn't say "Heil Hitler".'

It was true. The Jews really were on their own. Fritz's parents had lots of friends who weren't Jewish. Some lived in the same apartment building. There was Ludwig the coalman who lived downstairs and was close friends with Papa. And of course there was Mitzi; she was always grateful that Papa gave her work when he couldn't really afford to. And Olga Steyskal, who lived down the street; she had a market stall and was always warm and friendly to all the Kleinmann family. Fritz and Kurt knew lots of kids who weren't Jewish – including about half the gang who played in the Karmeliter market. Surely all those people would help their Jewish friends, wouldn't they?

There were others too. The men Papa did business with. Mum's relatives – some of them were married to non-Jews. Herta worked in a shop and knew lots of people. So did Edith, who was training to be a hat designer.

In Vienna there were lots of Jewish people, over a hundred and eighty thousand. That was far too many for the Nazis to bully and hurt, surely? They wouldn't dare. Fritz tried not to think about what Hans had told him about how the Nazis treated Jewish people in Germany. In German towns, they were outcasts, thrown out of jobs and schools, their most precious belongings stolen from them, even their houses taken. All anyone could do was hope that those things wouldn't happen in Vienna.

CHAPTER FOUR

The Connection and the Exclusion

'Come on, girls!' Mum called through to the bedroom, where Herta and Edith were getting dressed. 'If we're late, we'll miss our turn!'

Fritz and Kurt sat in the kitchen, dressed in their best outfits. The whole family were going to the photographer's studio to have their picture taken. Papa was in his only suit and Mum wearing her best dress and shoes. Fritz had on his smart jacket and the baggy knickerbocker trousers that Austrian boys often wore in those days. His boots were gleaming.

Kurt was in his sailor suit, which he only wore on special occasions. He swung his legs as Mum smoothed down his hair – he was happy just to be going on an outing. Hardly anything nice happened nowadays. Kurt was wearing Papa's wristwatch. It was much too big for him, but he was proud of it. It made him seem grown-up.

At last, the girls appeared. Edith knew how to dress with style, even though she had so little money. As for Herta, Kurt always thought of her as the very image of beauty and love.

But Edith looked scared. 'I don't know why we have to do this,' she said.

'We don't have a picture of all of us together,' said Mum. 'It'll be nice.' Quietly, she said to Papa, 'After all, we don't know how much longer we'll be together.'

Kurt held Mum's hand as they walked along the street. Everyone but him was nervous and trying not to show it.

Weeks had passed since Hitler came to Vienna. He'd gone back to Berlin and left his men in charge. Austria was now part of Nazi Germany's empire. They called it the 'connection' or the 'joining' – in German the word was *Anschluss*. Every day there seemed to be new laws, mostly to do with Jewish people. All the terrible things that Fritz's friend Hans had described seeing in Berlin had now started happening in Vienna.

Until now, Jewish people had lived their lives just like everyone else. Some were rich, some were poor, some owned businesses, some worked in jobs. A few lived in big houses, most lived in apartments. Jewish children went to school and played games and had all the pleasures and worries that kids usually have. But Hitler and his followers claimed that Jews were not like everyone else.

In the Nazi way of thinking, people like themselves were 'Aryans'. Aryans, according to them, were white, but not all white people were Aryans – Russian and Polish people were not Aryans, for example. Jews were especially ruled out. The Nazis believed that Aryans were better than *all* other people, but in their opinion, Jewish people had no place even living in an Aryan country like Germany. According to the Nazis, everything wrong in the world was Jewish people's fault. If Aryan people couldn't get work to pay their bills, it was because Jews took all the jobs. If Germany lost a war, Jews must have betrayed them. If there wasn't enough of something to go round – especially money – the Nazis said it was because Jews got more than their fair share. It was all a wicked lie, but it made the Aryan people feel good about themselves. Although a lot of things in the world were bad, they liked to believe that none of it was their own fault.

So Hitler had decided that the only way to make things better was to get rid of all the Jewish people somehow. Once they were gone, everything would be good again. The Nazis got to work on it right away.

Fritz was excluded from the trade school, and Kurt from his primary school. Edith and Herta were fired from their jobs. Papa was forced to close down his upholstery workshop. The same things had happened to all their Jewish friends.

And as for their non-Jewish friends, well, most of them were suddenly not their friends any more.

Fritz looked at his sisters as they walked beside him. It was amazing that they had the courage to be out like this. They had suffered worst of all. The streets were still covered in the painted slogans – SAY YES! AUSTRIA! The Nazis had ordered them to be scrubbed away, and Jews were made to do it as a punishment. Edith and Herta had both been caught up in it.

With Edith, it had happened one day when she was walking down the street. A mob was gathered there, led by some stormtroopers. Edith recognised one of them as an old schoolfriend named Viktor. The moment he saw Edith, Viktor yelled, 'She's a Jew!' and grabbed her. His stormtrooper friends gave her a bucket of bleachy water and a brush and forced her to scrub the slogans off the pavement. Several other Jewish people were also made to join in. As they knelt and scrubbed, their hands burning with the bleach and their good clothes dirtied and torn, the crowd laughed and shouted insults. 'This is proper work for Jews!' some of them jeered.

It happened all over Vienna – the stormtroopers called it 'scrubbing games', and the crowds loved it. The same thing happened to Herta, who was made to scrub the clock tower in the Karmeliter market.

Today, as they walked along the main shopping street heading for the photographer's, Edith and Herta bravely held their heads high.

In the main streets, most of the Jewish-owned shops were shut, and those that were open had signs hung up saying 'ARYANS, DO NOT BUY FROM JEWS'. Some had been vandalised and robbed by stormtroopers.

Mr Gemperle, the photographer, wasn't Jewish, and his studio at number 24 Tabor Street was doing business as normal. It was a posh place. Local celebrities came here to have their pictures taken.

'Welcome, welcome,' said Mr Gemperle as they entered the waiting room. 'Mr and Mrs Kleinmann, is it? Come in, please. And your lovely daughters and such handsome young sons!'

He didn't know them, and probably didn't guess that they were Jewish. If he had, he might not have dared to serve them.

They were ushered into the back room. It was plain, with a curtain and a few chairs all lit up by huge lights on poles. Mr Gemperle fussed about, arranging two chairs for Mum and Papa. 'Sir and madam, if you would be seated, and the young ladies like so. And the young fellows here. No, a little to the left . . . Perfect!'

Kurt perched on Papa's knee. Fritz stood in the middle. Herta and Edith stood by Papa and Mum.

'Smile, please!'

They all tried, but only Kurt and Herta succeeded. The flash popped and the picture was taken.

Mr Gemperle made copies for each of them. Mum was right, it was the last photo there would ever be of them all together. Each small crinkle-edged print was as precious as jewels and would go with them wherever they went. With it would go a feeling of home.

The sad goodbyes among friends and relatives started happening soon after. Many Jewish people who could afford to travel had decided to leave Austria and Germany. It was heartbreaking, but they couldn't stand life under Nazi rule. Getting out of the country was expensive, and the Nazis made it as difficult as they could. Although they wanted Jewish people to leave, they couldn't help being cruel about it. They made sure it cost them lots of money in 'taxes', which most people didn't have. And they ensured that if you did manage to get away, you would have to leave behind everything you owned.

It wasn't only the Nazis who made leaving difficult. The leaders of other countries, like Britain and America, had all said how angry they were at what Hitler was doing, and how sorry they felt for the Jewish people. But now that the Jews needed to escape, they said, 'Sorry, you can't come here. We don't have room.' There were people in cities like London and Manchester, New York and Washington, many of them Jewish themselves, who told their leaders, 'Let the German Jews come. Welcome them

in! They need us!' But their voices were drowned out by other people who shook their heads and said, 'No! We don't want refugees here. What if they take our jobs? What if they won't work and cost us money? Their ways are strange, not like ours. And what if they're really enemy spies? No, we can't have them here. We don't have room.'

Britain and America and a few other countries did allow in a few refugees, but they were strict about who they let in and didn't take many. Of all the multitude of Jewish people trying to escape from Austria and Germany, only a tiny number succeeded.

Among the lucky ones was Fritz's friend, Leo. His parents were taking him to France. It was hard for Fritz to lose one of the few friends he had left. Life wasn't the same any more. Jewish kids weren't allowed to swim in the local pool or play on the sports field or go to the gym or the cinema. There were signs everywhere saying 'NUR FÜR ARIER' and 'EINTRITT JUDEN VERBOTEN' – German for 'Aryans Only' and 'No Entry for Jews'. They couldn't even play on the street without being picked on.

Leo was lucky to be getting away from all that. When he and Fritz said goodbye, they hoped they would meet again before too long.

Kurt also lost a friend – his cousin Richard. Richard and his family weren't officially considered Jewish. Richard's father was Aryan and his mother was only half-Jewish, so

EINTRITT JUDEN
VERBOTEN

they were safer than most, but they had decided to leave anyway, just in case. They were sending Richard away first, to a boarding school hundreds of kilometres away in Belgium. His parents were planning to follow him later, when they would all set sail together on a ship to New Zealand.

It was hard for Kurt to lose Richard. He wasn't just a cousin, he was his best friend, and the two of them had grown up together. Now they might never see each other again.

Of all the old gang who used to play in the Karmeliter market, more than half were Aryans. Most of those weren't Fritz's or Kurt's friends any more. Some of them had joined Nazi groups – for the boys it was the Hitler

Youth and for the girls, the League of German Girls. The
Hitler Youth boys were training to become stormtroopers
and soldiers, and they joined the Brownshirts in attacking
Jewish people. The girls were being trained to be faithful
Nazi wives and mothers when they grew up – they would
make lots of babies and build strong Aryan families for
the Nazi empire. (In those days, girls in most countries
were discouraged from having their own careers, and the
Nazis were especially strict about this.)

It wasn't just the kids who turned against their
friends. Now that most of the Jewish-owned shops and
businesses had been shut down, some of the grown-ups
seized ownership of them. If they couldn't be bothered to
run them, they just took all the stock and the equipment
and gave it to the Nazi government – the cash registers,
the furniture, the scales and tools and materials and
machines.

To Fritz's dismay, Mitzi Steindl was one of the keenest
thieves. One day he and Papa saw her taking part in
robbing one of the Karmeliter market shops. She noticed
them watching and looked ashamed of herself, though it
didn't stop her. But at least she didn't take part in stealing
from Papa's workshop.

Well-known Jewish people were evicted from their
homes. In Island Street, just a few doors away from the
Kleinmanns, two families were thrown out. Rabbi Braun,
who was chief rabbi at the Orthodox synagogue, was

one. The other was Mr Mueller, who sang the chants at the city's finest synagogue, the Pazmaniten Temple.

Then, just when everyone thought it couldn't get any worse, it did. A frightening new word began to be whispered in Vienna. The word was *Dachau*. It was the name of a town in Germany where the SS had built a special type of prison called a *concentration camp*. People said it was a place of horror. Anyone the SS wanted to get rid of in a hurry (such as journalists or anyone who protested against the Nazis) began to disappear, and it was heard later that they had been sent to Dachau, never to return.

Little gangs of stormtroopers spent weeks going around the city, calling at every apartment building. Each building had a person living in it called a concierge, who was responsible for looking after it. The stormtroopers ordered each concierge to give a list of all the Jewish people who lived in their building. It was supposed to be for government records, but the Nazis used the lists to make Jewish people into slaves. At any time of the day or night, they could be called out to wash Nazis' cars or clean their toilets. If they wouldn't (or couldn't) go, they were punished. If they were seen as troublemakers, they might be sent to Dachau.

One day the stormtroopers came to Island Street and went from building to building. When they arrived at number 11, where the Kleinmanns lived, they hammered on the door. It was opened by the concierge, Mrs Ziegler.

She looked the stormtroopers up and down, from their shiny boots to their brown shirts and swastikas. 'What d'you want?' she said, scowling.

The leader held out a notebook. 'Write down a list of all the Jewish tenants in this building. Names and apartment numbers, please.'

Mrs Ziegler wasn't a particularly nice person; she was crotchety and unhelpful, no matter who you were.

'What?' she said.

'All the Jewish tenants,' the stormtrooper repeated loudly, and added: 'By order of the Gestapo.'

Everyone knew of the Gestapo, the SS special security police. It was a name that struck terror in all who heard it. There were nightmarish stories about what the Gestapo did to the people they investigated, stories of torture and murder in the prison cells in their headquarters. Being sent to Dachau was not the only awful fate that could befall people who caught their attention. Even some Nazis feared the Gestapo.

Not Mrs Ziegler, it seemed. 'I don't know what you're talking about,' she said, starting to close her door. 'There are no Jews here.'

'There are Jews everywhere,' said the lead stormtrooper.

'Not in my building. I've got things to be doing. Sling your hook.'

And she slammed the door in the stormtrooper's astonished face.

He wondered what to do. Looking up at the building, he reckoned there were at least twenty apartments in it. In this district, it was unlikely there would be no Jews here. He could order his men to force the concierge to tell the truth. But that would take time, and he had a long, long list of buildings still to visit . . .

He wrote 'No Jews' on his pad. 'Come on,' he said to his men, and they moved on down the street.

The Kleinmanns and their Jewish neighbours were safe from the lists. For the time being, anyway.

With no money coming in, Papa and Mum struggled to keep Fritz and Kurt and their sisters clothed and fed. They had a few non-Jewish friends who stayed loyal to them. Olga, the market trader, did what she could to help. And Papa had one or two Aryan friends with upholstery workshops who let him work for them sometimes. For a while, Fritz and Mum got a job delivering milk. The deliveries happened when people were still in bed, so they wouldn't know their milk was being brought by Jews.

But most of the time they had no money at all. Jewish charities set up a soup kitchen in the neighbourhood where families could get free food. Another charity set up a primary school for the little kids, so Kurt could carry on with his lessons. He began to learn a little English, such as *hello* and *yes* and *no* and how to sing, 'Pat-a-cake, pat-a-cake, baker's man, bake me a cake as fast as you can.' It sounded very strange when all he'd ever heard before was

German. And the thought of cakes was already like a memory of a dream. It was a long time since he'd had one.

The only nice things now were very small – things that had been everyday in normal life, such as a loaf of bread, or a pair of socks without holes in, or being smiled at.

The summer and autumn months dragged by. And then, in November, something truly terrible happened.

People called it the Night of Broken Glass – *Kristallnacht* in German. No Jewish person would ever forget that name.

It began with a murder far away in the city of Paris. There was a teenage Jewish boy living there, named Herschel, who had escaped from Nazi Germany and was extremely upset at the way his family had suffered. Herschel bought a gun, went to the Germany embassy, and shot one of the Germans working there.

When Hitler heard the news, he was furious. He was an angry man by nature, but this sent him into one of his most towering rages. A Jew had dared to murder an Aryan German! As far as Hitler and his followers were concerned, all Jewish people everywhere were to blame for what this boy had done in Paris.

And they must be made to pay for it.

CHAPTER FIVE

Night of Broken Glass

There were clouds in the sky over Vienna that November night. Clouds of smoke, thick and rolling, glowing orange from the fires burning beneath.

Fritz watched from the apartment window. He could hear the fire engine horns echoing, *Ta-raa! Ta-raa! Ta-raa!* Only a few months ago, he and his friends had chased after that sound, excited to see where the fire was. He still felt the urge to chase it. But now he knew where the flames were, and it made him feel sick.

All across Vienna, the synagogues were burning.

Huge gangs of Brownshirts and SS troopers went through the city with sledgehammers and axes. Every Jewish shop or business they came to, they broke down the doors and smashed the windows. They painted '*JUDE*', the German word for 'Jew', on the walls. The pavements in Jewish districts were carpeted in broken glass. There were many beautiful synagogues in Vienna, and the Nazis set fire to them all. When the firefighters arrived, the stormtroopers wouldn't let them stop the flames. All the firefighters were allowed to do was save the buildings near them.

The only synagogue the Nazis didn't burn was the City Temple, where Kurt used to sing in the choir. There were too many other buildings joined to it, so instead the stormtroopers went in and smashed up everything inside. The gold decoration and the sacred objects were broken and thrown to the ground.

Not satisfied with their wrecking of the synagogues and businesses, the stormtroopers forced their way into Jewish homes. They said they were searching for weapons, but that was just an excuse. They pushed people around and stole anything that looked valuable. Often they hurt the people and broke their belongings. All the Jewish men were dragged out. Fathers and sons and uncles and grandfathers. Hundreds of them were herded into the Karmeliter market. They huddled together as their Nazi-supporting neighbours joined in with the stormtroopers, yelling and laughing at the terrified Jews.

Fritz and Kurt, Papa and Mum, Herta and Edith all sat in the apartment and listened to the horrible noises coming from the street. Would they be safe here? The stormtroopers had no record of any Jewish people living in the building, thanks to Mrs Ziegler, the concierge.

But suddenly they heard loud voices and footsteps clattering on the stairs. Fists pounded on doors – *bam-bam-bam!* – and there were shouts of 'Open the door!' The stormtroopers were in the building. It sounded like they were going straight to the apartments where Jewish families lived. But how on earth could they know, without a list?

BAM! BAM! Fritz nearly jumped out of his skin as a fist hammered on their door.

'Open up!' a man's voice demanded.

Papa and Mum looked at each other. Mum's eyes were wide with fear.

'Come on, Kleinmann, open this door!'

They all recognised that voice. It was Ludwig, Papa's friend who lived downstairs. Had he come to save them? Papa went to the door and opened it warily.

Before Papa could speak, Ludwig had pushed his way into the room. Three other men came with him. One was Friedrich, another close friend of Papa's. Fritz was too confused to take it all in, but he recognised the fourth man forcing his way into the apartment. He was Mr Blahoudek, a local man who worked for the Nazis, keeping an eye on the neighbourhood for them. His eyes glittered with malice.

Papa spoke up. 'Ludwig, what's this all about?'

Ludwig ignored him. Instead, he pointed at Papa and said to Mr Blahoudek, 'Him. He's a Jew.'

Papa was stunned. Ludwig and Friedrich had been friends with him for years. They knew one another's life stories, they drank together, played cards.

Blahoudek glared at Papa and nodded. 'Take him.'

Ludwig gripped Papa's arm. 'Come quietly and you won't be harmed,' he said.

Mum couldn't believe her eyes or ears. 'Ludwig!' she said. 'What are you doing? How can you?'

But Ludwig didn't answer; his face was as blank as a mask, showing no trace of the friendly man they knew. Blahoudek glanced around at the family. He pointed at Fritz. 'Him too,' he said.

'No!' Mum shouted. 'He's just a kid!'

'Shut up, Jew!' Blahoudek spat out the words. 'Come on, boy. Go with your father.'

Fritz was grabbed. Mum was crying and protesting. Ludwig, Friedrich and the other men pushed Fritz and Papa through the door and down the stairs. Mum's cries echoed after them.

They were shoved across the road to the market to join the hundreds of other Jewish men.

Some local Nazi supporters had come out to watch. Fritz recognised a neighbour named Risa. She'd worked herself up into a furious state, calling the Jewish men every vile name under the sun and threatening them with

all sorts of terrible things. The other onlookers joined in with relish, and Blahoudek encouraged them.

Hours passed, and the dawn light was growing when cars and lorries began to arrive. The stormtroopers began loading the Jewish men into them. Fritz and Papa were pushed into the back of a truck with dozens of others. It set off along the street.

They drove through the city for just over two kilometres. Fritz recognised the Prater public park as the truck rumbled along Exhibition Street and past the park entrance. The Prater was one of his and Kurt's favourite places. There was a football stadium there, and an amazing funfair with a big wheel and a huge slide that you went down on mats. If you collected up everyone's mats and took them back to the start, you got a free go. Fritz and Kurt did that often, sliding down again and again, whooping with joy. Nowadays they weren't even allowed into the park – it was '*Nur für Arier*', for Aryans only. Fritz glimpsed the big wheel rising above the trees in the pale morning light.

The truck stopped at the main police station, where the men were ordered to get out. They were herded into an old stable building at the back of the police station. It was a big room, but there were already hundreds of men and teenage boys crammed into it, all of them Jews from different parts of the district. The police cells had filled up quickly, so the SS had started shutting people into any outbuildings that had space.

More prisoners kept arriving. Soon Fritz and Papa found themselves so tightly squeezed in that they had to stand with their hands raised to make room. They could hardly breathe.

Hours ticked by. Fritz was exhausted, hungry and thirsty, and his legs and arms were aching. All around him, frightened people groaned and prayed.

SS troopers appeared in the doorway and pointed to a few of them. 'You, you and you. Come this way.' The men they'd picked struggled to get out of the crowd and were then dragged away. Every few minutes the SS came back and took a few more people. Some had to climb over others to get to the door. If anyone was too slow they were shoved and hit and called horrible names. 'Jewish criminal' was one, and 'traitor to the people' another. But the name they used most, over and over again, was 'Jew-pig'. In German it was *Saujud*. The Nazis yelled and snarled it so often it became just noise, like dogs barking.

Fritz lost track of how long he and Papa had been standing in that awful room. At last, they were pointed to, and they elbowed their way to the door.

They were marched to another building and into a room upstairs. SS troopers and Vienna police guarded the doors. Sitting at a table were men from the SS and local Nazi leaders.

'Stand there, Jew-pigs.'

The men at the table fired questions at Papa. Who was

he? What did he do for a living? How much money had he stolen from true Germans? What illegal things had he done? What banned groups was he a member of? Papa answered truthfully – he hadn't done anything wrong. They asked Fritz the same questions, even though they could see he was only a child.

Fritz and Papa were then taken to another room and left to wait.

'Courage, Fritz,' said Papa softly. 'It'll be over soon enough.'

There was a window overlooking the stable yard. Down below, a gang of stormtroopers were forcing Jewish men to do exercises. Some were elderly, and a few were

wearing their best suits. The stormtroopers made them get down in the mud and roll around. They beat them with sticks and laughed and forced them to chant, 'We are criminals! We are Jewish pigs!' It was horrible to see such dignified men treated in this way. It shocked Fritz that anyone could be so cruel.

'We need to take care,' said Papa, who understood how bullies behave from his time in the army in the last war. 'The trick is to not wind these Nazis up. Follow what they say and be polite. Don't challenge them. Don't look them in the eye, but don't look at the ground either or show fear.'

After a while, Fritz and Papa were brought back into the room to hear what would be done with them. From what they'd overheard, they knew it was always either 'Return', which meant being sent back to the stable to be questioned again later, or 'Fit'.

'Fit' was the most frightening. Papa guessed it probably meant they were sending you to Dachau, the concentration camp. Or to the new camp he'd heard the SS had built, called Buchenwald. The name meant 'beech forest', conjuring up fairy-tale images of dark groves inhabited by dangerous creatures and evil spirits.

The man in charge nodded at Fritz. 'The boy's too young,' he said. 'Let him go free.' Then he pointed at Papa. 'Return.'

Fritz watched helplessly as an SS trooper grabbed

Papa's arm and started pushing him towards the door leading back to the stable. Fritz was dazed, exhausted, confused, hardly aware of what was happening. The next thing he knew, he was out in the street, alone.

It was evening. There wasn't much traffic, and hardly any pedestrians. There was nothing Fritz could do but head for home.

Walking along Exhibition Street, he passed the gates of the Prater park. He'd come this way so many times, heading home buzzing with the thrill of a day out. Now there was just fear and emptiness.

Along the deserted shopping streets, the pavements were carpeted with broken glass. Stormtroopers with paintbrushes had daubed the Jewish shops with the word 'JUDE' and the Jewish star. All the window frames were splintered and jagged with glass. It looked like a city that had been bombed.

After crossing the empty Karmeliter market, Fritz trudged up the stairs to the apartment and knocked on the door.

Mum opened it. 'Fritz!' She hugged him. 'Fritz, oh Fritz! I thought you were gone for good!'

Herta and Edith and Kurt all stared at him in astonishment. They could hardly contain their joy and relief.

Then someone said, 'Where's Papa?'

They all looked at Fritz.

He told them what had happened. 'They haven't decided what to do with him,' he said.

Fritz knew they were all thinking the same thing. *Dachau. Buchenwald.*

The family sat up waiting until late in the evening, and didn't sleep much that night. In the morning, there was still no news of Papa. All that day they waited and waited.

It was a Friday. As dusk was falling and Shabbos was beginning, Kurt went across the hall to switch on Mrs Neuberger's lights. Her husband had been taken with the other men.

Just after Kurt got back, there was a knock on the door. Mum opened it.

Papa stood there, pale and exhausted. His thin face was more gaunt than ever, but still he was their beloved, smiling Papa.

They were overjoyed. Fritz could hardly believe it after what he'd seen at the police station. 'What happened, Papa?'

'Those men questioned me again. They asked me about when I fought in the war. They didn't believe me when I said I had medals. But I was lucky. There was a policeman there who knows me. He told them it was true.'

The SS running the police station had been ordered to release women and children and the elderly, and they were also releasing any men who could prove they'd fought for Austria and Germany in the First World War. It seemed that some Nazis were reluctant to send war heroes to the concentration camps, even if they were Jewish.

But other men were not spared. Over the next few days, fleets of police vans began collecting them from the police stations. They were driven to the Westbahnhof railway station, where they were forced into wagons meant for cattle and goods. The locomotives steamed out of Vienna, pulling long trains of wagons packed with thousands of Jewish men, heading for Germany. Some went to Dachau, some went to Buchenwald. Most of the men were never seen in Vienna again.

As the weeks passed and winter set in, life became harder and harder for the Jewish people who remained. Most were women, older men and children.

Mum and Papa had been talking for a while about leaving for another country, like Richard's and Leo's parents had done. But they didn't have much money, and Mum hated the thought of leaving the only place she had ever known. Even so, she was willing to try. A friend of hers who'd gone to America years ago had put her in touch with people who could help. They were two Jewish American brothers called Philip and Samuel Barnet. They had plenty of money, and had offered to pay for the whole family to travel to the United States. All the forms were filled in and the applications were made, but although they waited for months, nothing happened.

After the Night of Broken Glass,* the leaders of other countries were horrified at what the Nazis had done. But they stood firm, and still wouldn't take in all the Jewish people who wanted to leave Germany and Austria. Members of the British parliament talked and talked about how the Jews were suffering under the Nazis and what might be done to help them. In the end, the politicians agreed to let a certain number of Jewish children come to live in Britain. The whole scheme was organised by charities and was known as the *Kindertransport* – German for 'children's transport'.

Fritz and Kurt were young enough to qualify for the Kindertransport, but there were far more children in Austria and Germany than there were places on the scheme. Fritz and Kurt were not among the lucky ones chosen.

Then Britain came up with the idea of letting Jewish refugee children go to live in Palestine. The modern country of Israel didn't exist during the 1930s; the land was called Palestine, and Britain was in charge of it. The British wanted healthy teenagers, and Mum applied for Fritz to go. But the scheme never happened.

Edith was the first in the family to find a way to

---

* Instead of *Kristallnacht* (Night of Broken Glass), many historians now call it the November Pogrom. *Pogrom* is an old Russian word which has been used in history to refer to attacks on Jewish communities.

escape. Britain started letting in Jewish refugees if they could get jobs (or at least the promise of a job) in the country before they travelled there. Adverts appeared in the British newspapers for maids, cooks, drivers, nannies, language teachers and gardeners. Edith didn't know how to do any of those things, but Mum helped her learn how to be a maid. There was a Jewish charity based in Britain that helped refugees find jobs. They promised to find a place for Edith.

But now Edith had to get permission from the British government to go there. Hundreds of Jewish families were applying for permission to move abroad, and all the foreign embassies in Vienna had queues out of the doors and down the street. They moved so slowly that people had to stand in them for days, even though it could be dangerous – gangs of Hitler Youth and stormtroopers sometimes went along the street beating up the people queuing. The Kleinmanns all took turns holding Edith's place, night and day.

At last, everything was arranged, and on a cold day in January, Edith said goodbye to her brothers and sister and to Mum and Papa, and set out for England. They were sad to see her go, but happy that she would be safe. A few weeks later, she wrote to say that she was working as a maid for a Jewish family in a city called Leeds, in the north of England.

Mum didn't give up hope for Fritz, Kurt and Herta.

And neither did the Barnet brothers in America. For months Mum scraped together what little money she could and wrote application after application. The Barnets did the same. But nothing worked.

In June, Fritz got his first identity card. All Jews in Vienna had to have one now. They called it a 'J-Card' because it had a big red 'J' for '*Jude*' ('Jew'). Fritz's photo was taken by the SS, and he had to strip to his underwear for it. His name was written as 'Fritz Israel Kleinmann'. It was a Nazi rule that all Jews had to take the middle name 'Israel' (for men and boys) or 'Sara' (for women and girls). In their J-Card photos, people often looked scared. Fritz felt more angry than afraid at the way he was being treated, and he stared into the camera with smouldering fury in his eyes.

That summer, the weather was hot in Vienna. There was a big international student sports festival in the city. Fritz loved sport, but of course Jews were banned. The neighbourhoods around the Karmeliter market were becoming a ghost town. Empty shops boarded up, men gone to Dachau or Buchenwald, homes with nobody living in them. It seemed like things couldn't get any worse.

But in the late summer of 1939, they did. Far away in Berlin, Hitler made a decision that changed everything. He decided to start a war.

His armies invaded Poland, the country next door to

Germany. Hitler had been threatening to do this for months, just as he had with Austria. His planes bombed Polish cities and his troops marched into them. He conquered the country quickly.

This time, the leaders of Britain and France agreed that enough was enough. They must try to stop Hitler. For a long time they'd been building up their military strength, and now they used it. Britain and France went to war against Germany.

For most Jewish people, the war didn't make much of a difference at first. But for some, it was the beginning of a new nightmare.

One Sunday in September, Fritz and Kurt were sitting in the apartment, trying to fill the time by reading or playing cards. Herta and Mum were sewing, mending old clothes. Papa had gone out to see a friend.

Suddenly there was a loud knocking on the door. They all looked at one another in surprise. Fritz stood up. Mum went and warily opened the door.

It was Ludwig. He had other men with him, and they pushed their way into the room. This time there were two SS troopers with them.

'What do you want from us now, Ludwig?' said Mum wearily. 'You know we've got nothing. We haven't even got food!'

'We want your husband. These men have orders.' Ludwig pointed to the SS troopers.

'Gustav isn't here,' she said. 'What do you want with him now?'

'They've got orders to arrest Polish Jews. That includes him.'

Mum turned pale with shock. 'But Gustav's Austrian.'

Ludwig smiled. 'You know as well as I do he was born in Poland.'

It was half true. When Papa was little, the town he'd grown up in was part of the Austrian Empire. He'd moved to Vienna to find work when he was a boy, about Fritz's age. After Austria and Germany lost the First World War, Papa's old home town became part of Poland.

'Where is he?' Ludwig demanded.

Mum shrugged. 'I don't know. He went out.'

'I see.' Ludwig then pointed at Fritz. 'In that case we have instructions to take the boy.'

Mum was stunned. 'What? No!'

Ludwig nodded to the SS men. They grabbed Fritz by his arms and started marching him to the door.

Mum pleaded. 'Stop! Don't take him, please! He's just a kid!'

'Look,' said Ludwig, 'we'll take Fritzy to the police station. When Gustav hands himself in, the boy can come home again. OK?'

Fritz was taken downstairs and put in the back of a police van. Several elderly Jewish men were already inside.

He sat on the bench seat and hugged himself, his insides feeling as if they were dissolving. It was like the Night of Broken Glass all over again, only this time he didn't have his Papa.

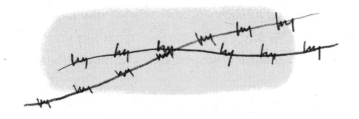

CHAPTER SIX

The Journey

After Fritz had gone, Kurt sat in a daze. He didn't know what to think. How could they just take his brother like that? Mum was in a state. Herta tried to comfort her, but she was just as terrified herself.

Hour after horrible hour went by. At last they heard the key in the lock, and then the door opened and Papa came in.

Mum rushed to him. 'Gustav, they took Fritz!'

'What? Why?'

Mum repeated what Ludwig had said. 'They think you're Polish.'

Papa had heard. Men were being arrested all over the neighbourhood. A lot of people his age and older had been born in that part of the old Austrian empire and had moved to Vienna when they were young.

'Ludwig said they'll let Fritz go if you hand yourself in,' said Mum.

Papa nodded. 'I see.' He didn't hesitate; he headed for the door.

'You're not going to, are you?'

'Of course! Tini, I'm not leaving Fritz in their hands!'

'Gustav, no!' Mum's voice was rising in panic. 'They'll send you to the camps! You have to run away. Go somewhere and hide! We'll get Fritz back some other way.'

But Papa had made up his mind. 'I'll sort it out,' he said. 'They'll understand I'm not Polish. I fought for Austria, remember.'

He left, and Mum fretted anxiously for half an hour. Then, to everyone's astonishment, Papa came back. Mum beamed in relief. 'Did it work? Will they let him go?'

Papa shook his head. 'They wouldn't let me do it. I went to the police station in Leopold Lane and told them I'd come to turn myself in. That the SS had taken my boy. The officer on duty knows me. He looked at me like I'd lost my mind. "Get the hell out of here," he said. So I did.'

'But what about Fritz?' Mum asked.

'I don't know. I'll try again tomorrow.'

'No. No, you can't. They'll come for you before then. You have to go, Gustav. Run away and hide somewhere.'

Papa shook his head. 'Not a chance. I won't leave my family!'

Mum was scared and desperate, as if the SS might come bursting in at any minute. 'Go!' she said to Papa. 'Go now and save yourself! If you don't, I'll turn on the gas and kill us all!'

Kurt and Herta had been listening in horror as their parents argued, but this threat was worse than anything they'd ever heard before – it was unbearable to see their mother so terrified and angry. At last, Papa gave in. Promising to find somewhere safe to hide, he left the apartment.

Mum, Kurt and Herta sat and waited for the SS to come looking for Papa. Hours dragged by. Darkness fell, and still they waited for the knock on the door. But it didn't come.

* * *

There were no windows in the police van, so Fritz couldn't see where they were going. It was a short journey, just a few minutes. When the doors opened and they were ordered to get out, Fritz recognised the place – it was the backstreet behind the Hotel Metropole in the city centre. The Metropole was the headquarters of the Gestapo. Fritz's heart shrank in terror.

He and the other prisoners were taken in through the delivery entrance and put into locked rooms. Dozens of other men were already there, and more kept arriving.

All of them were Jews who'd been born in what was now Poland. It consoled Fritz that as long as he was a prisoner, it must mean that Papa was still free. That was good.

The Gestapo cells were getting more and more crowded. After a short while, Fritz and some of the old men were hauled out. They were put in another van and taken to a police prison nearby. But that was getting crowded too. Into the van Fritz went, for yet another journey.

This time they went further. When Fritz was bundled out again, he found himself looking up in bewilderment at the massive concrete pillars of the football stadium in the Prater park. He and the other prisoners were herded in through the stadium entrance and along the echoing corridors under the grandstands.

Vehicles filled with prisoners kept arriving, until eventually there were over a thousand Jewish men in the rooms and hallways under the stands. SS guards stood at the entrances and exits.

Fritz found a place in the corner of a hallway where he could sit and lie down. He was tired and hungry. After a while the guards brought round dinner. It was just plain watery soup, a bit of bread and a mug of tea, but Fritz ate and drank gratefully.

Once he'd finished, he looked around at the other captives in the hallway. They were mostly grey-haired and old, although a few were about Papa's age. These were the ones who'd been released after the Night of Broken Glass – war veterans and the elderly. They were all wearing the clothes they'd been in when they were taken. Rich men and poor men, in business suits, Sunday-best overcoats, threadbare jackets, smart shoes and scuffed boots. Many of them had been allowed to bring suitcases or bundles of belongings.

When night fell, they were given thin mattresses stuffed with straw to sleep on. There was nowhere to wash. Fritz, too exhausted to care, lay down and slept.

After an uncomfortable night, a gloomy morning came. Fritz's bones ached, and he felt sick with misery waking up in that place. The building was cold, echoing with banging doors and the shouts of the SS police guards. 'Come on, you animals, wake up!' The men rose, bleary-eyed, scared. Breakfast was bread and tea.

Again Fritz wondered about his family. Was Papa safe? Would they be able to get Fritz released somehow? It worried him that he'd glimpsed boys his own age among the old men. Had Ludwig lied to Mum about releasing him if Papa gave himself up?

The day passed and nothing happened. Then another day passed, and another, and another. They were all the same, and they began to blur together.

Fritz found that the guards would let the prisoners roam a little way in the corridors, but not far. He got to know the faces of the few dozen men in his small part of the stadium, but most of the prisoners were being held in areas he couldn't visit. After a few days, some of the elderly men started getting ill from the damp, dirty conditions. Their coughing and groaning filled the darkness at night.

One day, a small group of men in white lab coats paid a visit. They were Nazi scientists from the city's Natural History Museum who were carrying out a scientific study of Jewish people. They picked out over four hundred of the prisoners and examined them as if they were animals in a zoo. (Fritz, luckily for him, wasn't one of the ones they picked.) The scientists took photos of the prisoners, measured their heads, took samples of their hair, and even made plaster casts of a few of their faces. Some of the prisoners guessed that the scientists were trying to prove that Jewish people looked like the nasty cartoons of Jews that the Nazis put in their posters and magazines. If that was their aim, they went away disappointed.

There were big windows where the prisoners could look out towards the road and the gates. Each day, people came to stand outside the fence, looking in. Fritz realised that they were the families of the men being held prisoner – mostly women searching for their husbands, their fathers, their grandfathers. A few were mothers looking for their sons. They walked up and down outside the fence, trying to see in, calling out names. They pleaded with the guards

to let them in to see their loved ones, but the guards refused.

One day Fritz was looking out when he saw his own mother.

Mum was staring hopefully through the fence. Fritz waved and banged on the window. Could she see him? His heart swelled with longing for her. His mum, his home, his beloved family. Her eyes were searching, but Fritz could tell that she couldn't see him among the faces behind the glass. At last she gave up and turned away.

Fritz looked out every day, but he never saw her in the crowd again.

It was hard to keep track of time when every day was the same. In fact three weeks had passed since they'd arrived in the stadium when, without warning, the guards ordered all the prisoners to assemble. Group by group, they were marched out of the building. Dozens of police cars and vans were waiting.

Fritz was pushed into the back seat of a car along with some other men. This time he could see where they were going. The convoy of vehicles crossed the Danube Canal, passed around the city centre, and drove to the Westbahnhof railway station.

The prisoners were taken out of the vehicles and herded into the station, where a train was waiting for them. It was long, made up of at least a dozen goods wagons. SS guards, swearing and yelling at the prisoners, forced them into the wagons as if they were cattle. Inside, Fritz found just a bare wooden floor and no windows. More and more men were crammed in around him until they could hardly move. Then the door slid shut with a clang.

After three weeks with no baths and no change of clothes, the smell inside the wagon was horrible. Men around Fritz muttered and prayed in fear. Many stood silent, scared half to death. Only a glimmer of daylight came in through cracks in the wooden walls.

Fritz could guess where the train would be going. He had heard the dreadful names said so often. *Dachau. Buchenwald.* He wondered if Mum knew where he was. She must be frantic with worry. And what on earth had happened to Papa?

The wagon jolted, and with a groan the train began to move.

* * *

Kurt was fast asleep in bed when a commotion suddenly pulled him out of his dreams. It was the middle of the night, the bedroom light was on, and there was a thunderous hammering on the front door. Confused, Kurt saw Mum shaking Papa awake.

'Gustav! Gustav, they've come!'

Papa woke up suddenly with a gasp.

As Kurt came wide awake, it all flooded back to him. It was two days since Fritz had been taken by Ludwig and the SS. Two whole days of waiting, two days of not knowing what was happening to his brother, two days of Mum worrying herself sick. Papa had gone away to hide for a while, but then he'd come back. He just couldn't leave Mum and Herta and Kurt to fend for themselves.

And now, the knock on the door they'd been dreading had finally come.

'Open this door now!' a voice yelled.

Mum went to the front door. Kurt got out of bed and followed her into the living room. So did Herta.

When the door opened, Ludwig and his SS friends came barging in. 'Where is he?' said Ludwig.

Papa came in from the bedroom, tucking in his shirt. 'I'm here, Ludwig.'

Mum was crying, but it was useless to plead with the Nazis. You might as well argue with the incoming tide or try to persuade storm clouds not to rain. As Kurt watched, dumbstruck, the SS men took hold of Papa.

'Wait,' said Mum. She hurried into the bedroom and came back with a brown paper package. She gave it to Papa. 'Here, my love. Some things I got ready, just in case. There's a sweater and a scarf and a pair of socks.'

She tried to hug him, but the SS men were marching him out of the door.

'Don't worry about me, my darling' he said. 'I'll be fine. They'll let Fritz go now!'

The door closed and he was gone.

* * *

The train rumbled slowly on and on, swaying. Fritz sat hunched on the floor, arms around his knees. He was surrounded by a forest of men's legs. It was impossible to stretch out, and when you got too cramped from squatting, all you could do was stand up, which was exhausting. The only toilet was a bucket, which didn't help the awful smell, and the only food was a bit of bread and water they'd been given at the start of the journey. From the light leaking in, Fritz had counted two nights and two days.

At long last, the train slowed down and shuddered to a stop. Fritz could hear voices outside shouting and dogs barking.

Suddenly, the wagon door slid open with a groan. Daylight flooded in, dazzling Fritz's eyes. An eruption of noise battered his ears. Dozens of SS men with guns and snarling, barking guard dogs surrounded the prisoners. After two days of nothingness, it was like being thrown into a raging storm of lightning and thunder.

'Out, Jew-pigs – now! Out! Out! Out!'

More than a thousand men came pouring out of the wagons on to the train tracks, scared and dazed. The

SS guards shoved and hit them with the butts of their rifles.

'Move, pigs! Come on, quickly, quickly!'

The prisoners had to run along the tracks to the train station, then through a tunnel to the road. The signs said they were in Weimar, a town in the middle of Germany – Fritz didn't know exactly where, but it was a very long way from home. Local people had come out to see the prisoners arrive. They stood behind the line of SS guards, laughing and calling out insults. They spoke German differently from Viennese people. To Fritz's ears they sounded barely any different from the snarling guard dogs.

'Run now!' yelled the guards. 'Let's see you run, you Jews!'

They began to run up the road. Most of the men were old and unfit. Some were carrying bundles they'd brought from home, or even suitcases, which they struggled to carry as they ran. The SS ran alongside with their rifles, hitting anyone who couldn't keep up.

These SS were different from the ones in Vienna. They had silver skull badges on their collars as well as their hats. They were from the SS Death's Head division, which was in charge of the concentration camps. They were louder, nastier and more brutal than any human beings Fritz had ever seen.

Fritz forced his cramped legs to run as hard as he could. The town was soon left far behind. The country road went uphill, making it harder and harder to keep going. His lungs felt as if they were catching fire.

As he ran, Fritz thought he saw a familiar figure ahead of him in the crowd. It was impossible, but it looked just like Papa!

Fritz ran harder, pushing through the crowd until he caught up. He was right!

'Papa! What are you doing here?'

'Fritz? My goodness, it's you!'

'How can you be here?'

Papa struggled to breathe and talk. 'Ludwig . . . lied, I guess. They . . . they had no intention of . . . letting you go.'

'You were at the stadium all that time?'

Papa nodded. Fritz thought of Mum outside the fence. She hadn't only been looking for him, she'd been looking for Papa as well! Fritz couldn't imagine the state she must have been in.

An SS guard noticed them talking and slowing down. But before he could swing his rifle at them, Papa steered Fritz towards the middle of the crowd, where the guards couldn't reach them.

The road turned left on to a wide track leading into a thick forest. Still it went uphill. Was there no end to it? Every so often Fritz saw men stagger and fall by the side of the road. He heard gunshots from somewhere behind, but didn't turn to look. He guessed that the guards were shooting the men who couldn't run anymore.

Oak and beech trees crowded either side, and Fritz knew that this must be the notorious beech forest of Buchenwald. What he didn't know was that the men who had come this way before him called it *Totenwald*, meaning 'Forest of the Dead'. The road through it was known as the Blood Road.

After a while they came to the top of the hill and saw a vast open area where the trees had been cut down. There were construction sites everywhere, with only a few finished buildings among them. The road led towards a wide, low building with a tall wire fence either side of it, and in the middle a great steel gate, which swung open as the running prisoners approached.

They ran through the gate and found themselves in a big open square that looked like a parade ground.

'Halt!' yelled the guards. 'Halt here!'

Fritz's legs felt like they could fall to pieces. He bent over, gasping to catch his breath. He and Papa held on to each other. Everyone was doing the same. The last of the prisoners were still struggling in through the gate.

Looking around, Fritz saw rows and rows of long, single-storey wooden buildings, like army huts, on the other side of the square. There were other buildings made of brick. In between were streets lined with grass verges, making it seem like a small, very orderly town, completely surrounded by the giant wire fence, which was three metres high, topped with barbed wire. At its corners and spaced out along it stood wooden watchtowers with machine guns. SS guards patrolled along the fence. If any prisoner went near it they would be shot. Fritz would learn later that the fence had 380 volts of electricity running through it, enough to kill anyone who tried to climb it.

So this was the place they had all learned to dread; this was Buchenwald concentration camp. As Fritz and the other prisoners took their first look at it, the gate clanged shut behind them.

CHAPTER SEVEN

The Little Camp

'Stand in lines! Come on, you animals, form lines!'

The prisoners stood, forlorn and frightened in their dirtied business suits and torn overcoats, their filthy shoes and crumpled hats. The SS guards went among them, yelling and hitting them with sticks and rifle butts. 'Come on! Quickly, or you'll get a beating! Form lines!'

Papa understood. 'We have to line up like soldiers,' he said to Fritz. 'Quick, before you get hit.'

With a thousand confused men, it took a while to get them organised. But at last they stood lined up as if they were on parade, row upon shabby row, clutching their bits of luggage.

A group of finely dressed SS officers appeared and inspected the new arrivals. Their leader was a chubby-faced man. Despite his fine uniform, he was an ungainly,

93

slouching figure. This was Commandant Koch, who was in charge of the camp.

Commandant Koch looked at the prisoners as if they were dirt. 'So, you Jew-pigs are here now,' he said. 'This is Buchenwald. You cannot get out of this camp once you are in it. Remember that – you will not get out alive.'

With that, he turned and walked away.

An SS sergeant barked, 'Now strip! We'll get you filthy animals cleaned up! Everything, all off. Quick now! What's the matter with you, don't you understand an order? You don't want to be clean?'

The men began undressing. With the guards staring at them, Fritz and Papa had to take off all their clothes – shoes, socks, underwear, everything. They stood shivering in the autumn chill. Then they had to queue to be registered. Tables had been set up on the parade ground, piled with forms.

Their names and addresses were written down. They had to hand over their clothes and any belongings. Every item was noted down on their forms. The package Mum had given Papa was seized – one sweater, one pair of socks, one scarf. Each man was given a number. Papa was 7291, Fritz was 7290. From now on, they would be called by their numbers; their names meant nothing to the SS guards.

'Now line up and march!' yelled the sergeant. 'Bath block this way!'

Naked and cold, they marched through the camp, past row after row of long, low barrack buildings. It was surprisingly quiet, with hardly anyone about. Here and there, prisoners were sweeping or cleaning or tending the grass verges. They wore the camp uniform – trousers, jacket and cap, the whole outfit in blue and white stripes. As the new arrivals marched past, they kept their heads down, eyes fixed on their work.

The bath block was a long brick building. Inside were huge shower rooms. Fritz and Papa flinched as the water poured down. It was incredibly hot, almost unbearable. Some of the older men collapsed from the shock.

There were no towels. Dripping wet, they had to hurry outside, where shallow tubs like paddling pools waited for them, reeking of disinfectant. After a plunge and scrub in the pools, they were made to sit on stools to have their heads shaved. Other prisoners in uniform did the disinfecting and shaving.

Fritz sat dripping and shuddering with cold, despite the sheet he was given to wrap around him while his hair was sheared. After clipping, his head was shaved with a razor, nicking and cutting his skin. The prisoner shaving him didn't look him in the eye or say a word. Fritz noticed he had two sewn-on badges, one with his prisoner number, and next to it a red triangle.

Finally the new arrivals had to run back to the square, where they were given their uniforms. Fritz

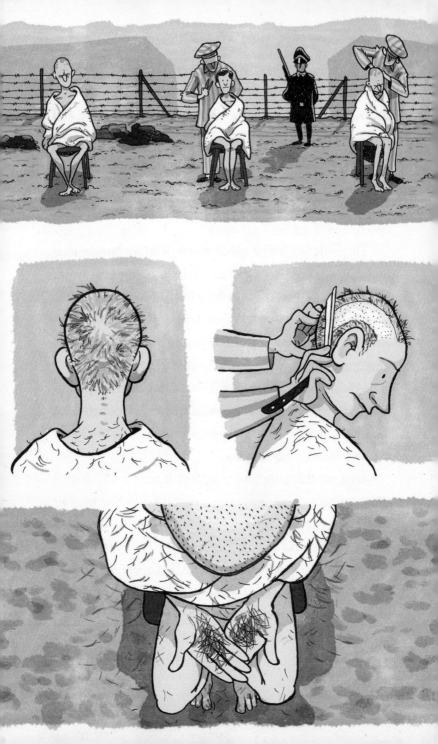

looked in dismay at the striped trousers and jacket, both too big for him. There was also a shirt, long underpants, socks, a pair of shoes and a striped cap. The shoes too were badly fitting and uncomfortable. He and Papa looked at each other in their baggy stripes, with the caps shaped liked squashed chefs' hats covering their bald heads. It would have been funny if it hadn't been so horribly frightening.

The prisoners were each given two badges, which they had to sew on to their jackets. Fritz looked at his. One had his number, 7290. The other was different from the one he'd seen on the man who shaved him. Instead of one triangle he had two, a red one and a yellow one, put together to make a star shape. It was meant to be a Star of David, a traditional symbol of Jewish identity (a bit like the cross for Christians or the crescent and star for Muslims). In Vienna, the stormtroopers had crudely painted Stars of David next to the word *JUDE* on the Jewish properties they vandalised. All the men who'd come to Buchenwald with Fritz were given the same star-shaped badges. He didn't understand why the other prisoners he'd seen had only a red triangle. Were they not Jewish too?

Dressed in their new uniforms, Fritz and the others all lined up again in rows. Another SS officer came to inspect them. He was an evil-looking man with a flat face like the back of a shovel. This was one of Commandant Koch's deputies. He looked at the new prisoners and shook his head in disgust. 'Jews!' he said to the sergeant. 'I can't believe such people have been allowed to walk around free until now.'

There was a barbed-wire enclosure next to the square, like a camp within the camp. The guards called it the 'little camp'. Instead of barrack buildings it had four enormous tents. This was where the new arrivals were housed. It was already crowded with prisoners, all wearing new uniforms with red-and-yellow stars. In the past few days, thousands of Jewish men had been brought to Buchenwald from all over Germany as well as Vienna. They were put in the little camp to keep them away from the other prisoners for now.

As Fritz and Papa and the other new arrivals walked in, the men already there stared sadly at them. Inside the tents were bunk beds, but not like any that Fritz had ever seen before. They were four levels high, and they looked more like shelves than beds. There was nowhere to wash, and the toilet was just a ditch with a plank over it to sit on.

As darkness was falling, Fritz heard the sound of marching feet, like an army approaching, and he looked out. The square was lit up by floodlights. The main gates opened and a long procession of prisoners came marching in. Thousands of them. As far as Fritz could see, they mostly had red triangles on their jackets. They got into lines on the parade ground. Loudspeakers crackled into life and an SS officer began calling the roll (like taking the register in school). No names, just numbers. It took ages. All the time, guards prowled with rifles and sticks, whacking a backside here and cracking a head there. Afterwards, the prisoners trooped off to the barrack blocks.

There was no food that evening for the men in the little camp. The bunks had no mattresses, just bare planks and one blanket each. There were so many prisoners that Fritz and Papa were crammed into a space two metres wide with three other men. Fritz's empty belly hurt, but he was so tired he fell asleep right away.

The next morning, before it was even light, there was another roll call out in the main camp. Then the prisoners went marching off again through the main gate. Fritz watched them in puzzlement. Where were they going?

That afternoon, the men in the little camp got their first warm food. Fritz was given a bowl of watery stew made from unpeeled potatoes and turnips, with a bit of fat and meat floating in it. It was horrible, but he was so hungry he wolfed it down.

There was nothing to do in the little camp but wait for the next meal. All day long, loudspeakers in the main camp played German radio from Berlin. It was all news about how brilliantly Germany was doing in the war and what a great leader Hitler was. They played his speeches, and in between there was a lot of German marching music.

Evening drew in, and the main-camp prisoners came marching back again for another roll call. In the little camp Fritz and his companions had their dinner – a hunk of bread and a small piece of sausage. The bread came in whole loaves. There were no knives, so they had to tear it up with their hands. The men were starving, and quarrels broke out over who had more than someone else. Fritz and Papa gathered what they could and shared with each other.

The next day was the same, and the day after. The main-camp prisoners marched out and marched back. Meagre meals morning, noon and evening.

Fritz and Papa got to know some of their fellow prisoners. Fritz had noticed a few boys his age among them. One, with the number 7225, introduced himself.

'I'm Jakob,' he said. 'Jakob Ihr. But people call me Itschkerl.'

'Why?'

Itschkerl shrugged. 'No reason. What's your name?'

'Fritz Kleinmann. Where are you from? Vienna?'

'Yeah, I live right by the Prater. What about you?'

Fritz told him about Island Street and the Karmeliter market. It all seemed so far away now, as if it was just a dream he'd had. 'I'm here with my papa. Are you?'

Itschkerl shook his head. 'No, just me. My father's gone. I live with my mother.'

Fritz could hardly imagine how terrifying this place would be if he didn't have Papa with him.

On the morning of the ninth day after they'd arrived, Fritz and the others were torn from sleep by an ear-splitting sound. A couple of men were striding between the rows of bunks, blowing whistles.

'Up! Up! Wake up, you lazy animals! Time to get out of your pits!'

The two men weren't guards but prisoners! They both had brutal expressions on their faces, as if they hated every person they looked at. Their badges were green triangles.

'Come on, let's be having you! You think you can lounge in bed all day?'

Fritz got down from the bunk. As usual, his shoes sank into the gloopy mud of the tent floor. The green-triangle prisoners carried short wooden clubs and lashed out at anyone who moved too slowly.

Everyone trooped outside. It was still dark, but the square was lit up. Fritz and Papa were swept up in a tide of men streaming out of the little camp. Prisoners from the barrack blocks were marching in orderly groups and lining up for roll call. With a lot of swearing and hitting, the green-triangle prisoners and SS guards forced the little-camp prisoners to line up with them.

Fritz and Papa found themselves standing to attention in the middle of a row. An SS officer stepped up on to a platform.

'Caps off!' yelled a guard.

All the prisoners whipped off their caps. Fritz and Papa copied them.

The officer started calling the roll. He spoke into a microphone, his voice echoing from the loudspeakers. It took well over an hour to go through all the numbers. Next, prisoners carrying big metal canisters came along the lines, doling out coffee in tin mugs. By the time Fritz got his, it was cold. It wasn't even real coffee – it was made from roasted acorns and tasted oddly sweet.

By the time they began marching out through the gate, the sky was getting light. At last Fritz would find out where the other prisoners went each day.

Outside the gate, the prisoners began splitting away in groups – lots of them went marching off towards the building sites. The rest kept on going down the far side of the hill, where a wide road had been cut through the forest.

They sang as they marched. It was a rousing tune, and the words went:

> *Oh Buchenwald, I cannot forget you,*
> *For you are my fate . . .*
> *Oh Buchenwald, we do not whine and moan,*
> *And whatever our fate may be,*

We will say yes to life,
For the day will come when we are free!

A space opened between the trees. It looked to Fritz as if the men were marching off the edge of the world, as the ground suddenly plunged down a steep slope to a vast rocky ledge cut into the hillside, as deep as a three-storey building and as wide as a football pitch. Beyond the far edge, Fritz had a bird's-eye view of misty fields and villages lit by the rising sun. The people down there wouldn't be having cold acorn coffee for breakfast, he guessed.

Here among the rocks, hundreds of prisoners worked, quarrying the stone that was used on the building sites. Fritz and Papa were put to work breaking up big rocks with hammers. They noticed how the guards and the green-triangle prisoners hit anyone who wasn't working hard enough.

'Take care, Fritz,' said Papa as he swung his hammer. 'Keep a lookout from the corner of your eye. This isn't so different from being in the army. If anyone comes near, don't look them in the eye, just keep your head down and work like mad!'

Fritz did as Papa said, and the guards left them alone. The work was hard, and there was nothing to drink. Fritz noticed other prisoners lapping at puddles. He got so thirsty that he did the same. The water was foul, but at least it was wet.

Around noon, lunch was brought to the quarry – thin soup served from canisters. Cold, of course, but Fritz was glad of it. He was tired out after the morning's work. He was sure he couldn't keep it up all day.

'Delicious, eh?' said a man nearby, watching Fritz lick his dish clean. 'Stay here long and you'll be thin, my lad! Got here in the last transport, did you?'

The man was about Papa's age. He had a red and yellow star, and his uniform was frayed and grubby.

'Yes,' said Papa. 'We came from Vienna. You've been here a long time?'

'Six years,' the man said. 'First Dachau, then here. I was one of the first inmates.' He touched his badge. 'Not because of the star, though. I'm a political.'

'What's a political?' asked Fritz.

'Political prisoner. See all the men with red triangles? They're political. They're in here because they opposed Hitler in one way or another. Me, I was in the Communist Party.'

Fritz knew about communists. They were very radical, believing that businesses and private wealth should be abolished and that everyone should be made to be equal, working together for their communities. They were against Hitler, who loathed and feared them almost as much as he did Jewish people. (The existence of communists was one of the many things for which Hitler blamed Jews.)

The man went on: 'You'll see four times as many red triangles as Jewish stars in here. The politicals were the first ones they rounded up. With me, being Jewish was just a bonus.' He smiled. 'Leopold Moses at your service.'

'Gustav Kleinmann,' said Papa. 'This is my boy, Fritz.'

'Father and son? Not many like you in here.'

'If red triangles are politicals, what do the green triangles mean?' asked Fritz.

Leopold scowled. 'Criminals. Thieves and thugs mostly. Steer clear of the green men. The SS use them as kapos.'

'Kapos?'

'Prisoners who work for the SS. The guards use kapos to beat down the rest of us. Saves the Nazi boys from getting their hands dirty. The green-triangle men are the worst of the kapos.' Leopold finished the last of his soup. 'One other thing. Whatever you do, don't cross the sentry line. See over there?'

Fritz looked. Surrounding the quarry was a line of SS guards, one every ten metres or so. They were armed with rifles and sub-machine guns.

'They'll shoot you if you go past them,' said Leopold. 'It's a game to them. They'll try to tempt you to cross the line just so they can gun you down. Don't fall for it.'

The kapos started shouting, 'Back to work, you lazy slobs!' Fritz and Papa picked up their hammers. A kapo yelled at them. 'You two! Put those down and follow me! Look alive, now – run, run, run! This way!'

Leopold glanced up from his work. His face fell in dismay when he saw where the kapo was taking them. In the middle of the quarry was the place where prisoners loaded blocks of stone and buckets of gravel into big wagons. The wagons ran on rails that led out of the quarry and up the hill. There were no engines to pull them; the work was done by prisoners.

'You're on my team now,' said the kapo, and he pointed at a wagon. 'Get to work.'

The wagon was made of steel and had been loaded with over four tonnes of stone. Long ropes were tied to the front end. A team of fourteen prisoners were getting ready to either pull on the ropes or push the wagon from behind.

Fritz and Papa found a gap and got ready to push.

'Go!' yelled the kapo.

The prisoners put all their strength into pushing and pulling, straining on the ropes. The wagon began to move, gradually picking up speed.

'Faster! Faster!' said the kapo, striding alongside. 'Left-two-three! Left-two-three!'

The rail tracks turned right and, to Fritz's alarm, went straight up the steep slope.

'Faster! Faster!'

They picked up just enough speed to propel the wagon a little way up the hill, but then, as it began slowing to a stop, they had to use every ounce of strength to keep it going. The men were all half-starved, and didn't have much left to put in. Fritz strained against the steel side of the wagon. His badly fitting shoes scrabbled on the loose stones. Slowly, painfully, the wagon went up the hill.

'Come on, you lazy animals!' the kapo shouted, lashing at them with his club. 'D'you think you're on holiday? Left-two-three! Left-two-three!'

At last they reached the top. The wagon rumbled along the rails and came to an unloading area near the building sites. The stone was tipped out, and prisoners from the construction team swarmed all over it, picking up lumps and running off while their kapos screamed at them.

'Now back down, double-quick!' said the kapo. 'You've lost us enough time already.'

They ran, the empty wagon clanging and bouncing on the rails. All the time, the kapo was yelling at them to go faster. The wagon went down the hill, jolting. Fritz was afraid it would jump off the rails and crash.

Back at the bottom, the men caught their breath and waited for the wagon to be filled. Then it started all over again, and again, and again, all afternoon.

It was dark when they marched back into the camp for roll call. Fritz could hardly stand upright. That night, still hungry, he fell asleep as soon as he pulled his blanket over himself.

Tomorrow would be the same. And the day after, and the day after that. It was impossible to imagine how he and Papa could survive it.

CHAPTER EIGHT

The Stone Crusher

'Left-two-three! Left-two-three!'

The kapo's voice hammered inside Fritz's head.

'Come on, you dogs! Onward, pigs! Isn't this fun?'

Fritz's starved muscles strained to push the stone-wagon to the top of the hill. The team had to do this journey twelve times a day. Up the hill, then racing back down at top speed, holding on for dear life.

He and Papa had been doing this work for a few days and had already seen accidents. Sometimes a speeding wagon would bounce off the rails and crash into one coming up. It was horrific. The injured men got little medical treatment. If they were Jewish, they got virtually none. Fritz and Papa had been lucky so far.

While the stone-carriers loaded up the wagon, Fritz and Papa watched the prisoners working. All day long the men in stripes dug stone, broke stone, carried stone, and were beaten by the kapos if they slacked. Each kapo knew that if he didn't please the SS, he would lose his job as a kapo. They'd put him back with the ordinary prisoners, who would take revenge on him.

In the middle of the quarry stood a huge machine for crushing stones. A massive roaring engine drove a series of wheels and belts. On one end was a huge funnel, into which prisoners shovelled stones. Inside, steel plates worked up and down and side to side like an iron jaw, chewing and crushing the stones to gravel.

'That's like us,' said Papa, pointing at the prisoners feeding stones into the monstrous machine.

'What do you mean?'

'We're the stones, Fritz. The Nazis are the machine. They shovel us into the camps and grind us down to dust.'

One of the prisoners feeding stones into the crusher was a tall, muscular man. He shovelled well. The kapo operating the machine saw a chance for a game. He turned the throttle up, faster and faster, until the machine was running at double speed, rattling and banging diabolically. The big prisoner shovelled faster and faster, grunting and sweating.

It was a contest between man and machine – the man panting, muscles straining, the crusher grinding and clattering, fit to explode.

All around, prisoners stopped working to watch. The kapos didn't say anything; they were watching too.

On and on the contest went, shovelful after shovelful, clattering plates, roaring gears, the man dripping with sweat, the crusher thundering and pouring out gravel. The man was strong and determined, but the crusher's strength was limitless, and little by little the man grew tired and slowed down. He was going to lose.

Summoning his willpower, he made one more massive effort, stretching his muscles, shovelling for his life. Even if the machine won, he would at least have tried.

Suddenly there was a bang and a groan from inside the machine. It shuddered, coughed, and then stood still. The kapo driving it delved into its insides and found that a stone had got into the gears.

There was silence. The big prisoner leaned on his shovel, gasping for breath. He had beaten the stone crusher.

Everyone thought the kapo would murder him for it. But instead the chief kapo in charge of the quarry workers burst out laughing. 'Come here, tall lad!' he called. 'What are you, a farmhand? A miner, I'll bet?'

'No,' said the big prisoner. 'I'm a journalist.'

'A newspaperman? Too bad. I've got no use for one of those.' The chief kapo turned away, then stopped. 'Wait, though, I do need someone who can write. Go and wait in the hut there. I have other work for you.'

As the hero laid down his shovel, the other kapos ordered the prisoners back to work.

Papa smiled. 'You see, Fritz? There *is* hope for us. Don't give up. They can't grind us down like this if we don't let them.'

As the days went by, Fritz tried to hold on to hope. But it was hard. He was seeing things that no human being should have to see, let alone a boy his age. Terrible things. Men tortured for not working hard enough, men killed, men left to die from injuries and illness.

A disease called dysentery had broken out in the camp. It was caused by the dirty conditions. Dysentery gave you stomach pain, fever and awful diarrhoea. If you were unlucky you could die from it. Many men in the camp were unlucky.

Everyone was hungry. Some prisoners in the little camp managed to steal food from the kitchens, but the SS found out about it. As a punishment, they stopped everyone's food for two days.

Then, suddenly, everything got even worse.

In the German city of Munich, someone tried to kill Adolf Hitler with a bomb. Hitler wasn't hurt, but he was furious. More furious than he had ever been. He knew who to blame. Nazis everywhere knew who to blame. *Jews.* In fact, Jewish people had nothing to do with it. The Gestapo found the man who had planted the bomb, and he wasn't Jewish, but in Hitler's mind, and in his followers' minds, everything bad was somehow the fault of Jews. In concentration camps across Germany, the SS took revenge on Jewish prisoners.

It was morning, and Fritz and Papa were at work. Everyone knew something bad was going on when Sergeant Blank, head of the quarry guards, came striding down the hill. Blank was a notoriously cruel man who enjoyed hurting prisoners. Of all the SS men in Buchenwald, none was more frightening than Sergeant Blank.

He ordered his guards to march all the Jewish prisoners back to the camp.

Once they were inside, the gates were closed and the prisoners were sent to their tents in the little camp. Those who'd been there longer, like Leopold Moses, were shut in their barrack blocks.

Inside the tent, Fritz and Papa had no idea what was going on outside. There was only silence. Someone said they'd seen Blank and his men round up about twenty Jewish men from the main camp and take them back towards the quarry. Suddenly they heard a crackle of guns firing far away, seemingly from the quarry. There was silence again, then another burst of gunfire.

After the firing had died away, Sergeant Blank came to the little camp. He and his SS guards came storming into the tents. 'Out! All of you Jewish pigs, get out! Out now!' They lashed about them with their rifle butts.

The prisoners all rushed to obey, keen to avoid being hit. Out on the roll-call square, they had to line up in rows, just as they did every morning and evening.

Then Blank ordered his guards: 'Take every twentieth man!'

The guards went along the rows, counting the prisoners. 'One, two, three, four ...' When they got to twenty, that prisoner was grabbed and dragged away. Then they moved on to the next man and started again. 'One, two, three, four ...'

Fritz and Papa stood to attention, watching from the corner of their eyes as a guard came along their row. 'One, two, three ...' He got closer, his finger pointing at each man. 'Seventeen, eighteen, nineteen ...' The finger pointed at Papa and moved on, then, 'Twenty!' It was pointing at Fritz.

The guards grabbed Fritz and dragged him towards the others who'd been picked out.

'Bring out the Horse!' said Blank.

There was a silent gasp from the prisoners; they knew what was about to happen. Two guards came on to the square carrying a heavy wooden table with a sloping top. This contraption was the Horse, and they were all terrified of it.

Sergeant Blank had a cane, and he swished it as he spoke. 'Fetch the first one,' he said. 'Now we'll teach you Jews a lesson.'

They picked out Fritz. His heart was hammering. There was nothing he could do. Papa had to watch in helpless horror, knowing that if he tried to save Fritz, the SS would kill them both. Fritz was pulled to the wooden table, and then he was pushed face down on to the top.

The cane whistled through the air. 'Count!' yelled one of the guards.

Fritz knew how it went. He'd seen it happen. You had to count the strokes. If you lost count, they started again from the beginning. On and on it went. Ten . . . eleven . . . twelve . . . Fritz concentrated hard to make sure he didn't lose count. Fifteen . . . sixteen . . . It seemed like it would never end. Twenty-four . . . twenty-five.

At last it was over. As Fritz staggered away from the Horse, the next victim was dragged to it.

The punishment went on for hours, one man after another. That evening, back in the tent, Papa did what he could to make Fritz comfortable. Fritz tried to be brave, to take away the worry in Papa's eyes.

The next day, everything went back to normal – woken before dawn, roll call in the square, work in the quarry. Fritz's pain had faded just enough for him to cope, but it was difficult standing to attention through roll call.

Fritz was too worried about Papa to pay much attention to his own pain. There was still dysentery in the little camp, and Papa had caught it. He was pale and weak, and only his toughness got him through the day's work. Leopold Moses had given Fritz some charcoal anti-diarrhoea tablets after seeing him drinking from puddles, and he still had some, which he gave to Papa. They helped a little, but Papa kept on getting worse. One morning at roll call, Fritz noticed him swaying. Suddenly, he collapsed.

'Papa!' Fritz shook him, but his eyes wouldn't open. His forehead was burning hot. 'Papa! Wake up! Don't be ill, please don't be ill.'

A kapo came along the row and saw what had happened. 'Take him to the Jew hospital,' he said. 'Quick now! Get him out of here.'

Fritz struggled to lift Papa, but he couldn't.

'Here, let me help,' said Itschkerl, who was standing nearby.

Together they lifted Papa up and carried him. The so-called hospital for Jewish prisoners was an ordinary wooden barrack block. The prisoners called it the Death Block, and few patients came out of it alive. The air inside was stuffy and stinking. The shelf-like bunks were filled with men groaning or just lying still. Simply being in here made you lose all hope.

They found a bunk space and laid Papa in it. His face was soaked with sweat and he was shivering. The doctor came to look at him. Dr Heller was a young Jewish prisoner. He was kind and did his best for the patients, but the SS gave him almost no medicines and allowed him very little time away from his labouring work in the quarry. Examining Papa, he looked grim. Men who were this ill rarely got better.

Fritz felt terrible leaving Papa in that place. If he died, Fritz didn't think he could go on without him.

Meanwhile, things were getting worse in the little camp. Somebody had done something or other to make the SS angry, and everyone's food was stopped again. Another two days of starvation.

Fritz and Itschkerl and the other boys got together and talked about what to do.

'We should beg the SS for food,' said one. 'I mean, look at us. We're just kids!'

'I agree,' said Fritz.

'Me too,' said Itschkerl.

One of the older men was listening. 'Don't do it,' he said. 'Getting yourself noticed just leads to punishment. You'll be lucky if they don't kill you.'

But Itschkerl was stubborn. 'I don't care,' he said. 'Even if we have to die, I'm going to ask Dr Blies for food.'

Dr Blies was the SS officer in charge of health and hygiene. He wasn't a nice man by any means, but he was less cruel than some of the other SS doctors.

'OK,' said Fritz. 'But I'm coming with you. And I'll do the talking. You just back me up.'

It was a brave thing to do – many would say it was foolish – and Fritz tried not to imagine what Papa would have said if he'd been there.

They didn't have to wait long for Dr Blies to make his next inspection. He was a funny-looking man, which did little to make him less frightening. Fritz knew the best way to speak to him – they had to make it seem like helping them would be good for the SS.

He stepped up to Dr Blies and, making his voice shaky and weepy, said, 'Sir, we have no strength to work because we're starving. Please give us something to eat.'

The doctor stared in astonishment. Fritz was small for his age, which made him look even younger. He could see Blies wavering, struggling to choose between his Nazi training and his humanity. The boy had a point. The

prisoners had to have the strength to work. His jaw clenched. 'Come with me,' he said sharply.

Fritz and Itschkerl followed Dr Blies to the camp kitchens. 'Wait here,' he said, and went into the food store.

He was gone for several minutes while the two boys waited nervously. At last he came out carrying a loaf of bread and a two-litre container of soup. 'Take this. Now – back to your camp. Go!'

Fritz and Itschkerl were greeted with amazement by the older prisoners. There was enough for six people, and the boys shared the soup and bread with their closest bunkmates. Soon after, it was announced that the hunger punishment was being stopped, on orders from Dr Blies.

The two boys were heroes in the little camp, and from that day on, Itschkerl and Fritz were best friends.

As the days went by, Fritz visited Papa whenever he could. The dysentery hadn't killed him, but he was extremely weak. Dr Heller spoke to Fritz. 'Your father has begged me to let him go, but I can't. He's far too weak to survive out there in the camp.'

But Papa was determined. He knew he was never going to get well in this awful, dirty, germ-filled place. When Dr Heller had gone, he gripped Fritz's hand. 'Please, Fritz,' he said. 'Help me get out. I'll die in here.'

Fritz helped him out of the bunk. He could hardly stand up, and Fritz had to support him. Dr Heller was busy with other patients and didn't notice them slip through the door. With Papa's arm around his shoulders Fritz guided him across the square to the little camp. He wasn't heavy. He'd lost so much weight with starvation and illness, that he only weighed 45 kilos.*

Even the muddy, crowded tent seemed fresh and healthy compared with the Death Block, and Papa said he felt better already. The next day, he was given light work to do around the camp. 'I like to work,' he said. 'It helps me forget where I am.'

With winter approaching, Fritz and Papa were surprised and delighted when a parcel arrived for them. It was from Mum! (Prisoners were allowed to receive letters and gifts from their families, but weren't allowed to write back because the SS didn't want people outside to know what the camps were really like.) Mum had sent some socks and gloves, which were very welcome. In her letter she wrote that she was still working hard to try and get permission for Fritz, Kurt and Herta to go to America. (There was no news of Edith, though. While the war was going on, Britain was cut off from the rest of Europe.)

'You see!' said Papa to Fritz. 'There *is* hope that we can get through this. The crusher won't beat us. We're strong. They can't grind us down!'

---

* 99 lbs or 7 stone, less than two thirds of the proper weight for a man of his height and build.

CHAPTER NINE

A Feeling of Hope

Another day, just like every other. Fritz was torn from sleep by the kapo's whistle. Rubbing his eyes ... lights switched on ... still dark outside.

He dropped down from the bunk and landed on a wooden floor. It was nice not to be in mud any more. He pulled on his uniform, still damp and smelly from the day before. The bunk room reeked of stale uniforms and dirty men.

Winter had come and gone. He and Papa were no longer in the little camp. Dr Blies said it was too unhealthy, and they'd all been moved to barrack blocks in the main camp. It was just as crowded, and had the same kind of hard, shelf-like bunks, but there were walls and a floor and the place was kept clean.

Papa had regained his strength and was back at work

in the quarry. He and Fritz had been taken off the wagons a while ago and switched to stone-carrying. It was even worse. The stones were heavy and made your hands raw with cuts and blisters. And the kapos were horrible.

'On, you shirkers,' they yelled all day long. 'Wagon number two! If you don't fill it quick, I'll beat you to a pulp!' The stones clattered and banged into the hollow iron belly of the wagon. 'Finished? You think you're free now? D'you see me laughing? Wagon three, at the double! Faster, or you'll get my boot. On, pigs!'

Every day, prisoners suffered in the quarry, and many died there.

Eventually, Fritz had been transferred to work in the camp's vegetable gardens. It was better, but still hard work. A lot of the time he was carrying buckets of filth from the camp toilet pits to fertilise the vegetable beds. You had to run with it, and the stuff slopped out of the buckets on to your legs. Their kapo was a Viennese man called Willy Kurtz. He let the boys take it easy as long as nobody was looking. When any SS were nearby, he made a big show of yelling ferociously and lashing out with his stick, but then he stopped as soon as they were gone.

On this spring morning, Fritz and Itschkerl guzzled down their cold acorn coffee. The barrack block had a table where they could eat, which was an improvement over the conditions in the little camp. Papa was in a different block now, and he and Fritz met up whenever they could. Fritz and the other boys had been put together in Block 3. They shared it with prisoners who'd been in the camps for years, like Leopold Moses. Mostly they were red-triangle men – politicals. They took pity on the boys, and gave them any extra bits and pieces of food they could lay their hands on.

With the warmer summer weather coming, roll calls weren't quite so awful. Today, though, something unusual and frightening happened. As roll call ended and Fritz was about to head off with the other garden workers, the camp's chief kapo announced over the loudspeaker: 'Prisoner 7290 to the main gate, at the double!'

That was Fritz's number. Fear took hold in the pit of his stomach. His friends glanced at him anxiously. The SS only called you to the main gate when you were in serious trouble. Those who were called usually ended up dead. Fritz hadn't done anything wrong, had he? But he knew it was always possible to be in deadly trouble without even knowing why.

He pushed through the mass of prisoners and ran to the gatehouse. Waiting for him was Lieutenant Hackmann, a slender officer whose charming smile hid a brutal nature. He always carried a hefty bamboo club, which he swung lazily as he spoke. 'Wait here,' he said. 'Face the wall.'

Fritz did as he was told, staring at the whitewashed bricks while the other prisoners marched out to work.

After a while, the SS sergeant in charge of Block 3 came to fetch him. 'Come with me,' he said, and led Fritz out of the gate. They went straight to the camp's Gestapo office. Fritz's heart shrank in dread.

'Cap off,' said a Gestapo clerk. 'Take off your jacket.'

Fritz did so, and the clerk handed him a dark suit jacket and a tie.

'Put those on,' said the clerk.

The jacket was far too big, but Fritz put it on, knotting the tie carefully. The jacket hung loosely on him, and his neck barely touched the shirt collar.

He was taken into a room with lights and a camera. He stared into the lens with deep suspicion as his photo was taken. What could this possibly be for? Nobody said a word to him.

Afterwards, they gave him back his uniform and ordered him to run back to the camp. He was even more puzzled when the block sergeant told him he didn't have to work for the rest of the day.

That evening, Papa came and found him. He'd been frightened half to death all day, thinking the SS must have done something terrible to Fritz. When Fritz described what had happened, nobody could make any sense of it.

A few days later, Fritz was sent to the Gestapo office again. He had to sign his name on a copy of the photo, and it was stamped by the clerk.

'Your mother's applying for you to be released,' the clerk said.

Fritz was bewildered. 'You mean . . . I can go?'

The clerk laughed nastily. 'Are you an idiot? Of course not. This letter here says Mrs Kleinmann has obtained the affidavit for you to go to America.'

An affidavit was one of the papers you needed to be able to go to America. Fritz remembered that Mum and Papa had often talked about it.

'This photo goes in her application,' said the clerk. 'If it's accepted, you'll be released and Germany can be rid of you.'

Fritz walked back to the camp feeling as if he was floating on air. For the first time since he'd arrived in Buchenwald, there was real hope in his heart.

* * *

Back in Vienna, Mum was working hard to get the paperwork in order for the children's applications for America. That meant another trip to the photographer's for Kurt and Herta. It was nothing like the last time – just the two of them with Mum, and they didn't wear their best outfits. Kurt didn't feel like smiling this time, and Herta looked scared. There was nothing in life to smile about any more.

Mum never stopped worrying about Fritz and Papa.

She sent them whatever little gifts she could. One day she'd got messages back from both of them. They weren't allowed to write proper letters – just an SS form with a few lines filled in. They were alive and well, and that was all it said. There was nothing about what it was like in the camp.

The stories brought back by people who'd been released from the camps were terrible. The Nazis had also been sending Jewish families from Vienna to live in Poland, which was now part of the Nazi empire. A few came back to Vienna saying that lots of people had been killed there. Mum was determined to send Kurt, Herta and Fritz somewhere safe. It was too late for them to join Edith in England now that Britain was at war with Germany. All Mum's hopes were pinned on America.

She spent most of her time trekking from one Nazi office to another, filling in forms and being insulted. Every message that came through the door was an anxious moment. Would it be another disappointing refusal from America? Or a letter saying they'd been accepted? Or an order that they were all being sent to Poland?

Mum had cousins and friends who'd gone to live in America years ago. One of her friends had put her in touch with the Barnet brothers, who were still trying to arrange to bring the kids to America. But the American government was still only letting a tiny number of refugees into the country.

Kurt knew how worried Mum was, and that she worried especially about him. He was ten years old now. He'd always been a *Spitzbub* – a rascal, a tearaway, with lots of energy for being naughty. Mum told him he must behave. It would be terrible if he did something bad that got them all into trouble with the Nazis. Just the littlest thing could do it.

She went on about it so much that it scared him. Kurt missed his friends. He had classmates still, at the Jewish school, but it wasn't the same as the old days, before Hitler came, when they were all in the big gang, playing in the marketplace. The thing Kurt had loved best was when they used to go on expeditions across Vienna. Their mums would pack sandwiches in their backpacks and off they'd go for the day, exploring the huge city – the parks and the palaces and the river. Now all the nice places had those nasty signs up: NUR FÜR ARIER ('Aryans Only'), or EINTRITT JUDEN VERBOTEN ('No Entry for Jews').

One day, Kurt noticed some of his Aryan friends from the old gang hanging around in the market, and it made him long for those days when he could have joined in. But these kids weren't his friends anymore.

While Mum was busy, Kurt crept down the stairs to the street. One of the boys, Hannes, had a scooter and seemed to be taking it apart.

Kurt couldn't stop himself; he went along the street and joined the group. They didn't seem to mind him being there. Hannes, who was the leader of the group and a bit of a bully, still seemed friendly. Everything was OK for a while. They chatted while Hannes fiddled with his scooter. Then something changed. Hannes looked at Kurt, and he had the nasty smile in his eyes that bullies get when they feel like picking on someone.

'What are you doing here, Jew?' he said. 'You're not supposed to be here.'

Kurt didn't know what to say.

Hannes started pulling at the buttons on Kurt's coat. 'Your dad's gone to the camps, hasn't he?' He twisted the buttons, trying to tear them off. ''Cos he's a Jew-pig like you.'

Kurt had been bullied before by Nazis – last winter, a big Hitler Youth boy had shoved him to the ground and pushed his face in the snow. But this was worse – this was a friend calling him vile names and ripping the buttons off his only coat.

Something snapped in Kurt. Without warning, he lashed out and punched Hannes in the face.

Hannes was astonished and enraged. He grabbed a metal bar from his scooter and hit Kurt on the head with it. Kurt tried to shield himself, but Hannes swung the bar again and again.

The beating stopped at last. Hannes was panting for breath and Kurt was bleeding. The other boys yelled and jeered as Kurt staggered away.

When he got home, Mum and Herta stared in horror at his bruised, bleeding face. Mum tried to clean him up, but he was too badly injured. He needed to go to hospital. She took him to the Jewish clinic, where a doctor tended his wounds and gave Mum some medicine for him. There wasn't much of it, because the Nazis kept most medicines for non-Jews.

The next day, an SS policeman came to the apartment. Hannes's parents had made a complaint against Kurt.

They said that he had attacked Hannes. Kurt knew it wouldn't do any good to tell the policeman what had really happened. The SS would never believe a Jewish boy. In their eyes, Kurt had committed the worst kind of crime – a Jew attacking an Aryan.

'He's just a little boy,' said Mum to the policeman. 'Can't you have mercy on him?'

'Your boy's got to answer for what he's done,' said the policeman. 'But if the parents agree, he can apologise and be let off with a caution.'

Mum was relieved, and thanked the policeman.

Kurt and Mum had to meet with Hannes and his parents. Kurt's head and face were bandaged and purple with bruises. Hannes stood there without a mark on him.

'It is wrong for a Jew to attack an Aryan,' said Kurt, as he'd been told to say. 'I am sorry for what I did, and will never do such a thing again.'

With that, the matter was closed. Kurt was glad that he hadn't got the family into trouble, but the unfairness of it gave him a pain inside, worse than the cuts and bruises. He would never forget it as long as he lived.

One day, Mum was ordered to take Kurt and Herta for an interview with the SS for their application to go to America. Kurt sensed Mum's and Herta's fear, and he wanted to protect them. He had a bone-handled knife, which he'd got from a cousin long ago, in the days before Hitler. He slipped it into his pocket. The Nazis had taken his father and brother away, tormented his sisters, bullied and beaten him and then made out it was his crime. He was determined to defend Mum and Herta against them.

They set out for the police station. Kurt touched the knife blade in his pocket as he walked. He knew that when Jews were ordered to report to the SS, they were sometimes sent away. He could tell that Mum was getting more and more worried as they approached the police station. He showed her the knife. 'See, Mum, I'll protect us,' he said.

Mum was horrified. 'Get rid of it!'

'But –'

'Kurt, throw it away before someone sees it!'

He protested, but she was furious and terrified at the same time. Reluctantly, he tossed the knife away. They walked on, Kurt feeling heartbroken. How could he defend the people he loved now? What would become of them?

Winter was coming again. After months of waiting, Mum was finally given the result of the applications she'd made for the children to go to America.

They'd all been turned down by the American government. There weren't enough places for them right now.

After all her hard work, Mum was devastated. But there was one little ray of hope. The German Jewish Children's Aid charity that helped arrange for children to leave Austria was making a special effort for Kurt. It had a transport of children going to America in the New Year, and it had granted him a place on it.

CHAPTER TEN

The Road to Life

It was evening in Buchenwald. Fritz and the other boys sat in the common room of Block 3, listening to Stefan Heymann read to them. Stefan was one of the politicals who'd been in the camps for years. Like Leopold Moses, he was also Jewish. They both looked after the boys and tried to protect them and teach them.

Stefan had a thin face. Behind his thick, round glasses his eyes were wide, as if he was constantly surprised by something. He loved books, and had a little collection he kept hidden from the SS.

The book Stefan was reading from was called *The Road to Life*. It told the story of a group of boys in Russia who'd got into trouble and were sent to a camp. But not a camp like Buchenwald.

'*We transferred to the new colony on a fine, warm*

day,' Stefan read. '*The leaves on the trees had not yet begun to turn, the grass was still green.*' Stefan's voice filled the room. The only other sound was the rustle as he turned a page. '*There were many shady mysterious corners here, in which one could bathe, mingle with pixies, go fishing, or share secrets with a friendly spirit. Our main buildings were at the top of the steep bank, and the boys could jump right out of the windows into the river, leaving their clothes on the windowsills.*'

Hearing stories of a better world gave Fritz and his friends a sense of joy that they never got in their real lives anymore. They could hardly remember what it was like to swim and play and be happy. Most of the boys listening had lost their fathers, who had either been killed by the SS or died of illness, so Stefan and Leopold and a few other older prisoners tried to be like fathers to them, doing what little they could to bring comfort and protection.

One evening Stefan came into the block with a mysterious air. Telling Fritz and the other boys to be quiet, he led them across the camp to the clothing store. It was dangerous to be out. If a kapo or a guard saw them, they'd be in trouble.

The store building was next to the shower block. This was where the SS kept all the clothes and other belongings they took from prisoners when they arrived. Stefan led the boys inside.

It was quiet and still, with rows of hanging racks and shelves stuffed full with prisoner uniforms and stolen clothing. It smelled musty. They squeezed between the racks until they came to an open space. Some prisoners had gathered here. They welcomed the boys and gave them each a piece of bread and a mug of acorn coffee. Fritz still had no idea what they were there for.

All was revealed when a little group of prisoners appeared with violins and other instruments. In the warm, dusty silence, they started to play music. Fritz was spellbound. He'd never heard such lovely music before. They played a piece called 'A Little Night Music', a cheerful tune that made everyone smile with delight. They even laughed. Fritz would remember that magical evening as long as he lived.

Such moments helped Fritz to get through life. Months had passed since the photograph had been taken, and he'd heard nothing more about it. Hope had faded away again.

At least life was a little less dangerous now that he worked in the vegetable gardens. And Papa wasn't in the quarry any more. He had a less arduous job working on the transport column, pulling road wagons around the building sites. Papa and his friends were made to sing as they worked, and the other prisoners called them the Singing Horses.

'It's hard work,' Papa said to Fritz. 'But it's more

peaceful than the quarry, and the kapos don't kill us. We're creatures of habit, we humans – you can get used to anything, I suppose.'

Fritz wasn't so sure. They had a new SS man in charge of Block 3, Sergeant Schmidt. He stole from the prisoners and loved to punish them. He looked for the slightest thing wrong in the barracks – bunks a bit untidy, floor not quite clean enough. Of course, there would always be something, and when he found it, he flew into a rage and ordered all the prisoners in the block to go outside, where they had to do exercises.

'Run! March! Lie down! Get up!' he yelled. 'Not good enough! Lie down again! Stand up! Now run!' He called it 'punishment sports'. *Thwack!* went his cane on their backsides if they moved too slowly.

In hot sun or freezing rain the prisoners of Block 3 spent miserable hours doing punishment sports. Afterwards, starving, they would sit down to the only warm meal of the day – turnip soup. If they were lucky, they might get a little scrap of meat with it.

One evening Stefan gathered the boys together and told them, 'I have to talk to you.' When they were sitting, he went on. 'You boys mustn't run so fast during the punishment sport. When you run fast, the older men can't keep up and they get beaten by Schmidt.'

The boys were ashamed, but what could they do? Stefan showed them: 'Run like this – lift your knees higher, take smaller steps. That way, you look like you're running with all your strength, but you go slowly.'

It worked well enough to fool Sergeant Schmidt. As time went on, Fritz learned lots of little tricks. Silly things, some of them, but they could mean the difference between safety and pain, or between life and death.

The SS kept thinking up more and more bizarre ways to be cruel. In the evenings, Major Roedl, who was one of the most powerful officers, made the prisoners stand out on the roll-call square singing. The camp orchestra (including the men who'd played the secret concert in the clothing store) played while the prisoners sang. Major Roedl pranced about on top of a gravel heap, conducting them and yelling instructions through the loudspeakers. Sometimes they had to lie down in the mud and sing. Guards walked between the rows, kicking anyone who didn't sing well enough.

Outside the fence, Buchenwald kept on growing. Stone came from the quarry, bricks and cement arrived in lorries, trees were cut down, and more and more buildings rose out of the forest. Buchenwald was an SS base, with offices and huge barracks. There were nice houses for the officers and their families, and even a zoo. All of it was built by prisoners.

Leopold Moses was friends with the chief kapo of the building team. He persuaded him to let Fritz come and work there. It was known to be safer than most work teams.

The chief kapo's name was Robert Siewert, and he was completely different from most of the other kapos. He was a good man, and the SS had only made him the chief building kapo because he was such a good builder. Robert Siewert was a German red-triangle prisoner, about Papa's age. He was thickset, with a large face and small eyes under dark, heavy brows. He looked stern and scary, but he had a kind heart.

Working on the building sites was extremely tough. Fritz had to carry bricks and bags of cement that were heavier than he was. But nobody got beaten or abused by the kapos. The SS needed builders more than anything, so Robert Siewert was allowed to protect his workers.

He gave Fritz the same advice Papa had given him. 'You have to use your eyes. If you see an SS man coming, work fast. But if there are no SS about, then take your time.'

Fritz became so good at watching for SS guards that he could spot them long before they noticed him. Then he would throw himself into his work, heaving and pulling and lifting and running. Whenever the chief guard showed up, Robert would point to Fritz and say, 'Look how hard this Jewish boy works!'

One day, an SS officer named Lieutenant Schobert came to inspect the building work. He was a nasty-looking man with a perpetual sneer. Robert called Fritz over and showed him to Schobert.

'Look at this lad, sir,' he said. 'He's one of my best. Hard-working, clever. There are more boys like him in the camp. I'm thinking it might be good for us if you'd let me train them up as bricklayers.'

Lieutenant Schobert looked down his nose at Fritz. 'Train Jews to be builders?' he said with disgust. 'All that expense to train *Jews*? You're joking.'

'Sir, we're really short of skilled men. And with all the new projects coming up –'

'Absolutely not!' Schobert snapped. 'Now get back to work!'

Robert didn't give up. He really needed bricklayers, and he wanted to do something to help the Jewish boys. Once they had a skill the Nazis really needed, they'd be much safer from harm. Robert went to Commandant Koch himself and said, 'I just can't get all the building work done without new bricklayers.' But the commandant gave the same answer: '*No Jews*.'

Still Robert didn't give up. He decided to show the SS what his boys could do. He made Fritz his apprentice. He taught him how to lay bricks to make a simple wall, with a string set up as a guide. Fritz learned how to 'butter' a brick with mortar and lay it neatly, all in a straight line, brick after brick, layer after layer.

Fritz had inherited Papa's knack for working with his hands, and he learned quickly. Robert taught him how to build corners, then pillars, then window openings, fireplaces and chimneys. Then he learned how to plaster a wall. It didn't take long before Fritz was quite good at his trade – the only Jewish builder in Buchenwald.

When Robert got Fritz to demonstrate his skills to the SS, Commandant Koch at last gave his permission for the training scheme to go ahead.

Along with Fritz, Robert chose as many boys as he could, most of them Jewish. A few were Roma. The Roma – short for Romani – are travelling people (often called Gypsies, though many Roma dislike that name) with their own culture and long history. The Nazis hated them just as much as they hated Jews, and just as unfairly, and they mistreated them every bit as cruelly. But there were far fewer Roma than Jewish people, and since much of the rest of the world shared the Nazis' prejudice against travelling folk, little notice was taken of the Roma people's terrible mistreatment.

The boys spent half of each day working on the building sites, learning the same things as Fritz. The other half of the day they sat in their block learning about the science of building. They wore green armbands with 'Bricklayers' School' written on them. They got extra food, including bread and meat that was better quality than the normal rations.

To Fritz, Robert Siewert was a hero. He stuck up for his workers if the SS picked on them, and he spoke to the boys patiently and kindly, becoming like a father to them.

Fritz wondered how long his own Papa would last. Working with the 'Singing Horses' on the transport gang was easier than the quarry, but still extremely hard. Fritz saved as much of his extra food as he could, and gave it to Papa when they met in the evenings.

Papa didn't seem to be worried. 'We'll get through this,' he said, although he looked thin and frail from hunger. 'We have good friends in Robert Siewert and Leo Moses. And you're popular now, Fritz. I'm proud of you.'

At least they weren't in the quarry any more. More and more prisoners were being killed there, especially Jewish ones. Many of them were friends of Fritz's and Papa's – some were men Papa had known in Vienna in the old days. With German troops fighting the war on the front lines, the Death's Head SS in the camps felt they were fighting a war within Germany against Jews and Roma and politicals.

The war was going well for Germany. France had surrendered, and only Britain was still fighting, with help from its Empire and Commonwealth countries, such as India, Jamaica, Canada, New Zealand, Australia and many more, plus volunteers who'd escaped from Nazi-occupied countries such as France and Poland. The Royal Air Force fought to defend the British homeland from German bombers, while dropping its own bombs on Germany. But people in Britain feared that German forces – only a handful of kilometres away in France –

would soon invade them, just as they'd invaded Poland, Austria, France, Belgium and the Netherlands. Hitler assured everyone around him that the British would soon be beaten.

At least Fritz was safe, for now. And Papa was staying alive, for now. But how much longer could that go on? So many prisoners were dying in Buchenwald that the SS built a crematorium inside the main camp. Its chimney pumped out smoke all the time, and the vile smell of it was always in the air.

CHAPTER ELEVEN

The New World

Kurt sat on the edge of the kitchen table, his legs dangling. Mum took a leather wallet and hung it round his neck on a string.

'Now, my darling, you have to take good care of this,' she said. 'Everything important is in here. Your identity papers, your permission papers, your travel papers and your money. Whatever happens, don't lose it.'

'No, Mum.'

The day had come for Kurt to leave for America. Mum's eyes were anxious and she fussed nervously with the wallet and string.

'You'll be good, won't you?'

'Yes, Mum.'

'I mean it, Kurt. Please behave yourself. Don't give them any reason to send you back. It breaks my heart that you're going, but I couldn't bear it if you had to come back here.'

Kurt's heart was breaking too. 'I'll be good, I promise.'

She smiled, but there were tears in her eyes. 'I got you a present,' she said, and took out a harmonica, brand new and shiny. When he blew into it, the sound was sweet and sharp, like the taste of lemonade. How she'd got the money to buy such a thing, Kurt couldn't guess. He clutched the precious gift in his hand.

Suddenly, everything vanished. The room, the table, Mum and Herta, even Kurt himself all disappeared, and there was nothing but darkness . . .

And then it was as if he fell into a dream.

Kurt opened his eyes and saw the sky, blue and shimmering through leaves and white blossoms. He was in the Prater park, in the long, long avenue under the trees.

Looking ahead, Kurt saw the rest of the family. Mum and Papa were walking arm in arm. Fritz was sauntering along with his hands in his pockets. Herta and Edith were strolling elegantly. It had been a wonderful day. They'd had a picnic, and Fritz and Kurt had lost count of the number of times they'd gone down the big slide, collecting up the mats and racing back to the start for a free go.

Trailing behind the family, Kurt was walking with one foot on the path and the other on the grass bank, up and down, up and down. He hummed to himself and didn't notice how far behind he was getting. When he looked up again, everyone had gone.

Fear clutched at his heart. He ran to the end of the avenue, where it opened on to a huge roundabout teeming with traffic. People passed by on the pavement, but Kurt didn't recognise any of them. And he didn't know how to get home.

'Are you lost?'

Kurt looked up and saw a woman smiling down at him. He didn't know what to say. Then a policeman appeared and led Kurt to the police station. He sat him on a chair in the office. All around were more policemen, busy at their desks. It was filled with the sounds of *typewriters, chatter and paper rustling, and it smelled of wood and dust and tobacco smoke.*

In his pocket Kurt had a roll of caps – a paper strip with little blobs of gunpowder on it, rolled up in a coil. All boys had rolls of caps in those days. You put them in a special toy pistol, and they made a loud bang when you pulled the trigger. One of the policemen chatted to Kurt and let him use his spare belt buckle to make the caps go bang! *He was enjoying himself so much, he hardly noticed the time going by . . . Then suddenly:*

'Kurt!' He spun round, and there were Mum and Papa. 'There you are!' Mum said.

Kurt's heart lit up with joy. He jumped up and ran into her open arms . . .

And then he woke up, staring, shaking, his heart beating fast. At first he didn't know where he was. There was a rush of noise in his ears – thumping, clattering, rushing.

He was on a train.

There were strangers all around him. Reading, snoozing, looking out of the window. The seat was one of the hard wooden benches they had in third-class carriages. How had he got here? He noticed the leather wallet on its string round his neck, and he remembered. The train was taking him to the sea, where he was going to get on a ship to America.

He couldn't remember saying goodbye to Mum and

Herta. It was as if part of him had been torn out. He was all alone in a huge, scary world filled with strangers. It was worse than being lost in the Prater. He might never see Mum or Herta again. Or Fritz or Papa or Edith or his friends.

The train was taking him a long, long way, further than he could even imagine. To get to the sea, he had to cross the whole of Austria, then Germany, then all of France, then Spain, and finally reach the city of Lisbon in the country of Portugal, which is west of Spain, with a coast on the Atlantic Ocean.

Outside, frosty February countryside went by. That was France, Kurt knew, but in his mind, Vienna seemed like the real world, and he was travelling deeper and deeper into an imaginary realm.

Crowded around him were Jewish refugees, all hoping for a better life in America. Most were grown-ups; some were old, and some were lucky families who'd come with their children. Mothers spoke softly to their kids while the fathers read or talked or dozed. Old men with hats pulled down over their eyes snored into their beards.

As the journey dragged on, they had to change trains often. Police and German soldiers herded the refugees along the platform. Sometimes Kurt found himself in luxurious first-class carriages, sometimes in second class, but more often on the hard wooden benches of third. He preferred the benches because he could sit properly. The

first-class seats had armrests which the kids had to perch on, squeezed between the grown-ups. Frustrated, Kurt climbed up on the luggage rack to sleep lying down.

At one station somewhere in France, a terrible thing happened. France had been conquered by Germany, and the Nazis controlled most of it now. Some German soldiers stopped Kurt and teased him. 'What's this?' said one, finding the gleaming harmonica in his pocket.

'That's mine,' said Kurt. 'My mum gave it to me.'

The soldier blew into it, playing a little tune.

'Can I have it back, please?' said Kurt.

The soldier smirked at him. 'This is too nice for a Jew boy. It's mine now.'

Before he could do anything, he was swept along by the crowd of refugees trying to get to their next train. In an instant the soldier and the harmonica were out of sight.

It was like a stab in the heart. Kurt pictured Mum giving the harmonica to him, and the love that had come with it, and the scrimping and saving she must have done to buy it. And now it was gone forever.

After that, the kilometres went by in a blur. France ended, then there were mountains, and then days and days of Spain going by the windows. A terrible storm had ravaged the whole country, wrecking bridges and railways. It seemed to take forever to travel across it. For Kurt it was all dozing, staring through the window, dreaming.

Kurt remembered getting lost in the Prater, the police

station and the roll of caps. Caps reminded him of his Aunt Jenni, who used to buy them for him. Kurt loved Aunt Jenni. She made dresses for a living and lived alone with her talking cat. At least, Jenni *said* it talked. It had an odd *miaow*, and when Jenni said, 'You can talk, can't you puss?' the cat went, 'Mmyeaah.'

Aunt Jenni loved animals, and hated the Vienna pigeon-catcher. There were thousands of pigeons in the city, and the catcher's job was to trap them and kill them. Jenni gave Kurt money for him and his friends to buy caps. Just as the pigeon-catcher was about to pounce with his net, the boys fired their cap-pistols – *bang! bang! bang!* – and the birds fluttered up in the air.

Those were the good old days, before Hitler came and spoiled everything and took away Kurt's friends.

On the train, there were only two other children who were travelling alone. One was a boy called Karl, a few years older than Kurt. Karl was from Vienna. He wore thick glasses and didn't seem very healthy. The other was a girl called Irmgard from Germany. Although she was Kurt's age, Irmgard was taller than either of the boys.

As train after train carried them further from their homes, Kurt, Karl and Irmgard became friends. The journey started to feel like an adventure.

At last they reached Lisbon, a city on the coast of Portugal. They'd been told that there would be dozens of other Jewish children joining them for the voyage to America. But although they waited a few weeks in Lisbon, no other children came. Eventually, Kurt and his new friends and the refugee families were taken to the docks, where their ship was ready to sail.

Its name was *Siboney*. It towered over the dockside, taller than a house, topped by smoking funnels and rows of lifeboats. Huge ropes held the ship in place, and gangways connected it to the dock. Kurt had never seen anything like it. On the side, in huge letters it said AMERICAN EXPORT LINES, with the flag of the United States of America painted beside the words.

Inside, *Siboney* was a maze of corridors and stairs. Kurt and Karl went in search of the cabin number shown

on their tickets. At last they found it, down lots of stairs –
a big bunk room in the depths of the ship's stern. It was
stuffy inside, and the noise from the engines came through
the wall.

The boys dumped their things and ran back up on
deck to watch *Siboney* set sail. The funnels belched steam,
the water churned to foam, and the horn blared out a
long blast as the ship began to move, turning slowly to
point west.

Kurt stood on deck for three hours. Lisbon shrank
until it was just a smear, then the whole coast disappeared
over the horizon, so that in all directions, there was
nothing to see but ocean waves.

Somewhere beneath that ocean, German submarines
were prowling, hunting for merchant ships carrying
supplies to Britain. That was why *Siboney* had huge
flags painted on the side – so that the submarines would
see it was American. America wasn't in the war – at
least, not yet.

Kurt was tired out, but he couldn't sleep in the hot,
noisy bunk room. The next day he started feeling seasick,
and the only food he could stand to eat was fruit. He
couldn't face another night in that cabin, so he said to
Karl, 'Why don't we sleep outside?'

'You mean, up on deck? Are we allowed?'

'Nobody'll know,' said Kurt.

There was a nurse on the ship, an American woman

called Miss Sneble, who was supposed to look after the children, but she was too busy with the elderly passengers, or too busy being seasick herself. She wouldn't notice if they sneaked out.

In the back of Kurt's mind was his mother's anxious voice: '*You'll be good, won't you? Please behave yourself.*' But his *Spitzbub* spirit didn't listen.

They crept up the stairs and out into the chilly night air. The sky was deeper and blacker than Kurt had ever seen it in Vienna, dusted with unimaginable glittering stars. It was cold, but the boys had brought their blankets. They found deckchairs and lay down, wrapped up warmly, and fell asleep under the strange new sky.

The next morning, they were woken by a dash of cold, wet spray across their faces. It wasn't sea spray, just the splashing of sailors washing the deck. Rolling up their blankets, they went back inside.

Somehow Miss Sneble found out about their little night out. 'You won't be doing *that* again!' she told them. 'From now on, you'll sleep in your cabin, do you hear?'

Kurt and Karl didn't understand a word she was saying. English was just gibberish to them. Kurt's school lessons in 'Pat-a-cake' and 'yes, no, thank you' didn't help him much. But he and Karl knew they were in trouble and nodded obediently.

There was no more sleeping in the fresh air, but in the daytime the two boys and Irmgard were free to explore the ship, playing games and making friends with the sailors.

The voyage went on for ten days. Then, at long last, *Siboney* sailed into New York harbour. All the passengers crowded on deck to watch. Kurt and Karl squeezed through to get to the rail, to see the Statue of Liberty grow from a tiny grey spike to a towering figure, proud and magnificent. The children had been given American flags, and they held them up, fluttering in the wind, as the ship sailed by Manhattan, an incredible sight, with its skyscrapers like glittering porcupine spines.

So this was America! Kurt gazed at it in wonder. He could hardly believe that he was meant to live here.

Every passenger (other than Americans returning home) had to be inspected by a doctor to see if they were bringing any diseases into the country. Then they were allowed to gather their things and walk down the gangway. Kurt clutched his suitcase in one hand and in the other held on to the leather wallet, still dangling round his neck. It was as if he was holding his mother's hand. It had brought him safely all this way. What strange new wonders were waiting for him here?

CHAPTER TWELVE

Child of Fortune

New York City was vast, towering, teeming, deafening, dazzling. Bright yellow taxis beeped and thundered angrily in the streaming traffic, battling for road space with bell-ringing trams. Kurt clutched the hand of the woman from the Aid Society as if she was a lifebelt in the river of people crowding the pavements – their skirts and overcoats, swinging umbrellas, flapping newspapers and flying cigarette ash.

Kurt had grown up in a big city, but New York was different. Super-modern cars and glass and concrete and people and people and people and still more people, always rushing.

When Kurt and his friends had come down the ship's gangway, they'd been met by the woman from the Aid Society that looked after Jewish refugees coming to

America. She was here to help the kids get to the families they would be staying with.

Kurt had to say goodbye to his new friends. Irmgard was staying here in New York and Karl was going to a faraway city called Chicago. The Aid Society woman would be taking Kurt to his new home.

He got to see the sights of New York on the way to the train station. He was amazed by the Empire State Building. In those days it was the tallest building in the world, stretching far above everything else, piercing the clouds.

The train from New York travelled north, then east. Kurt was going to a place called Massachusetts, where he'd been told he would be staying with an old friend of Mum's called Mrs Maurer.

America was a country built by immigrants like Kurt. Many had been poor people seeking better lives, and some had been refugees like him, escaping from cruel governments. The lands that the train went through had been settled long ago by people who'd made the long sea voyage here from England. Homesick, they'd named their towns after the places they'd come from – Greenwich, Stamford, Stratford, New London and Warwick were just a few of the place names that passed by the windows of Kurt's train.

At last, the train reached a place called Providence, where Kurt and the Aid Society woman disembarked.

Mrs Maurer was there to meet them. She was about Mum's age, but far more expensively dressed.

'Hello, Kurt, it's wonderful to meet you,' she said in German. 'My name is Alma Maurer.' For Kurt it was a huge relief to hear his own language again. 'There's a gentleman here I want you to meet,' said Mrs Maurer.

A man was standing with her, regarding Kurt with a rather stiff smile. 'This is Judge Samuel Barnet.'

Kurt knew the name – he was the man who had provided the precious affidavits for him, Fritz and Herta, promising to pay for their journey to America and for all their needs when they arrived. He was short and stocky, with grey hair and a large nose, bushy eyebrows and piercing eyes. At first sight, he didn't *look* like an especially kindly man. He seemed extremely serious and a little frosty.

'Judge Barnet will be looking after you,' said Mrs Maurer. 'Isn't that nice?'

There was another woman there, short and stocky like the judge. 'This is Miss Kate Barnet,' said Mrs Maurer. 'Judge Barnet's sister. She'll be helping to take care of you.'

Neither Judge Barnet nor his sister spoke any German, but Kurt understood 'hello' and their polite smiles. Kate's smile was rather warmer than her brother's.

Mrs Maurer said, 'Judge Barnet and I are trying to arrange for your sister, Herta, to come to America soon. We hope we can have all your family brought here.'

After they'd said goodbye to the Aid Society woman, Kurt, Mrs Maurer and the Barnets all squeezed into Judge Barnet's car, a beautiful, shiny American one. Leaving Providence, they drove through the Massachusetts countryside to the town of New Bedford. It was even less like Vienna than New York had been – a town of river ferries, small, smart buildings, and long avenues lined with trees and modest houses.

Judge Barnet was an important man in the town, especially in the Jewish community. But when the car drove along Rotch Street, the house it turned in at – number 91 – was not the mansion you might have expected for someone in his position. Instead, it was an ordinary detached house, almost, but not quite, identical to the others, all of which were almost, but not quite, identical to each other.

Waiting in the hallway to greet Kurt were two women who turned out to be more of the judge's sisters, Esther and Sarah. Judge Barnet's wife had died years ago, and none of his sisters had ever got married, so all four lived together in this house.

After Mrs Maurer had gone, Kurt was all alone with these strangers, who stood smiling down at him. They seemed friendly, but Kurt felt bewildered. They couldn't understand anything he said, and he couldn't understand them. They showed him his room. He'd never had a room of his own before, or even his own bed. They put his little

suitcase down and he unpacked the few things that Mum had been able to give him.

That night, Kurt slept his first proper sleep in America, a world away from everything he knew. What was happening to Mum and Herta? And to Papa and Fritz? And to Edith in England? It wrenched at his heart that they were all so far beyond his reach. It was as if he'd been blindfolded and spun round and round, and when the blindfold was gone, there was nothing familiar in sight.

The next morning, Kurt woke to find a tiny, very smartly dressed boy standing by his bed. He was about three, and he was staring at Kurt in amazement. The little boy opened his mouth to speak, and out poured a stream of English gibberish. He looked at Kurt as if he was expecting a reply. When none came, his face fell, and he burst into tears.

'Kurt won't talk to me!' the boy wailed. The Barnet sisters explained to him that Kurt didn't speak English. All Kurt knew was that there was a strange, screeching little boy in his room.

After Kurt had washed and had breakfast, they began explaining to him who everyone was. It was difficult to understand, with everyone using little bits and pieces of simple German and English. One sister, Esther, was a teacher at the high school. The little boy was David, and his father was Judge Barnet's brother, Philip. Philip and

21

his wife and children lived next door, and the two households made up one big family. David called the judge 'Uncle Sam', and the sisters were Aunt Kate, Aunt Esther and Aunt Sarah. Kurt was told that he should call them that too.

They couldn't have been nicer to him. Even Judge Barnet – Uncle Sam – was friendly, but he wasn't warm like Kurt's papa was. Kurt's new aunts were always around, and he was never alone. Even if he felt like being naughty, he wouldn't get much of a chance.

* * *

Kurt sat and gazed at the letter that had come from Mum. Months had passed since he'd last seen her or heard her voice, or been held in her arms. She'd touched this precious sheet of paper, filled it with her words, and lovingly tucked it inside the envelope to make its long journey across Europe and over the ocean to end up here, with him, in Massachusetts.

'*My beloved Kurt*,' the letter began. Mum's handwriting was so familiar, it made Kurt's heart beat faster. '*I just have some time to drop you a line. I'm so happy that you are doing fine and that you are well. I am really curious to hear about your summer holiday. I envy you; we can't go anywhere any more here. I would be so glad if I could be there with you.*'

Kurt felt the same. He longed for his mum. Looking out of the window of the hut, he saw Camp Avoda – the lake, the baseball field, the boys playing and shouting in the summer sunshine. It was a new, different world from anything he'd known before. He'd been in America for four months now, and the German words in Mum's letter were already starting to look a little strange to his eyes. He thought back on his time there so far.

Uncle Sam had quickly got Kurt started at school. He was sent to the local primary school, but because he couldn't speak English, they put him in a class of eight- and nine-year-olds, even though he was eleven now. Everyone looked at him as if he'd arrived there from outer space. They were all fascinated by 'The Boy Who Came All The Way From Germany'. Everyone knew about the war, even though America wasn't involved in the fighting. Lots of Jewish people lived in the west end of New Bedford, and they were well aware of what Hitler was doing over there in Europe.

Kurt did well in maths, so after a few weeks they moved him up a year. Then, less than a month later, he went up again, so now he was with kids his own age. By this time, he had learned just enough English to be able to do his lessons.

Kurt didn't make any friends. He didn't feel ready for that. His heart was still in Vienna, still with Fritz and the friends he'd had in the old days. He spent most of his time alone in his room, looking through magazines and comics.

One day he came home from school to find a young woman in the house, sitting chatting to the Barnet sisters.

Aunt Esther introduced her. 'Kurt, this is Ruthie. She's our niece.'

Ruthie held out her hand. 'Hello, Kurt. It's lovely to meet you. I hear you're learning English really well.'

Kurt took her hand shyly. 'Hello. I am please I meet you.'

Ruthie smiled. 'That's very good, but it should be "I am pleased *to* meet you."'

'I am pleased to meet you,' Kurt repeated.

'Perfect!'

Esther said, 'Ruthie's a teacher. She's going to come live with us. Isn't that nice?'

'I just finished college,' said Ruthie. 'I got a job teaching at the school over in Fairhaven. Tell you what, Kurt – I could help you with your English. Would you like that?'

As it turned out, Kurt liked it very much, even though he didn't have his own room any more (Ruthie had his bedroom, and Kurt had a bed in Uncle Sam's room). Each day when he came home from school, Kurt sat with Ruthie for an hour, and she helped him to get better at English. She was an excellent teacher, and he quickly grew very fond of her.

Once he could talk properly with American people and tell his story, Kurt became famous in New Bedford. He was interviewed by the local newspaper and the radio. When the time came for school to break up for the summer, they had a class photo. The teacher was so proud of Kurt that she got him to stand in front of the rest of the class, as if he were the star of the school.

The whole town seemed proud that they'd given a home to a Jewish boy who had escaped from Hitler. So why couldn't they give homes to Herta and Fritz and Mum and Papa? And to all Kurt's Jewish friends from the Karmeliter market?

The answer was that they wanted to. But not every town in America was as welcoming as New Bedford, and some people didn't want to help at all. They thought it was Germany's problem, not America's. And there were some who just didn't like Jews. Kurt didn't know it then, but many of the other Jewish children who'd come from Europe didn't have a happy time at all in America.

When the summer holiday started, Uncle Sam decided that Kurt should go away to summer camp. It was a thing that lots of American boys and girls did. Kurt would go to Camp Avoda, a special place for Jewish boys.

The only camps Kurt had ever heard of were like the one that Papa and Fritz were in. He'd heard horrible rumours about them, and he hoped Camp Avoda wouldn't be anything like that. Of course, it wasn't. If Fritz had been able to see Camp Avoda, he'd have thought it was just like the boys' camp that Stefan had read to them about in *The Road to Life*. A paradise on earth.

Camp Avoda was on the shore of a lake called Tispaquin Pond. In among the trees were big huts with bunk rooms, classrooms and art and craft workshops. In the middle of the camp was a baseball field. Kurt had the time of his life. He played baseball, did crafts, and swam in the warm, shallow waters of the lake. In Vienna he had learned to swim in the Danube Canal, with a rope tied round his waist and a friend on the bank holding the other end. At Camp Avoda, he learned to swim properly.

Before coming to the camp, he'd written to tell Mum how he was doing, and now her reply had arrived. (Uncle Sam had sent it on from New Bedford.) He sat with the letter, looking up from time to time at the lake and at the boys playing baseball, trying to believe that Camp Avoda and Vienna and Buchenwald were all part of the same world.

Mum's words and handwriting were so familiar, it made his heart ache. He continued to read:

I'm so happy that you are doing fine and that you are well. I am really curious to hear about your summer holiday. I envy you; we can't go anywhere any more here. I would be so glad if I could be there with you. Here, life is getting sadder by the day. But you are our sunshine and our child of fortune, so please write often.

Fritz and your dear Papa wrote last week. They want to hear news of you, especially Fritz.

Stay healthy. Please be obedient and be good for your Uncle Sam so that they will have good things to say about you. Be well-behaved.

Hugs and millions of kisses from Herta, who is always thinking of you. A thousand kisses from your Mum. I love you.

Kurt didn't know it, but Mum had also written to Uncle Sam. Herta's application to come to America had been refused by the American government, and Mum begged Judge Barnet to help. He was doing everything he could, but there was little hope of Herta or Fritz ever escaping.

When winter came, the war came with it. In December 1941, far, far away, at a place called Pearl Harbor, Japanese planes attacked the United States Navy. America was now at war with Japan. Hitler was Japan's friend, and since he feared and despised America, he jumped at the chance to declare war on the United States as well.

Germany had already attacked Russia, so now the three big world powers – Great Britain, the United States and the Soviet Union (as Russia's empire was called) – became the 'Grand Alliance', or just 'the Allies'. Their shared enemy was made up of the so-called Axis Powers of Germany, Italy and Japan.

It had truly become a World War. The forces of the Allies and the Axis came from all parts of the globe and were fighting on nearly every continent and every ocean. There was now no question of any more refugees getting out of Germany or Austria.

CHAPTER THIRTEEN

The Final Solution

There was a new officer in charge of Buchenwald. The flabby figure of Commandant Koch had gone, and in his place came the brutal-looking Commandant Pister.

'From now on a new wind blows in Buchenwald,' he bellowed over the loudspeakers at roll call.

It was true. The place became crueller than ever. On Pister's orders, the prisoners had to get up half an hour earlier and do exercises before roll call. There were no more letters home. Men were dying all the time. Everyone thought to themselves, *Tomorrow it could be my turn.*

Fritz and Itschkerl, as members of the building team, had a safer life than most of the other prisoners. Papa was still with the 'Singing Horses', but he was now in charge of his team. They were working in the forest, carrying logs. Papa liked being among the trees, where there was a breeze in the leaves and birds singing. 'My lads are true to me,' he said. 'We stick together.' If one was too weak or ill to work hard, the others made up for him so he wouldn't get picked on by the SS.

But it was getting harder for Jewish people to survive in concentration camps. Now that Germany was at war with almost the whole world, Adolf Hitler's hatred of Jews grew even worse. On orders from Hitler's deputy, the heads of the SS and other senior Nazis got together and talked about what to do. They came up with a plan that they called 'the Final Solution to the Jewish Question'.

The chief Nazis kept the Final Solution secret, but Jewish people everywhere began to hear terrible rumours. Fritz and Papa and their friends heard of special camps being built where Jewish people were murdered. Not like in Buchenwald, where the SS killed prisoners randomly. It was said that in the new camps Jews were killed hundreds at a time, by being shot or poisoned with gas.

There were other rumours too. The Jewish families who were still at home – the women and children and older men – were being sent away. Hundreds at a time were transported to the vast lands that Germany had conquered in Poland and Russia. It was known as the *Ostland*, which means 'East Land'. The Nazis said the Jews would have new homes in the Ostland, to make space in Germany for the Aryans. But some people suspected that that was a lie. People who went to the Ostland were never heard from again.

The number of Jewish men in Buchenwald had dwindled. Hundreds of them had died from sickness, hunger, accidents and murder, so that the survivors made up only a small fraction of all the prisoners.

Fritz was desperately worried about Papa. An SS sergeant called Greuel accused him of not driving his wagon-men hard enough. Papa was put on punishment, which meant that every Sunday he had to work and go without food. His friends in his block secretly slipped him morsels of food, but he lost weight. He'd always been thin, but now he was starting to look like a skeleton. Only Papa's bravery and spirit kept him going. He still believed that the Nazis couldn't beat him.

One evening in summer, Fritz was sitting at the table in his block. They'd finished their dinner – a small bowl of turnip soup and a piece of bread. The older men sat and talked, and Fritz, who felt too shy to join in, just listened and learned. They talked about politics a lot, and about the world. They loved to conjure up grand visions of the Nazis losing the war. They imagined what the future would be like without them, with freedom for everyone!

Fritz noticed Robert Siewert in the doorway, beckoning to him. He got up and went outside.

Robert looked very serious. 'You know I have friends who work in the camp offices?' he said.

Fritz nodded. Robert knew prisoners all over the camp. Some worked as assistants in the SS offices, some worked in the kitchens, and so on. Robert gathered valuable information from them.

Robert went on: 'One of my lads in the mail room told me there's a letter come from your mother. The SS won't let you see it, but my friend read it and told me what was in it.' Robert paused, looking grave.

'What does the letter say?' Fritz asked impatiently.

'Your mother says that she and your sister have been notified for resettlement.'

Despite the summer warmth, a horrible chill crept into Fritz's bones. 'What does that mean?' he asked.

'It means your mother and sister have been arrested. They're being sent to the Ostland.'

Fritz's heart pounded. Before Robert could stop him, he ran off between the barracks, until he reached Papa's block. Some men were hanging about outside.

Prisoners weren't allowed in any blocks other than their own, so Fritz begged them, 'Please, tell my father I need to see him!'

He waited, shaking with impatience, while one of the men went inside, calling out, 'Gustav! Your boy's here!'

After a few moments, Papa appeared. 'What is it?' he asked.

Fritz turned to Robert Siewert (who had caught up with him) and said, 'Tell my father what you told me.'

Robert repeated what was in Mum's letter. Papa's face turned pale with shock.

Nobody knew anything for sure about what went on in the vast, unknown obscurity of the Ostland, but they could guess. One thing was certain – there wouldn't be any more letters from Mum and Herta.

From that moment on, Fritz was haunted by a feeling of dread. It seemed to him that they were all doomed. Papa still had faith that they could get through this, but Fritz couldn't believe it any more.

Autumn was coming. Fritz and his workmates were helping to build a new factory on the edge of Buchenwald. Once it was finished, it would make weapons for the German army. Most of the walls had been done, and Fritz was building the openings for the huge windows. It took a lot of skill. High up on the scaffolding, the builders were well away from the SS guards. Fritz felt safer up here.

Fritz finished the brickwork and his workmate helped to raise the lintel – the heavy concrete beam across the top of the window – into place. Fritz adjusted its position, tapping it with his trowel. Satisfied, he took a moment to stretch his muscles. There was a beautiful view over the forest from up here. The leaves of the oak and beech trees were dappled with autumn colours of gold and copper.

Birds were singing. Far away he could see peaceful-looking farmlands.

'Fritz Kleinmann!' a voice called out from below.

He looked over the edge of the scaffolding. 'What is it?'

'Fritz? Come down here. Kapo wants you.'

Fritz climbed down the ladder and went looking for Robert Siewert. When he found him, Robert was wearing the same grim expression Fritz had seen before.

'Come here,' said Robert, and put his arm around Fritz's shoulders. He'd never done anything like that before. 'One of my pals saw a document in the camp office,' he said. 'It's a list of Jewish prisoners who are being sent to Auschwitz.'

The name *Auschwitz* was enough to make anyone's heart quail. It was one of the new camps, and if the stories were true, being sent there meant certain death.

'Fritz, your dad's name is on the list.'

'What? Why?'

'It's basically all the Jews still in Buchenwald. The only reason you and Itschkerl and the others aren't on it is because you're building this factory. The SS need you here.'

'But Papa does useful work!'

Robert shook his head. 'That doesn't matter. It's been decided – all Jews except for builders are going to Auschwitz.' He squeezed Fritz's shoulders. 'Fritz, be thankful. You're one of the lucky ones.'

'Lucky?! I can't be without my papa! I'll go with him!'

Robert looked at the devastated expression on Fritz's face. 'Fritz, if you want to go on living, you have to forget your father.'

Fritz pulled away, struggling to speak. 'I can't forget my papa,' he said. 'That's impossible.'

He turned and scrambled back up the ladder, up, up the scaffolding, and went back to work. Half-blinded by anger and tears, he dug his trowel into the mortar bucket, scooping and spreading, laying brick upon brick upon brick upon brick.

A few days later, all the Jewish prisoners had to

assemble in the roll-call square. They knew what to expect. It was exactly as Robert had said. An SS officer read out a list of prisoner numbers. Fritz heard his own number, 7290, and recognised some of the others. All of them were builders working on the factory.

The officer announced: 'Prisoners whose numbers have been called, return to your blocks.'

Fritz and his workmates had no choice but to walk away. Papa and four hundred others were left standing.

The officer went on, blaring out over the loudspeakers. 'The rest of you are being transferred to a different camp. Go now to Block 11.'

Block 11 had been cleared out ready for them; the prisoners who normally lived there had been moved to different blocks. The guards herded the four hundred Jewish men inside, then the door was closed.

From that moment, the doomed men weren't allowed to see any other prisoners. They could only wait for the transfer to Auschwitz to begin.

That night, Fritz was haunted by the memory of his papa standing with the others. And he couldn't stop thinking about all the time they'd spent together and the things they'd been through. The thought of being parted forever was more than Fritz could stand. He knew Robert was right. He knew he had to forget about Papa if he wanted to survive. But how could he? His fears about what had happened to Mum and Herta filled him with despair. How could he live without Papa? How could he stand by and let him be taken away?

By the next morning, Fritz had decided what he needed to do. Before roll call, he went in search of Robert Siewert.

'I need you to get my name added to the Auschwitz list,' he said.

Robert was appalled. 'You're not serious! Those men will all be killed! Gassed! I told you, you have to try to forget your father.'

'I can't. I want to be with my papa,' said Fritz. 'No matter what happens. I can't go on living without him.'

Robert argued with him, but Fritz wouldn't change his mind.

Without Robert, Fritz might have been dead long ago, so he felt guilty about throwing his life away like this. But what choice did he have? With a heavy heart, Robert gave up and went to speak to Lieutenant Schobert.

As roll call was ending, the loudspeaker bellowed: 'Prisoner 7290 to the gate!'

Fritz went to the gatehouse, where Schobert was waiting for him with his usual sneering look. Fritz explained that he needed to go with his father. Schobert shrugged. It was all the same to him – as long as Jews were sent to be disposed of, he didn't care. 'Very well. I'll tell them to add you to the list.'

And that was it. There was no turning back.

An SS guard marched him across the square to Block 11. The door opened and he was pushed inside.

The block was only meant to hold two hundred people. With four hundred inside, it was crammed to bursting. As the door slammed behind him, Fritz found himself looking into a mass of striped uniforms – standing, sitting on the few chairs, squatting on the floor. Dozens of faces turned to stare at him. One was the thin, bespectacled face of his friend and teacher, Stefan Heymann. There were other friends there, too.

As soon as they realised why Fritz was there, they pleaded with him, just like Robert had. They told him he was being crazy, that he had to save himself while he still could.

Fritz took no notice. He pushed through the crowd, searching for his papa.

And there he was, the familiar thin, lined face with those gentle eyes. Fritz and Papa threw their arms around each other and hugged, both sobbing with joy.

They were going to die. But for them it didn't matter, as long as they were together.

The next day, the doomed prisoners were marched out to the square. They were ordered to take no belongings with them. Food was handed out for their journey. Fritz and Papa had just a lump of bread each.

Even the SS were in a sombre mood. Usually they shouted abuse at prisoners being transferred. But not today. It was as if even they understood that this was different.

Outside the main gate, buses were waiting. The prisoners travelled down the Blood Road in far more comfort than they had run up it three years ago. Fritz had seen and learned so much since that day.

At Weimar train station, they were loaded into goods wagons, forty men in each.

'They're all saying it's a journey to death,' said Papa to Fritz after the wagon door had clanged shut. 'But we won't let our heads hang down, will we, Fritz? Remember, a man can only die once.'

The train groaned and began to move. They were on their way to Auschwitz, probably the last journey any of them would ever make.

CHAPTER FOURTEEN

Let's All Fight!

Kurt whipped back his fishing rod and flicked it, sending the hook and line flying out over the lake. The chilly water lapped around his knees. He was wearing rubber waders that came up to his thighs, but he could still feel the cold.

Uncle Sam was standing further out, deeper in the water, laden with a bag of fishing gear and a big net, as well as his own rod.

Kurt was happy fishing. It brought back some of his best memories of Vienna. His aunt Helene used to take him and his cousin Viktor fishing on the river Danube. Kurt loved those trips. He and Mum used to catch the tram to Aunt Helene's house, out in the suburbs. It was from Viktor that Kurt had got the bone-handled fishing knife that he'd wanted to use to protect Mum.

Kurt had been in America for well over a year now. He hadn't heard from Mum in a very long time. He hoped she and Herta were all right. In one of her last letters, Mum had mentioned those old fishing trips. '*Aunt Helene is always thinking of you when she goes fishing,*' she wrote. '*She would like to give you her wonderful fishing gear that she uses to catch trout.*'

He wished he could still write to Mum, like he had before America joined the war. He would have loved to tell her how well he was doing at school. That he could speak English, that he'd made friends, and that he was being good.

Despite doing well, he was still like a stranger here. Uncle Sam and aunts Sarah, Esther and Kate were good to him, but he missed Mum and Papa and Fritz and Herta and Edith. And deep down there was a feeling of anger that never went away – at Hitler and his Nazis and all the people who were helping them. The anger was buried, like a fire smouldering under a lid, and Kurt didn't let anybody see that it was there.

Uncle Sam reeled in his line and waded to the bank. 'That's enough for this morning,' he said. 'We've got a busy afternoon ahead of us, young Kurt! Come along!'

Kurt knew what to expect. After lunch, they both changed into their good clothes and went into town. They were going to sell war bonds.

It was costing America a vast amount of money to

fight the war. War bonds were the government's way of borrowing money to pay for all the planes and tanks and trucks and weapons. The idea was that you gave the government eighteen dollars and they gave you a war bond. Then, in ten years' time, you would give the bond back and the government would pay you twenty-five dollars for it. The more war bonds you bought, the more money you would get back later. There were posters everywhere showing an American soldier saying: BUY WAR BONDS – LET'S *ALL* FIGHT.

Judge Sam Barnet had volunteered to help sell bonds, using his high status in the community to persuade people to buy them. Kurt too had become so well known in New Bedford that he made a great helper and salesman. Uncle Sam knew all the bosses of the companies in the town, and took Kurt to their offices, factories and shops and introduced him.

'Go sell bonds!' Uncle Sam said, and he would push Kurt through the door.

When the bosses and the workers heard Kurt tell his story – how he'd had to flee to America all alone to be safe from the Nazis – they truly understood how important it was to beat Hitler and win the war. They got out their wallets and bought lots of bonds.

Most weekends and holidays, Kurt and Uncle Sam went out selling. After a while, Kurt sold so many war bonds that he was awarded a medal by the government.

As the weeks and months passed, little by little Kurt was growing more American and less Viennese. But all the while, the secret feelings of sadness and anger never went away.

Sometimes these feelings came out when he was at school. Kurt was twelve now, and had lots of good friends. Each day they got their lunch at a deli. (In America, a deli – or delicatessen – is a shop where you can buy certain kinds of nice food. Many of them sell food that Jewish people particularly like, such as special beef sandwiches and dumpling soup.) One day, as Kurt and his friends were getting their lunch, they were chatting. Something Kurt said made one of them, James, laugh and say, 'Ha! You Jews are all the same!'

Kurt's mind seemed to freeze, then catch fire. The memory of the boy Hannes pulling off his coat buttons . . . the memory of Papa and Fritz being taken . . . people screaming '*Jew-pigs! Jew-pigs!*'

Before he even knew what he was doing, Kurt punched James in the face. The deli had a big pyramid display of cans, and as James staggered backwards he fell through it with a huge crash. Cans went clattering and rolling all over the shop.

The other boys stared in amazement. Kurt was shaking with anger and shame as James sprawled among the cans, struggling to pick himself up.

The outburst had astonished even Kurt. What had he

done? What if they sent him back to Vienna? Mum had never stopped worrying that he would behave badly. '*Please, Kurt, be a good boy,*' she'd written in her last letter. '*Hopefully you are a pleasure for your uncle and aunts, and you keep your things and your bed in order and you are nice. Please do not bring shame on your Uncle Barnet and me.*'

He didn't get into too much trouble. Even James forgave him. But Kurt's feelings never went away, they just got buried even more deeply in his heart. They had to, otherwise how could he live?

Mum's last letter had ended like this:

All the kids here envy you being at summer camp. They don't even get to see a garden, only the walls of the Jewish school. You look so nice in the picture you sent, handsome and radiant. Darling, you are my only consolation.

Well, darling, I wish you all the best. Herta sends kisses. I love you – Mum.

Those were the last words he had from her. The war had cut her off from him completely. He wondered if he would ever see her or hear her voice again.

CHAPTER FIFTEEN

A Town Called Auschwitz

In one corner of the train wagon stood a bucket, which all forty men had to use as their toilet. Fritz's nostrils were never free of the stink of it. He sat in the darkness next to Papa as the long hours dragged by, their stomachs hurting with hunger. It was two days since they'd left Buchenwald.

Suddenly the train slowed and jolted to a stop. The door squealed open.

'Everyone out!'

Fritz and Papa helped each other down from the wagon, both of them in pain from being unable to move for so long. It was night time. Torches dazzled their eyes, and they could hear dogs snarling and the groans of four hundred men with stiff limbs. They were in a station rail yard, standing among the tracks. They were kept there for hours. SS men with their guard dogs prowled around them, and whenever they came near, Papa hugged Fritz to him.

At last the order was given: 'Form ranks and march!'

They'd all been thoroughly trained to obey orders in Buchenwald, and quickly fell into line. They were led over the tracks and on to the road.

Papa had been to this town before. He was born in the village of Zablocie, less than fifty kilometres away. Back then, this town had just been an ordinary place, old and rather pleasant, where people came to sell and shop at the market. In those days it had been called by its Polish name, Oświęcim. Under the Nazis, it was known by its German name – Auschwitz. When people said that name, they meant the SS concentration camp just outside the town.

Fritz didn't know it, but Papa had been to the camp before as well. As a young soldier in the last war, Papa had been wounded in battle. There had been an Austrian army base at Oświęcim, and they'd brought him to the military hospital there. That army base had now been taken over by the SS and they had made it into the main part of their concentration camp.

After a short distance, the marching prisoners reached a tall wire fence with a gate. Above it was a sign in German, *ARBEIT MACHT FREI* – meaning 'work brings freedom'. Like many things the Nazis said, it was a lie. Nobody believed it.

Inside the fence stood rows of two-storey brick buildings – far better made than anything in the main camp at Buchenwald. This was the old Austrian army base. Now it was the centre of Auschwitz concentration camp, the most cursed and terrifying place on earth.

The prisoners marched through the camp until they came to a building in the corner, where they were ordered to go inside.

'Remove your uniforms,' said an SS sergeant. 'Underwear too. Put it all over there. There will be a medical inspection, followed by showers.'

There was a nervous murmur among the prisoners. They'd heard the rumours of mass killings here, and that the chamber where they pumped in the deadly poison gas was disguised as a shower room. But with the guards pointing guns at them, they had to do as they were told.

They were inspected by a doctor, then their heads were freshly shaved and they were examined for lice. Fritz noticed a sign painted on the wall saying EINE LAUS DEIN TOD – 'One louse means your death'. After that, the first group of men were ordered to go through to the shower room.

Fritz and Papa waited anxiously with the other men, who started muttering in fear. When their turn came, would they obey, and just walk into the gas chamber?

Suddenly, a face appeared at the door, dripping wet and grinning. 'It's all right! It really is a shower!'

Relieved, Fritz and the others went through. Afterwards, their uniforms were returned, along with fresh underwear. They reeked of the chemical used to disinfect them.

They were put in Block 16A, in the middle of the camp. It was nothing like the very basic blocks in Buchenwald – it had two storeys, with its own toilets and washrooms.

The block was already full of hundreds of red-triangle prisoners. Most of them were young Polish soldiers who'd fought against the German invasion. Most of them were suspicious of the German Jews, or even hostile. Some of Fritz's friends were robbed of the few little keepsakes they had to remind them of home. When the meal was served, the Poles, led by the block kapo, who was a German green-triangle prisoner, gave the Jewish men the worst helpings, with no meat. Anyone who argued was beaten up.

Papa could still speak Polish from his childhood in Zablocie, so the Poles treated him a bit better. They told him that everything he'd heard about Auschwitz was true. The gas chambers. The mass murders. He told Fritz what he'd learned, and Fritz felt certain that their lives here would be cruel and short. But Papa refused to give up hope.

After three days, the Buchenwald men were given their prisoner numbers. In Auschwitz, your number was worn on a badge and also tattooed on your arm. Fritz's new number was 68629. It was scratched into his left forearm with a needle and coloured with blue ink. The prisoner doing the tattooing wasn't very skilled – Fritz stiffened with the pain, and the 2 and the 9 came out wonky.

Then they were taken back to the block. The SS wouldn't tell them what was going to happen to them, and their fears returned and grew.

Papa learned from the Poles that the camp they were in was only a small part of Auschwitz. A couple of kilometres away was another camp, called Auschwitz-Birkenau. It was vast, built to hold a hundred thousand prisoners. That was where most of the killing happened.

If you ever heard that you were being sent to Birkenau, it meant you were going to the gas chambers.

But here in the main camp – which was called Auschwitz I – you were far from safe. In Block 11, known as the Death Block, the SS carried out punishments and torture. In the yard was a wall they called the Black Wall, where thousands of prisoners had been shot. The Buchenwald men had only been in Auschwitz for nine days when two hundred Polish prisoners were shot there.

'Lots of scary things here,' said Papa to Fritz. 'But we have good nerves, don't we? We can stand it.'

Fritz wasn't so sure. The days passed, and still the SS didn't reveal what would happen to them. Fritz couldn't stand the suspense.

'We have to tell them we're skilled workers,' he said to Papa.

Stefan Heymann and some other friends were listening.

'Don't do that,' said Stefan. 'You know the first rule of survival – never draw attention to yourself.'

'I have to. If they know I can build, they might spare us and give us work.'

'It's too dangerous,' said Papa. 'Don't do it, Fritz.'

'If I don't, they'll kill us anyway.'

They couldn't argue with that, although Papa still tried to persuade him not to risk it. But Fritz was determined. He just couldn't stand waiting any longer. He found the SS block chief. Nervously, Fritz spoke to him.

'I'm a skilled builder,' he said. 'I'd like to be given work to do.'

The SS man stared at Fritz in surprise, and glanced at the star badge on his uniform. 'A Jewish builder?' he said. 'There's no such thing!'

'It's true, I swear.'

Fritz braced himself, expecting to be hit. But the block chief just shrugged and said, 'Follow me.'

He took Fritz to SS-Sergeant Palitzsch, who was in charge of the prisoner register. Palitzsch was handsome, with a charming smile and an air of cheerfulness. But his appearance was deceptive. Sergeant Palitzsch was the most ruthless murderer in Auschwitz. The number of prisoners he had shot was beyond count. He would whistle happily while he did it, and even his own SS commanders were wary of him. This was the man Fritz had chosen to get noticed by.

Palitzsch smiled at Fritz and said, 'Yes?'

'Sir, I'm a skilled builder,' Fritz repeated. 'I'd like to work.'

Palitzsch reacted the same way as the block chief. 'I've never heard of a Jewish builder.' He looked Fritz up and down. 'I'm intrigued. Let's put you to the test.' He said to the block chief, 'Take this prisoner away and make him build something.' He added to Fritz: 'By the way, if you're trying to fool me, you'll be shot.'

Fritz was taken to a building site nearby. The site

kapo didn't believe Fritz's story either. Hoping to make a fool of him, the kapo ordered him to build an upright section between two windows. It was a tricky task even for a good bricklayer.

Despite the danger he was in, Fritz felt completely calm. For the first time since leaving Buchenwald, he knew what to do. Taking a trowel and a brick, he set to work. His hands moved quickly, scooping up mortar and slapping it in place, shaping it with the trowel, laying down the bricks neatly. The wall rose, straight and solid. The kapo's mouth hung open in astonishment.

Fritz was brought back to Sergeant Palitzsch.

'He really can build,' said the block chief.

Palitzsch's smile turned to a scowl. He'd been hoping for an excuse to shoot another prisoner. He made a note of Fritz's number and sent him back to the block.

Nothing happened for a couple of days. Then, one morning, all the new prisoners had to parade together. As well as the four hundred men from Buchenwald, there were over a thousand Jews from camps all over Germany.

Guards surrounded them, and a group of SS officers arrived. What was about to happen was something the SS called a 'selection'. The prisoners were ordered, 'Take off all your clothes!'

In single file, the naked prisoners had to walk slowly past the officers, who looked them up and down. The one

in charge held up his clenched fist, and as each prisoner passed, he pointed his thumb left or right. Prisoners who seemed young and fit had to go to the right and wait. Those who looked old or unhealthy had to go to the left. About half were sent left. Everyone could guess what fate would be in store for them: the gas chambers.

Fritz's turn came. The officer in charge took a look at him. The thumb jerked to the right.

Waiting with the other healthy men, Fritz watched anxiously as Papa's turn came. Papa was over fifty years old now and his health had suffered badly. Hardly anyone his age managed to stay alive for long in a concentration camp. By the time his turn came, dozens of men younger than him had been sent to the left.

Fritz's heart thumped. He held his breath as the SS officer looked Papa up and down. The officer hesitated – and then the thumb pointed to the right. Papa walked over and stood beside Fritz.

By the end of the parade, over six hundred people had been sent to the left, including a hundred of Fritz and Papa's friends from Buchenwald. They were marched out of the gates.

'Going to Birkenau,' said someone.

He was right. Those men were never seen again.

Fritz thought to himself, *So this is Auschwitz. We're all doomed to death.*

But not just yet. The eight hundred men who were still alive were also ordered to march out. But instead of heading west towards Birkenau, they were marched east. The SS had work for them to do. They were setting up a new camp about seven kilometres away called Auschwitz-Monowitz, and they needed skilled builders to do it.

The prisoners crossed the river, passed the town of Oświęcim, and marched on into the countryside. They were happy that, for now, they were still living.

'Everyone admires you,' said Papa to Fritz. 'They all understand what you did. You've saved us all. I'm proud of you.'

CHAPTER SIXTEEN

The Day Will Come
When We're Free

An aeroplane flew overhead, so high that its engines sounded no louder than the buzzing of a fly. Fritz glanced up. *Imagine how free it must feel to be up there!*

'Faster! Faster!' The voice of Boplinsky, the Polish kapo, drowned out everything. 'Tempo, tempo! Faster!' That was all they ever heard from him – that and 'Five on the bum!' followed by five loud *whacks* of his cane on somebody's backside.

Fritz kept his head down, laying bricks. Boplinsky passed him by.

They'd been in Monowitz for two weeks. It was worse than anything in Buchenwald. When they arrived, the new camp was nothing but fields with a couple of basic wooden barrack blocks. They had no heating, no lights and no kitchens. Food had to be brought each day from the main Auschwitz camp, and was stone cold by the time it arrived. There were no fences, so the prisoners were surrounded by armed guards. There were no facilities for the SS yet, and the guards were always in a foul mood. They took out their anger on the prisoners.

When they first arrived, Fritz and the others were made to dig roads. It rained all the time, sticking their sodden uniforms to their skins and turning the ground to gloopy mud. During that first week, Fritz worried about Papa all the time. At his age, he wouldn't be able to survive these conditions for long.

Fritz went to the SS sergeant in charge. 'Please, sir, I'm a bricklayer.' He spoke quickly, getting his words out before the sergeant could react. 'We're from Buchenwald. Lots of us are skilled building workers.'

The sergeant stared at him, then called the kapo over. 'Find out which of these Jews are builders.'

And that was that. Most of the Buchenwald men claimed they were builders, even though they weren't. Papa was good at woodworking, so he claimed to be a carpenter. They joined in building the new barrack blocks. Fritz helped lay foundations and floors, and Papa helped put up the wooden walls.

It was all a frantic rush. The Nazis were building factories near the Monowitz camp to make fuel and chemicals for the war. The factories were called the Buna Works. The orders to build them came straight from Heinrich Himmler, who was the head of the SS and one of Hitler's most powerful henchmen. The Monowitz camp – once Fritz and the others had completed it – would house the prisoners working in the factories.

As the camp grew and was fenced in, hundreds and hundreds of new prisoners arrived. Mostly they were Jewish men who'd never been in concentration camps before. They didn't know how to survive. The terrible work, the hunger and the brutal treatment quickly wore them out. The worst thing was to be sent to labour on the building sites at the Buna Works. Every day, injured men came back on stretchers. Every day, dozens of them were sent to the Birkenau gas chambers.

Some of the transports brought old friends who'd been transferred from Buchenwald months ago to another camp called Natzweiler. Fritz heard from them that Leopold Moses had died. Remembering what a kind friend Leopold had been, Fritz grieved for him.

One by one, the men who'd come from Buchenwald with Fritz were dying, many of them good friends. The death that upset Fritz the most was of Willy Kurtz, the garden kapo who'd been so kind to the boys who worked for him.

Fritz was safe for the time being, but Papa had to use all his wits to stay alive. Each day, when the SS read out the list of the kinds of workers they needed for building the camp, Papa raised his hand and said, 'I can do that.' Putting up roofs, fitting windows, building beds, making mattresses – the list gradually changed as the days passed and the camp grew. The SS men and the kapos didn't seem too bright – they never noticed that every week Papa claimed to be an expert in some different kind of skilled work. He could turn his hand to many things, and even when he couldn't, he had an amazing ability to fake it.

Terrible rumours were heard in Monowitz about what was happening in Birkenau. All the time, transports of Jewish people arrived from countries conquered by Hitler – France, the Netherlands, Poland. The young men were brought to Monowitz to work, while the SS forced their wives, little children and grandparents straight into the gas chambers. The new young men were the saddest sight. Some were so depressed and hopeless they didn't even try to survive. Losing their families had broken them. They quickly wasted away to skin and bone, until they couldn't even stand up. Their eyes were lifeless, their spirits gone.

Another winter came, another new year. Within a few months, most of the men from Buchenwald had died from beatings or accidents. Papa and some of Fritz's friends were still alive, including Stefan Heymann. But Fritz had nobody his own age. Itschkerl and the other

Jewish boys in Robert Siewert's building team had stayed in Buchenwald.

Fritz was starting to give up hope. He was sure his friends were all going to die, every last one.

'Hold your head up high, Fritz,' Papa said. 'It's heartbreaking, I know, but these Nazi murderers will not beat us! The day will come when we're free. We still have good friends by our side.'

For the time being, their work kept them safe. Stefan worked in the camp hospital, another friend called Gustav Herzog worked in the SS office, and Papa did upholstery work for the SS. It was indoor work, and once the heating was installed, Papa was even able to keep warm.

The camp grew. The electrified fence was up, the blocks were finished, and the buildings for the SS guards were under way, with the headquarters located by the gate.

So many builders were needed for the camp and the Buna factories that, in addition to the prisoners, the SS began to bring in German civilians. Because they weren't prisoners, they were paid for their work. Fritz found himself laying bricks alongside some of them. They never spoke to the prisoners, not even to say 'hello'. Some of them acted as if the men in striped uniforms weren't even there.

One civilian bricklayer who worked next to Fritz was like that. Never a word or a look. But then, one day, the man leaned close and whispered, 'I was in Esterwegen.'

Fritz was startled, but the man just went on working as if nothing had happened. Fritz had no idea what 'Esterwegen' was, and didn't dare to ask. That evening, he asked Papa and Stefan about it.

Stefan knew. 'It was one of the first concentration camps. A lonely place on the moors. Your friend must have been a political prisoner – one of the lucky ones who were set free.'

The civilian never said another word to him, but each morning Fritz found little presents left by his mortar tub – like a piece of bread or a couple of cigarettes. Fritz's heart was warmed.

Cigarettes were valuable to him now. In those days, most people didn't know how dangerous it is to smoke. And anyway, the concentration camps were so terrible and deadly that even if Fritz had known how unhealthy smoking was, it would still have seemed trivial. It passed the time, and even if you didn't smoke, cigarettes were like money to the prisoners – you could trade them for other things.

The last three years had taught Fritz to see danger and death as part of everyday life. Sometimes it was almost as if he'd stopped caring what terrible thing might happen next. He and a friend sometimes played a risky game. 'You go and ask that guard for a cigarette,' said the friend. 'If he gives you one, you win. If he hits you, I win.'

It wouldn't take much for the game to turn deadly.

Some guards weren't nasty, and they'd hand over a cigarette if they felt sorry for you. Most of them would hit you for being cheeky. But there were some who wouldn't stop hitting you until you were lying unconscious on the ground. The trick of the game was to know which guards were which.

Papa didn't take up smoking – perhaps because he truly believed they would get through this alive. He had faith, and maybe that was why he didn't feel any need for false comforts. Fritz didn't have the same faith.

One day, Fritz was at work on the scaffolding, laying bricks and thinking about his grandfather, who had died when Fritz was little. Grandpa, whose name was Markus, had worked in a bank and considered himself rather posh. He didn't think that Jewish people should work with their hands – in his opinion, they should study and get good jobs, like he had. What would Grandpa Markus have thought if he could see Fritz now?

Just then, a friend who worked on the wagon team arrived with a load of cement. 'Hey Fritz, what's new?' he called up.

Fritz leaned over the rail. 'Oh, hi. Nothing new,' he said. 'I was just thinking about my grandfather. He used to say, "A Jew belongs in the coffee house, not on a builder's scaffolding!" Now look at me!' He laughed.

A voice roared, 'You! Jew! Come down here now!'

Fritz's heart raced. He rushed down the ladder and

found Lieutenant Schoettl glaring at him. Schoettl was the director of Monowitz, a nasty-looking brute with eyes like a snake and a face like a blob of dough. He was the type that could either pat you on the back with a friendly chuckle or kill you, depending on what mood he was in.

'What are you laughing at, Jew?'

Fritz stood to attention and took off his cap. 'Just something my grandfather said.'

'What did your grandfather say that was so funny?'

'He said that a Jew belongs in the coffee house, not on a scaffolding.'

Schoettl stared at Fritz, who hardly dared to breathe. Then the doughy face split, and Schoettl guffawed. 'Ha-ha! That's a good one! Clear off, Jew-pig,' he said, and walked away laughing.

Fritz was sweating as he climbed back up the ladder. That had been a close call.

As time passed, Fritz started to gain the trust of some of the German civilian workers, and a few even talked to him and gave him extra food. Some of them were almost as frightened of the Nazis as the prisoners were. They feared that if the building work ran out, they'd be forced into the army and sent to fight. A couple of them even admitted to Fritz that they hoped Nazi Germany would lose the war.

It was beginning to look as if that might happen. At the start of the war, Germany had seemed unbeatable.

The Nazis appeared to have the toughest soldiers and the best planes, tanks and guns, and they were some of the angriest people in the world. Angry, determined people often succeed in wars. But now they weren't doing so well. There were rumours of German forces losing battles in Russia. A worker who'd come from France told Fritz about the French Resistance – secret fighters who launched raids against the German army in their country. In North Africa, the British and American armies were beating the Nazis.

In the evenings, Fritz repeated all this news to Papa and their friends. It was encouraging to hear, but all these places seemed very far away from Auschwitz.

Fritz learned that there was a secret resistance here in the camp, too. They were like the French Resistance, but without weapons. His friend Stefan Heymann was a leading member, and another of their Buchenwald friends, Gustav Herzog, was also deeply involved.

The Auschwitz resistance couldn't fight the SS, but they could make life difficult for them, and did everything in their power to protect their fellow prisoners from harm. Men like Stefan and Gustav, who both worked in the offices, acted as spies, gathering information about the SS. They listened for news from prisoners who were transferred there from the other Auschwitz camps. Often the resistance members could warn their friends when something bad was about to happen. In the Buna factories, they performed little acts of sabotage, such as disabling vehicles or leaving a hose running in a lorry-load of cement mix. Sometimes they even planned escapes.

Construction of the Buna factories was behind schedule. This was partly because of sabotage and partly because the prisoners were too starved to be able to work hard enough. The chiefs of the SS in Berlin sent a team of officers to investigate what was going on.

They were given a tour by Lieutenant Schoettl. The visitors did not like what they saw. Only half the factories had been built, and not a single one of them was ready to start making anything. It would take months, maybe a whole year, before they could begin their vital work.

The Berlin SS officers were frowning when they arrived, and their frowns grew deeper and darker with every word Lieutenant Schoettl told them and every half-built wall they saw.

But the thing that made them most angry was that some of the kapos on the building sites were Jewish. The officers demanded to know why. Lieutenant Schoettl explained that nearly all the prisoners sent to Monowitz were Jews. The visitors scowled and said it would not do. Hitler would be outraged. They ordered Lieutenant Schoettl to do something about it – no more Jews in important jobs!

All the prisoners heard about what had happened and

were terrified. When the SS were angry about something, Jewish people usually ended up hurt or dead.

One evening at roll call, Lieutenant Schoettl got up on the podium. With him was an evil-looking officer from the main Auschwitz camp. Everyone recognised him as Captain Aumeier, the deputy commandant of Auschwitz.

Schoettl's face looked deathly serious as he announced: 'The following Jews will take one step forward.' He read out the numbers of seventeen prisoners. One of them was 68523. Fritz's blood froze. That was Papa's number.

The seventeen men took a step forward. All of them were Jewish, and all had important jobs. A few were kapos, some worked in the office and hospital, and some did skilled work for the SS, such as Papa with his upholstery.

Captain Aumeier went along the line, studying each man. He had a face like a bad-tempered goblin, with close-together eyes and a mouth with no lips. He looked at the star-shaped badges with disgust. At the end of the line, he turned to Lieutenant Schoettl.

'Get rid of them,' he ordered.

Everyone expected the seventeen men to be shot or sent to the gas chambers. But instead, a kapo appeared with scissors and began removing the men's star badges. He pulled apart the red and yellow triangles that made up each star and handed back the red one.

'You are now political prisoners,' Captain Aumeier announced. 'Red-triangle men. There are *no Jews* in

important jobs in this camp. I will not allow it. Remember that. From this moment, you men are Aryans.'

And that was that. As far as the SS were concerned, Papa and the others weren't Jewish any more. In one moment, Captain Aumeier had shown up the whole stark stupidity of Nazi ideas. If you could live happily with Jews once you'd decided to pretend they were Aryans, what was the point of hating them in the first place?

From that moment on, life for the Jewish prisoners in Monowitz changed. The seventeen new 'Aryans' weren't totally safe – they were still prisoners in a brutal camp, after all – but the SS treated them better and trusted them more. With their jobs as kapos and clerks and craftsmen, they could help make their Jewish friends' lives less hard. The strangest thing was that the SS really believed that these men weren't Jewish any more. That meant they could sometimes speak out to prevent beatings with less risk of being beaten themselves. They had slightly better food, and could stick together to protect their friends from the brutal green-triangle kapos.

Most of the seventeen 'Aryans' were also members of the resistance, which now became more active than ever. One of them was Gustav Herzog, who had worked as a journalist in Vienna before the Nazis came. Now he ran the Monowitz records office for the SS, and had dozens of prisoners working for him. Another old Buchenwald friend, Jupp Hirschberg, became kapo of the SS garage, and got to hear all kinds of news and gossip from around the Auschwitz camps.

With the resistance growing, Fritz was determined to get involved, if only they would let him. But they wouldn't. He was too young, they said. But Fritz longed to do something against the Nazis. He just had to find a way to prove himself.

CHAPTER SEVENTEEN

A Man Far From Home

The time had come for one of the most important days in Kurt's life. He'd had his thirteenth birthday, so now it was time for his bar mitzvah.

In Jewish custom, when a boy or girl reaches thirteen years old (sometimes it's twelve for girls), they become grown-ups in the eyes of their religion. This is called their bar mitzvah – or bat mitzvah for girls. In preparation, they have to attend lessons in Judaism,* study holy books for months and go to prayers. After the bar mitzvah ceremony, there's a celebration with the family and the Jewish community.

Kurt's bar mitzvah was on a Saturday, which is Shabbos. He wore a smart suit, double-breasted and very

---

* 'Judaism' is the name of the Jewish religion.

grown-up, which had been bought specially for the occasion. For the ceremony he also wore a traditional prayer shawl (called a tallit) and cap (called a yarmulke or kippah). The party afterwards was small, with his new family – Uncle Sam Barnet, aunts Kate, Sarah and Esther, Uncle Sam's brother Philip and his kids, David and little Rebecca – and their close friends. It should have been a joyous occasion, but part of Kurt was sad. The Barnets were good to him, and he had a lovely life, but they weren't his real family.

A photo was taken of Kurt, Uncle Sam and the two young children. Rebecca sat on Uncle Sam's lap, Kurt

perched on the chair arm, and David sat on the floor. Kurt had vivid memories of the family photo taken in Vienna with Mum, Papa, Fritz, Edith and Herta. He'd worn Papa's watch and sat on his knee, beaming happily. At his bar mitzvah party, his face in the photo didn't beam. He managed a smile, but it was a faint one.

Kurt had been in America for two years. He knew how lucky he was to be there, far away from the terrible things happening in Europe. People told him all the time how fortunate he was, and it was true. Lots of children hadn't been so lucky. But at the same time, it wasn't only danger that Kurt had left behind. He was also far away – achingly far – from everyone he loved.

Two years in America! He was becoming an American boy, and in the Jewish community he was becoming a man. The little *Spitzbub* from the Karmeliter market now spoke English like an American. He was even starting to forget how to speak German. Mum's letters, which he'd kept carefully, were beginning to look strange. Perhaps one day he would no longer be able to read them.

Were Fritz and Papa still in Buchenwald? Were Mum and Herta still living in the apartment? The only person Kurt knew about with certainty was Edith, because America and Britain were allies in the war. They wrote to each other from time to time. Edith was still living in Leeds. She was married now, to a man named Richard who had also moved to England to escape the Nazis.

They had two little children – a nephew and niece for Kurt.

Edith had sent Kurt a copy of a photo of Mum that she'd taken to England with her. Mum looked beautiful in it, calm and healthy, not half-starved and stressed like she'd been the last time Kurt saw her. He kept it with his copy of the family photo, and the one he'd brought with him of lovely Herta. He missed her, and knew how much she had missed him after he left. Did she still miss him? He wished he could tell her how good things were here in America. He wished she could come here and join him.

Kurt followed the news about the war, studying all the newspapers he could get his hands on, eager for every detail of what was happening. At school they had air-raid drills – an alarm would sound and the kids had to hide under their desks. But no bombs ever fell. In Leeds they'd been bombed by the Germans, and Kurt's little nephew, whose name was Peter, had been sent away to live on a farm in the countryside to be safe.

As the new year of 1943 got under way, Kurt was still busy selling war bonds, trying to help America win. From the reports in the papers, it seemed that the Allies – America, Britain and Russia – would beat Hitler in the end. But how many years would it take? Kurt tried to believe that, however long it took, he would see his family again.

CHAPTER EIGHTEEN

The Resistance

Fritz and Papa were living in different blocks again. Every evening they met up. They talked about the camp and about how the war was going, and they wondered how their family and friends were doing. Was Kurt all right in America? Was Edith still safe with German bombs falling on British cities? And they wondered about Mum and Herta. That was a dark, upsetting subject. Maybe they were still alive somewhere in the Ostland. Or maybe the terrible rumours about what happened to people who were sent there were true.

One evening, Fritz and Papa were so engrossed in their talk that they didn't notice an SS guard watching them. To him, it looked like a Jewish boy talking to an Aryan as if they were equals.

Fritz was in the middle of speaking when he was suddenly shoved so hard he nearly fell over.

'Jew-boy!' yelled the guard. 'What d'you think you're doing, talking to an Aryan like that?'

'He's my father,' said Fritz.

The SS man's fist slammed into Fritz's face. 'He has a red triangle! He can't be a Jew's father!'

Pain pulsed through Fritz's face. He'd never been punched right in the face like that. 'But he *is* my father,' he insisted.

'Liar!' The guard punched him so hard that he fell over.

Fritz was totally confused. Papa was horrified, but he couldn't do anything to help. If he tried to intervene, it could make things worse for both of them. With a Nazi this angry, being 'Aryan' wouldn't help.

'Get up, Jew,' said the guard. 'And go back to your pigsty.'

Fritz picked himself up, his face bruised and bleeding. As he started to walk away, he heard Papa say, 'He really is my son.'

The SS man stared at Papa as if he was crazy. Papa gave up arguing. He had long understood that you couldn't reason with Nazis, so there was no point in trying.

Building work on the Monowitz camp was now complete. It had barrack blocks, workshops, kitchens, a roll-call square, a small hospital block and a double electrified fence around it all. There were even grass verges and flower beds. The careful way these were looked after, in contrast with how the human beings were abused, was one of the things that drove some prisoners mad.

Fritz had helped to build all this. That was another thing that could make a person despair. Prisoners had to build their own prison, and many died doing it. It was hard to live knowing that you had helped make a place where people would suffer and die.

Every day in Monowitz was a dreary nightmare. Once a week they had showers. They had to strip in the bunk room, then run to the shower block, even in freezing weather. There were only a few towels, so only the first men to finish got dry ones. The towels quickly became soaking wet rags, which meant that most of the men had to walk back to the block dripping and shivering. Prisoners got ill, and the hospital, run by cold-hearted SS doctors, was badly equipped. Anyone who didn't get well quickly enough was sent to the gas chambers.

At dinner, there weren't enough bowls for everyone. The men who got their helping of stew or soup first had to gobble it down while the others waited impatiently for the bowl. There was no toilet paper, so they used torn-up cement bags. Newspaper was better if you could get it, and became so valuable that it could be traded for food.

If your shoes were too big or too small, you'd get

blisters, which got infected. Socks were hard to come by, so some men cut pieces off their shirts and wrapped them around their feet. If the SS caught you doing that, you'd get whipped or starved.

Every week your head was shaved. The razors were blunt, and they nicked and scratched your scalp. These cuts could get infected. Unlike the others, Fritz was too young to need his face shaved, which was a small consolation.

On top of all that, there was the constant terrifying horror of the whole Auschwitz system. The gas chambers, the murders, the beatings.

Now that Monowitz was complete, Fritz no longer had a safe job. The Buna factories were also mostly finished, so there wasn't much building work to do there either. He was in terrible danger now; soon he'd be just another prisoner, with no useful skills, who could be driven like a beast and worked to death.

His friend Stefan Heymann had other ideas, though. One day, he tapped Fritz on the arm. 'Come with me,' he said. 'I want a chat.'

Stefan led him to a quiet corner behind the blocks, where some men had gathered. Gustav Herzog was there, and a few other old Buchenwalders who Fritz knew well.

'We've got a task for you,' said Stefan.

Fritz's skin tingled. Was this going to be his chance to be in the resistance?

'You're good at making friends with the civilian workers,' said Gustav. 'They trust you.'

'I suppose so,' said Fritz.

'There are lots of civilians working in the Buna factories,' said Stefan. 'Hundreds of them. Gustav's arranged for you to be transferred to one of the factory work teams. You'll have plenty of opportunity to get to know the civilians. Chat to them, get them to trust you.'

'OK. And you want me to report to you on what they tell me?'

'Exactly,' said Gustav. 'Good lad. We want info on the SS, news from outside, that kind of thing.'

It was all arranged. Fritz was assigned to Locksmith Team 90. The next morning, after roll call, he joined the work teams going to the factories. It was the first time he'd left the camp since they'd arrived.

As they marched out through the gate, the camp orchestra played rousing tunes. The musicians were all prisoners – a Dutch political, a German Roma on violin, and the rest were Jewish. They had a little building near the gate, where they sat and played every morning. The music was meant to put the prisoners in the mood to work. Most of the tunes were Austrian marches. In the last war, when Papa was a soldier, he'd marched to these same tunes at parades in Vienna.

The prisoners crossed the main Auschwitz road to the entrance to the Buna Works. The size of the place was

breathtaking – it was a vast grid of roads and railways crammed with buildings. There were factories, workshops, chimneys, depots, chemical tanks and pipes and conveyors snaking all over the place like fairground rides. If you stood at one end of the Buna Works, you could barely see the far end, nearly three kilometres away. Thousands of men and women worked in the factories. Two thirds of them were civilians, and the rest were prisoners from Monowitz.

Locksmith Team 90 was one of the nicer work groups. The kapos were decent men who let their workers take it easy as long as no SS guards or factory managers were nearby. Fritz found himself working in one of the main factories, helping to do repairs and maintenance on locks and bolts and the like.

Stefan and Gustav were right – there were lots of German civilians working there. Fritz began his task right away. He got to know the civilian foremen who ran various parts of the factory, and soon gained their trust. Fritz was a bright, innocent-seeming boy, and the civilians appeared to like him.

There was one foreman who was particularly friendly, a man named Oskar. He took pity on Fritz, just like the man on the building site had, and secretly gave him little presents of bread and cigarettes, or sometimes a newspaper.

Oskar would stop to chat if nobody was looking. Fritz

listened eagerly to the news he brought from the outside. Things were going badly for Germany. The Russians were hammering the German army in the East. In North Africa, they'd been defeated by the British and Americans, who were now fighting them in Italy. Oskar hoped Germany would lose soon and the war would end. He also told Fritz about things happening in the area around Auschwitz. Each day, Fritz took this information back to his friends, along with the gifts of bread and newspaper to share.

The local information was important to the resistance in planning escapes. They needed to know what was going on outside in order to figure out how they might get help from Polish people.

Fritz had little idea just how big the Auschwitz resistance was. It spread across all the Auschwitz camps, including the Poles in Auschwitz I, who were in contact with the Polish resistance in the nearby countryside and cities. The groups in each camp passed messages to each other and supported each other's spying and sabotage activities.

Of all the things they did, talking to German civilians was one of the most dangerous. The Auschwitz Gestapo officers were always trying to spy on the resistance to find out who its members were and what they were up to. Fritz had to be careful in case the civilians he talked to were Gestapo spies. But he felt sure that Oskar was trustworthy.

It was a Saturday in June. At this time of year it was

still light at evening roll call. Fritz stood in place, uniform buttoned up neatly, cap on straight – then whipped off smartly when the officer in charge appeared. Everything was normal, the same as every other day.

The officer finished the roll-call and the prisoners put their caps back on. Just then, a little group of people marched noisily into the square. Nobody turned to look. That wasn't allowed. But from the corner of his eye, Fritz saw two SS guards pushing a man along. He was stumbling and staggering, the guards shoving and hitting him like they would a prisoner. But he wasn't a prisoner; he was a civilian. His face was bruised and bleeding.

As they came to the front of the square, Fritz got a clearer view. He recognised the two SS men – Sergeant Taute and Sergeant Hofer from the Auschwitz Gestapo. A little shiver of alarm passed through the ranks of prisoners at the sight of them. Sergeant Taute turned the civilian to face the prisoners. Fritz's heart froze. It was Oskar.

'Point out which prisoners you've been in contact with,' Sergeant Taute ordered him.

Oskar peered into the crowd, but Fritz was far back, well out of sight. The sergeant pushed him in among the ranks, up and down each line. Oskar looked reluctantly at each face. They came to Fritz's row. Fritz stared straight ahead, trembling, his heart thumping. Oskar stood in front of him. His bruised, bloodshot eyes looked at Fritz. His hand rose and pointed.

'This one,' he said.

Powerful hands gripped Fritz's arm and force-marched him away. Past his friends, past the horrified, helpless eyes of his papa, and out of the square.

A truck was waiting in the street between the barrack blocks. Fritz was bundled into the back. The engine revved and the truck drove out of the gate. Fritz knew this road – he'd marched along it months ago, with four hundred Buchenwalders who were now mostly dead. It led to Auschwitz I, the main camp.

The truck stopped outside the Gestapo building, which stood outside the electrified fences and next to a small underground gas chamber. Sergeant Taute and Sergeant Hofer dragged Fritz down from the truck and marched him into the building, along a corridor and through a door.

Fritz found himself in a large room. There was a table with leather straps attached to it, and hanging from the ceiling above were evil-looking hooks. Fritz had been in the camps long enough to know what these things were for.

Minutes ticked by. Fritz felt his insides churning.

Eventually an SS officer entered the room. The two sergeants snapped to attention. The officer was smart and upright, with the badge of a lieutenant on his collar. His face was intelligent and friendly, and he looked at Fritz with a gentle smile – like a kindly uncle or a nice doctor.

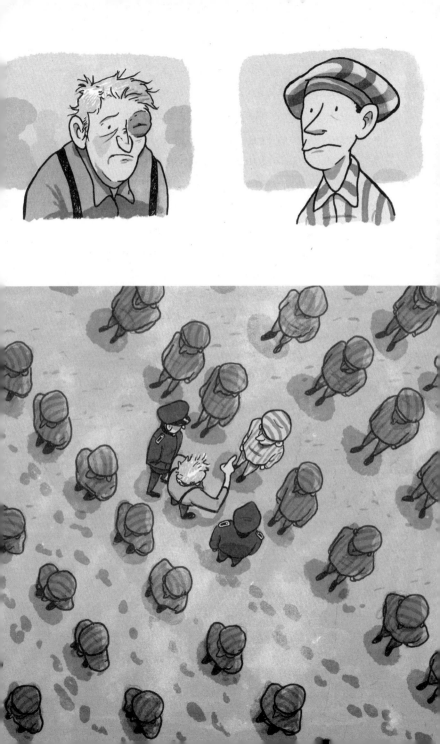

Fritz had never seen him before, but he knew his name and his reputation. He was Lieutenant Maximilian Grabner, head of the Auschwitz Gestapo, and his true nature was the exact opposite of how he appeared. Maximilian Grabner was a cold-blooded killer, with no more kindness in him than a snake. Over two thousand prisoners had been murdered on his orders. Even the other SS officers were afraid of him.

He studied Fritz's face for a moment, then said, 'Prisoner 68629, I know that you are involved in planning a major escape from the Auschwitz-Monowitz camp.'

Grabner's voice was eerily soft. He spoke with a rural Austrian accent, like the country people from around Vienna who brought their produce to sell in the Karmeliter market.

He went on: 'Sergeant Taute's men have been keeping an eye on that civilian you've been conspiring with. Isn't that right, Sergeant?'

'Yes, sir,' said Taute. 'I thought he was up to something.'

Grabner stared into Fritz's eyes. 'What do you have to say about that?'

Fritz didn't know what to say. He didn't know anything about any escape plan. Of course he knew that was the purpose of his mission, but there was no actual escape plan yet. Or was there? Would Stefan and Gustav have told him if there was?

Grabner took out a notebook and pencil. 'You will

now give me the names of all the prisoners involved in this plot.'

The faces of Stefan and Gustav and the others swam through Fritz's head. He tried not to think about them. He kept his mouth firmly shut.

'Well?' said Grabner, his pencil poised ready to write.

When Fritz said nothing, Grabner nodded to the sergeants. Taute hit Fritz with his club, knocking the breath out of him.

'Feeling shy, son?' said Grabner. 'My chaps will help you find your voice.'

Taute and Hofer grabbed Fritz's arms, bent him face down over the table and caned him. It was exactly like the Horse in Buchenwald. 'Confess what you've done,' Grabner said. 'Give me the names of the prisoners you were planning to help escape.'

Fritz still kept his mouth shut. Again the cane whooshed through the air.

By the time the caning stopped, Fritz could hardly stand, he was in so much pain.

'Tell me the names,' Grabner repeated.

Fritz knew he wouldn't be able to stand this much longer. He knew they wouldn't stop hurting him. And he knew that eventually the agony would get so bad that he would say anything to make it stop. All he had to do was name his friends in the resistance. The Gestapo would torture them and kill them. But they would let Fritz go – wouldn't they?

No, they wouldn't, and Fritz knew it. The Gestapo would kill him along with his friends.

He kept his mouth shut.

The torment carried on. They tied Fritz's wrists together and hung him up from the hooks. 'Give me the names,' Grabner repeated in his soft voice, over and over again.

As the ordeal went on and Fritz still wouldn't talk, Grabner's voice began to get impatient and lost its softness. It was Saturday night, and he wanted to get home for the weekend. At last, the sergeants let the rope go, and Fritz dropped to the floor.

'Take him back to the camp,' said Grabner. 'We'll continue on Monday.'

CHAPTER NINETEEN

A Trusted Friend

Fritz was in a terrible state when they drove him back to Monowitz. They dumped him in the camp street. 'We won't forget you,' said Sergeant Taute. 'Monday morning we're taking you back, and you'd better have more to say for yourself.'

With that, Fritz was left to get himself back to his block.

Two of his old Buchenwald friends, Fred and Max, found him struggling to pick himself up off the ground. They lifted him and carried him between them.

Gustav Herzog appeared. He took one look at Fritz and said, 'Take him to the hospital. I'll go and find Stefan.'

The hospital was a little group of wooden buildings in the corner of the camp. The SS doctor in charge was hardly ever there. The staff were mostly prisoners. Fred and Max carried Fritz to the medical ward, and a prisoner doctor came to examine him. Fritz's back was bruised and bleeding, and his whole body was in terrible pain. The doctor gave him some painkillers and massaged his numb arms.

After a while, Gustav Herzog came in with Stefan and another friend, Erich, who was also in the resistance. (Fritz's papa wasn't told; Stefan and the others thought it safest to keep him out of it, at least until they knew what had happened.) They stood looking at Fritz with pity and worry. As soon as the doctor had gone, Stefan asked what the Gestapo had wanted with him.

'They took me to Grabner,' said Fritz. It was a struggle to even speak.

'Why?' asked Gustav.

'He thinks there's an escape being planned. A big escape. He thinks I know about it.'

The resistance men looked at each other in alarm. 'Did you tell him anything?' asked Stefan.

'Of course not. I don't know anything.'

Stefan wasn't satisfied. 'You know the resistance. You know our names. Did you tell him *anything*?'

Fritz shook his head.

Despite the state Fritz was in, his friends kept on questioning him. They were suspicious of the fact that Grabner had sent him back to Monowitz. Normally he'd have been put in a cell in Auschwitz I. They wondered if

Fritz had betrayed them and been sent back here to spy on them.

Eventually they were convinced that Fritz was telling the truth. But they were still worried. 'Grabner won't let it lie,' said Erich.

Stefan agreed. 'He'll take you back there, Fritz, and keep on at you until you either talk or die.'

Erich added, 'If you do talk they'll kill you afterwards anyway.' Then he put his hand on Fritz's shoulder and said more gently, 'But you will talk in the end. Everyone does.'

'We've got to do something,' said Gustav Herzog. 'We can't let Grabner take Fritz back.'

They moved Fritz to the ward where patients with infectious diseases were kept. The SS doctor almost never set foot in there. Fritz would be safe for the time being, as long as he didn't catch anything.

But that wouldn't be enough. It was impossible to hide Fritz for more than a night. They couldn't put his name in the hospital register because the Gestapo could use that to find him. But if his name wasn't in the hospital register, they'd raise the alarm when he didn't show up at roll call the next morning. (It was impossible for someone else to answer 'present' for him at roll call because the block kapos and SS guards did headcounts, and whenever the numbers didn't add up there was always a thorough search.)

Stefan, Gustav and Erich racked their brains, but there was no other way around it.

'There's only one solution,' said Stefan. 'Fritz has to die.'

'What?' Fritz stared at him in alarm.

'We write in the register that you died. Then we hide you somehow.'

Gustav Herzog made sure that 'Fritz Israel Kleinmann, 68629' was written in the hospital register and that the entry was marked to show that he'd died. Then, as head clerk of the camp records office, he recorded Fritz's death in his prisoner file. Fritz was moved to a room away from the other patients so that he could begin to recover from his injuries. Whenever the SS doctor made an inspection, Fritz would be helped out of his bed and hidden in a storeroom.

It was all kept a total secret. Other than Gustav, Stefan and Erich, nobody outside the hospital was allowed to know that Fritz was still alive. It was too dangerous. Not even his father could know. That was the hardest thing of all for Fritz, having to let Papa believe that he was dead.

Papa was devastated by the news. With Fritz dead, the hope that had kept him going through all these years of suffering was gone. He and Fritz had been inseparable, living for each other.

Now he was all alone. He was nobody's Papa any longer.

* * *

Three weeks went by. Gradually Fritz got better. The resistance discovered that Lieutenant Grabner, believing Fritz to be dead, had given up his investigation. It was time for Stefan and the others to come up with a new plan – Fritz couldn't hide in the hospital forever. He needed a new identity.

Finding him one wasn't difficult, but it was a sad and terrible thing. Fritz's friends gave him the name and number of one of the Jewish prisoners who'd died in the hospital that day from typhus. They wrote in the hospital register that, rather than dying, the man had got better, and Fritz was given the dead man's jacket with its numbered badge. It was a terrible thing to do, to take a fellow prisoner's identity like that. Fritz and his friends felt bad about it, but it had to be done if Fritz was to survive.

There was some danger in pretending to be someone else, but not very much. To the SS, the ordinary prisoners were nameless and faceless. As long as Fritz answered to the other man's number at roll call and wore his jacket, there were no guards who would recognise him as Fritz Kleinmann. He just had to hope he didn't bump into the Gestapo sergeants who'd tortured him, and that nobody checked the number tattooed on his arm. There was no way to change that, so he put a bandage over it and hoped for the best.

Before Fritz left the hospital, Stefan spent hours with him discussing all the precautions he'd have to take, such as keeping his face hidden whenever he could, and not speaking unless he had to. Stefan found him a place in a new block where the prisoner in charge was a member of the resistance. Fritz was also given a new work placement in a different part of the Locksmith Team.

Since the early days at Buchenwald, Fritz had trusted Stefan with his life, and during his weeks in the hospital the trust between them had grown deeper. Even so, Fritz was afraid when he ventured out of the hospital for the first time. But he followed Stefan's rules, and nobody noticed him. At roll call and on the march to the Buna factories, he kept away from people he knew. His new kapo at work, a man named Paul, was also in the resistance and helped protect his secret.

There was no question of Fritz being involved in the resistance any more. His dream of resisting the SS had given him hope and energy, and now, with that gone, he grew depressed. Having to hide himself like this sucked away his spirit. There no longer seemed to be any hope for him.

* * *

One evening, Papa was sitting in the common room of his block when Gustav Herzog came looking for him. 'Follow me,' he said.

Gustav was excited, and he had an air of mystery about him. He led Papa between the blocks to the shower building. The bathing attendant was standing in the shadows of the doorway. Papa recognised him as a friend of Fritz's named David Plaut. Glancing around to see that no guards were about, David beckoned to Papa and Gustav to come inside.

The building had a damp, musty smell. Papa looked around, wondering what was going on. Then, from the door of the boiler room, a small, skinny figure with a familiar outline stepped forward. As he came closer, dim light fell on his face.

Papa couldn't believe his eyes. 'Fritz?'

'It's me, Papa.'

Papa had always lived in hope, but this was incredible, beyond anything he could have imagined. To have come back to life! How was it possible? Papa hugged his boy to him, and hope was kindled again for them both.

After that evening, they met up whenever they could, always secretly in the shower building. Ever since Papa was 'Aryanised', it had been risky for them to be together, but Fritz's new situation made it even more dangerous. Now that he knew Fritz was alive, Papa was terribly worried about him. Although Gustav Herzog and Stefan were doing everything they could to keep him out of danger, it might not be enough.

But the months passed and Fritz's secret stayed safe. Then, as autumn was turning to winter, good news came from the main Auschwitz camp: Lieutenant Grabner had been fired from his job as Gestapo chief. He'd been caught thieving. There were whole buildings in Birkenau filled with all the clothes and luggage and belongings that had been stolen from the Jews who had been gassed. Grabner had been taking gold, jewels and other valuables for himself, and the SS had caught him. The commandant of Auschwitz had been involved in Grabner's stealing and was fired too. So had some of Grabner's henchmen.

Around the same time, a mysterious fire broke out in the Gestapo offices, destroying the evidence of Grabner's crimes as well as all the details of his investigations.

For Fritz, this meant that the worst of the danger was gone. There was no need for him to pretend to be a different person any more. Quietly, the camp records were altered by the resistance, and Fritz Kleinmann, 68629, came back to life.

Papa pulled strings to have Fritz moved to his block so that they could spend time together in safety.

Winter was coming again – their fifth since being taken from their home in 1939. They'd been through many horrible experiences since then, and they'd seen things that should never exist outside of nightmares.

But neither Papa nor Fritz knew that they had still not seen the worst. That was still to come.

* * *

For the time being, each day in Auschwitz-Monowitz passed in the same awful way. Each morning, Fritz was torn from his dreams by the screeching of the kapos' whistles. He woke to the stench of three hundred unwashed men and their musty, sweaty uniforms. The men on coffee duty got up first, while Fritz tried to lose himself again in his dreams.

An hour later he was woken a second time by the bunk-room lights turning on. 'All up! Up, up, up!'

Instantly, the bunks sprouted legs, arms and bleary faces clambering down, treading on each other, struggling into their damp uniforms. Fritz and Papa pulled their straw-stuffed mattresses down and shook them, then laid them back with their blankets folded neatly on top.

After washing their faces in cold water, they cleaned their shoes with greasy polish from a barrel, then lined up in the bunk room for their acorn coffee. They had to drink it standing up, as sitting on the bunks wasn't allowed during the daytime.

At quarter to six, they trooped outside in the darkness and stood in rows in front of the block. Along the street, five thousand other prisoners were filing out of their blocks and doing the same. The block kapos counted to check they were all present. Even men who'd died in the night had to be accounted for. Most mornings there were a few, and they were counted along with the rest of the prisoners.

Once that was done, the prisoners marched along the street and turned smartly into the roll-call square, which was lit by floodlights.

They got into formation while SS block chiefs prowled up and down, looking for untidy rows and counting the men. If they saw anything they didn't like, or if anyone was missing, somebody would get a beating. When the block chiefs were satisfied, they reported to the officer in charge, who was standing on the podium, and went through the register.

By the time Lieutenant Schoettl arrived to double-check the register, the prisoners had been standing to attention for an hour. 'Caps off!' yelled a sergeant's voice over the loudspeakers as Schoettl appeared. Five thousand hands whipped off five thousand caps and tucked them under their arms. Now they stood and waited for Schoettl to go through all the numbers on the register, the reports from the block chiefs, the count of deaths and the reports of new prisoners arriving.

It seemed to drag on forever, while drizzle fell and the cold ate into Fritz's bones.

At last the loudspeakers barked, 'Caps on! Work teams, move!'

Fritz and Papa split up, heading for their teams. Then they all marched out through the gate while the orchestra played a thumping, cheerful tune.

The sky was getting light when they reached the factories. Depending on which factory they worked in, some of them still had as much as four kilometres left to march. Then they would work for twelve hours, followed by the long march back to camp, and more hours of roll call in the rainy evening darkness. Day after day, the same routine. It only stopped when you died, which could happen at any moment. Sometimes you could tell which ones would be next – the ones who'd lost all hope, their eyes lifeless, staring blankly at nothing. But not always. Anyone who annoyed an SS guard or had an accident could be killed.

Fritz went to the warehouse where he worked, for another dull but reasonably safe day of moving boxes around. He didn't know that today, something was about to happen which would change everything.

As Fritz was chatting to another Jewish prisoner, one of the civilian workers who happened to be nearby said, 'It's nice to hear people speaking German.'

Fritz and his friend looked round. The civilian was a welder, working on some metal shelves. Fritz hadn't seen him before. He was younger than most of the civilian workers.

The man said, 'I haven't met many Germans since I came to work here. Most of you lot are Poles or other foreigners.' He pointed at their camp uniforms. 'What are you in for?' he asked.

Fritz said, 'What do you mean?'

'What crime are you in here for? If you don't mind me asking.'

'Crime?' said Fritz. 'We're Jews.'

'OK, but what crime did you commit?'

'We didn't commit any crime. We're Jews, that's all. The Nazis put all Jews in camps.'

The man didn't believe Fritz. 'Mr Hitler would never lock up anyone who hasn't done anything wrong.'

'This is Auschwitz concentration camp,' said Fritz. 'Do you know what Auschwitz is?'

The man shrugged. 'I've been in the army, fighting the Russians. I don't know what's been going on at home.' Fritz had noticed that the man moved stiffly, as if he had a disability. He must have been badly wounded, and been transferred to a civilian job.

Pointing to his badge, Fritz said, 'This is the Jewish star.'

'I know what it is,' said the man. 'But they don't put you in a camp just for that!'

Fritz couldn't believe his ears. 'Of course they do!'

It was dangerous to argue with a German civilian, but Fritz couldn't help himself. How could someone be so ignorant? The man stared at Fritz, at his shaved head, his youth and his half-starved body. Then he limped away and went back to work. But he was obviously troubled by what Fritz had said. Later that day, he came and spoke to him again.

'Look, we've all got to pull together, haven't we?' the man said. 'We've got to defend Germany and work for the common good. Even you lot, the Jews, you've got a part to play.'

Fritz bit his tongue, seething inside, while the man went on and on about duty and patriotism and the good of Germany.

At last Fritz couldn't stand it any longer. 'Can't you see what's happening here?' he said angrily. 'This is Auschwitz! Look at it!'

Still the man didn't understand. He kept coming up to Fritz and saying the same things about duty and Germany. But Fritz noticed that he sounded a bit less sure of himself. Eventually he left Fritz alone.

For a few days, the man went about his work without saying anything. Then one morning, as he was passing Fritz, he quietly handed him a chunk of bread and a big piece of sausage. Then he walked off without saying a word.

Fritz smelled the bread. It was half a loaf of Wecken, a special type of Austrian bread. Fritz tore off a piece and put it in his mouth, closing his eyes in bliss. He hadn't tasted Wecken since the old days in Vienna. It was delicious, a taste of home. It brought back memories of the bread and cakes the baker used to hand out to him and his friends at the end of the day.

Tucking the sausage and the rest of the bread inside his uniform, he looked forward to sharing it with Papa and Stefan and his other friends. Later that day, the man limped by again and stopped.

'There aren't many Germans here,' he said. 'It's nice to have someone to talk to.'

'I suppose so,' said Fritz.

The man hesitated. 'I saw something this morning on my way to work, when I went past your camp over the road.' The man described what he'd seen. A prisoner who'd lost all hope had run into the electric fence, and his dead body was still hanging there. 'The SS guards told me he'd done it on purpose.'

Fritz nodded. 'That happens pretty often. The SS leave them on show for a few days to frighten the rest of us.'

The man looked angry and scrunched his mouth as if he was trying not to cry. There were tears in his eyes. 'This is not what I fought for,' he said. 'Not this. I want nothing to do with it.'

Fritz was amazed. Here was a German ex-soldier, a man who used to wear the Nazi uniform and salute Adolf Hitler, in tears over a dead concentration camp prisoner.

The man told Fritz his story. His name was Alfred Wocher. He'd been a sergeant in the army and had won a medal for fighting the Russians. He was still a soldier, but his injury was so bad he'd never have to go back to war. They needed welders at the Buna factories, so he'd been sent here. Alfred's wife lived in Vienna – she'd sent him the Wecken bread.

Fritz didn't tell him that he was from Vienna too. Now that Alfred had begun to be friendly, Fritz wasn't sure whether to trust him. If he *was* trustworthy, he'd be an excellent contact for the resistance. Even after what had happened with Oskar and the Gestapo, Fritz still wanted to help the resistance in their struggle against the SS. He decided to ask Stefan for advice.

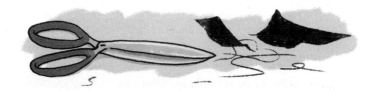

CHAPTER TWENTY

Fighting Back

'He could be an informer,' said Stefan. 'He could be spying for the Gestapo.'

'I know, Stefan,' said Fritz. 'But he might not be.'

'You can't trust the Germans, Fritz. And this one's a soldier, for goodness' sake. A *Nazi soldier*.'

'Ex-soldier. I think he's genuine.'

Stefan shook his head. 'You always go your own way, Fritz. It makes no difference what I say, does it? You should do what you think is right.'

A couple of days later, Alfred Wocher mentioned to Fritz that he had some days of holiday time coming up. He was going to Vienna to visit his wife.

Fritz thought of Vienna with longing. There were people there who knew him. A few relatives who weren't Jewish, a few friends of his parents who'd stayed loyal when the Nazis came, like Olga from the market. A part of Fritz even hoped that Mum and Herta might still be there. What if he gave Alfred a message to deliver to Olga or one of his relatives?

It would be dangerous. If Alfred was with the Gestapo, he'd give the message and the addresses to them.

Fritz had an idea to test him. Making sure nobody was nearby, he asked, 'Will you be passing through Prague or Brno on your way to Vienna?'

Alfred nodded. 'Yes, both of them. Why?'

'Could you deliver some letters to my family? One in Brno, one in Prague?'

'Yes, of course. I'd be happy to.'

Fritz came to work the next day with two envelopes. He'd written made-up names and addresses on them. If Alfred was a spy, he'd hand them over to the Gestapo and pretend to Fritz that he'd delivered them.

Alfred put the envelopes in his pocket. 'I'll deliver them by hand. The postal service is full of spies.'

'Thank you,' said Fritz.

A few days later, when Alfred came back to work after his short holiday, he was furious. He'd tried to deliver both letters, but couldn't find the addresses. He'd walked and walked and asked people, but the addresses didn't exist.

'Were you trying to make a fool of me?' he demanded. 'What for?'

Fritz hung his head. 'I'm sorry. I don't know why I did it. I'm really sorry, Alfred.' He kept on apologising, but inside he was delighted and relieved. He knew now that Alfred wasn't a spy.

Eventually Alfred forgave him. Now that they could trust each other, Fritz began to tell him more about what Auschwitz was really like.

He described how thousands of Jewish people were transported there from countries the Nazis had conquered – Poland, France, the Netherlands, Russia. He described the selections in Birkenau, how children, the elderly, unhealthy people and most of the women were sent to the gas chambers, while the others became slaves.

Alfred had seen the long trains of closed wagons passing near Monowitz on their way to Birkenau. Now he understood what they were. He was beginning to realise how ignorant he'd been.

It was hard to miss what was going on. Like a cancer, Auschwitz was spreading and growing. It had dozens of camps. Monowitz had become the centre of its own network of smaller sub-camps, which were springing up all over the countryside like sores, filled with prisoners taken from the Birkenau selections. Monowitz now had its own commandant, more powerful than Lieutenant Schoettl. Commandant Heinrich Schwarz was a fanatical Nazi who hated Jews as fiercely as any Nazi could. He loved to see the trains pass through, knowing that they were heading for the gas chambers.

Sometimes the selections happened right by Monowitz, beside the train tracks. Hundreds of bewildered people got down from the wagons, laden with luggage, thinking they were coming to new homes and a new life. The healthy men were sent into the camp, still carrying their belongings. Their families were loaded back on the train and went on to Birkenau.

Fritz watched those men go through the same ordeal that he and Papa had endured in Buchenwald. They were robbed of their belongings, stripped and shaved and put in uniforms. Some of the men were from Vienna. They'd been sent to ghettos in the Ostland, then brought here. (A ghetto was a part of a town that was fenced off and made into a kind of prison camp for Jewish people to live in.) Fritz begged them for news of home, but they had little to tell. He learned that virtually all the Jews had gone from the city now. The Nazis had begun picking on people who were half Jewish or a quarter Jewish. Nobody knew anything about Fritz's own relatives.

Christmas was coming. When Alfred announced that he was going to Vienna again for the holiday, Fritz jumped at the chance to find out what was happening there. He gave Alfred the names of some of his and Papa's loyal non-Jewish friends. Fritz also wrote a letter to Mum. He couldn't let go of the hope that she and Herta were still alive in Vienna. Perhaps they'd returned from the Ostland, or had never actually gone there in the end. He gave the letter to Alfred, addressed to 11 Island Street, apartment 16, their old home.

Fritz waited anxiously as the days dragged by. Christmas in Auschwitz was no different from any other day. The Jewish festival of Hanukkah, which often happens at the same time as Christmas, also passed by with no change in routine. Religious prisoners did what they could to observe the holidays, holding little secret services in their blocks. Fritz didn't take part. Papa still held on to his faith, but Fritz could no longer believe in a God who loved Jewish people. Whether you believed in God or not, the days came and went in the same horrible way.

At last, the holidays were over and Alfred returned to work. He brought news that lifted Fritz's spirits but also broke his heart.

Alfred had gone to Island Street and climbed the stairs to the old apartment. There was nobody there. He knocked on some of the other doors and eventually found Karl Novacek, an old friend of Papa's who hadn't sided with the Nazis. He was overjoyed when Alfred told him that Fritz and his father were still alive.

Karl took Alfred to meet Olga, who lived in the building next door. Olga told another loyal friend, Franz. They were all delighted to hear the news about Fritz and

Papa. Right away, they hurried across to the Karmeliter market and returned with baskets of food for Alfred to take back to Auschwitz. Fritz's cousin Lintschi – who had become non-Jewish by marriage – donated food as well. She wrote a letter to Fritz and Papa, enclosing photos of her children. Olga wrote Papa a letter too. She'd always been very fond of him.

When Alfred left Vienna, he was weighed down with gifts. Back at Auschwitz, he smuggled the letters and packages of food into the factory and passed them secretly to Fritz. Fritz was deeply grateful for the kindness of their old friends, and of his new friend, Alfred.

But Alfred also had terrible news. Everyone he'd spoken to had said the same thing – Fritz's mother and sister had been sent away to the Ostland with thousands of other Jewish people. Nobody had seen or heard of any of them since. Fritz's letter came back unopened. Some of his other relatives had also been sent away. His aunt Jenni, the animal lover with the talking cat, was one of them.

Fritz was bitterly disappointed, but he still clung to the faint hope that Mum and Herta might be alive somewhere in the Ostland.

He hid the food inside his uniform and smuggled it into the camp to share with Papa and their friends. There was plenty to go round, and it was luxurious compared with what the SS gave them.

Papa was thrilled to read the letters, especially the one from Olga. Other than his family, 'Olly' was one of the dearest people in the world to him. Despite the news about Mum and Herta, he wouldn't give up hope. And it gave him joy to know that he could write to people he loved.

When Fritz told his resistance friends what had happened, they weren't at all happy. 'It was a foolish thing to do,' said Gustav Herzog. 'You put yourself and all of us in danger.'

Fritz disagreed. 'I trust Alfred. He's a good man.'

'It was too much of a risk,' said Stefan. 'You cannot trust a German. Not ever. You shouldn't have anything more to do with him.'

Fritz looked up to Stefan. He knew what he was talking about, and Fritz owed him his life. But Fritz longed for his family and the old world as it had been before Hitler ruined it. His yearning was as deep and wide as an ocean, its waves crashing against his heart.

Right away, Papa wrote back to Olga. He told her how thankful he was to her and their other friends. He wrote:

The years have been hard to me and Fritz. Being in touch with you and your dear ones makes up for what I have been missing. For two and a half years I have had no news about my family. But I'm not letting my hair turn grey over it, because some day I will be reunited with them. Dear Olly, I am still the same old Gustav, and intend to stay that way. With the fondest wishes and kisses, your Gustav and Fritz.

Fritz took the letter and gave it to Alfred, who saved it for his next visit home.

Word quickly spread among his closest friends that Fritz had a way to send messages to Vienna. Soon Alfred had a little pile of letters, mostly from Jewish men who had Aryan wives at home. He faithfully delivered each one and brought back replies from the astonished, delighted families.

All the while, Alfred showed no sign of betraying Fritz or any of them to the Gestapo.

* * *

As spring turned to summer, Auschwitz began to change, getting worse by the day. Until this time, the trains packed with Jewish people had unloaded in the open area in front of Birkenau. But now the trains came in such numbers that the SS built tracks right in through the gates, and a long platform for unloading inside the camp. People who failed the selection were herded straight from the platform into the gas chambers.

These new arrivals were nearly all Hungarian Jews.

The country of Hungary had been an ally of Nazi Germany. But Hitler and the leader of Hungary had fallen out, and without warning, Hitler sent his armies to take over the country, just as he had taken over Austria six years earlier. There were hundreds of thousands of Jewish people in Hungary, and they all suddenly came under Nazi rule. The SS rounded them up and put them on trains to Auschwitz. Most of them had no idea what the Nazis would do with them – and those who'd heard rumours couldn't believe that anything so terrible could be real. And so they walked, unsuspecting, into the 'shower rooms' that pumped in deadly gas.

There were so many victims that the gas chambers were running twenty-four hours a day. The smoke from the crematorium chimneys drifted all over Auschwitz and the surrounding countryside.

Those men and women who passed the selections were either kept in Birkenau or sent to other Auschwitz camps to work. Thousands of them came to Monowitz, which was becoming extremely overcrowded.

Fritz and Papa felt sorry for the Hungarians. Many of them already had the familiar look of despair, their eyes hollow and blank. Fritz guessed that most of them wouldn't survive for long. What made it so hard to bear was that there was nothing he or anyone else could do to help them. With such a vast, never-ending multitude, there was no hope of teaching them the usual tricks of scavenging and scheming for an extra bit of bread or soup. Most of them couldn't speak German, which added to their bewilderment and fear.

Life was very different for Fritz now. Papa was running an upholstery workshop at the Buna factories, and Fritz had been transferred to work for him. Once again Fritz was learning his father's trade – the training that had been halted by the Nazis invading Vienna.

But they still weren't safe. Nobody could ever be truly safe in Auschwitz. In February, Papa had caught one of the terrible, deadly diseases known in Auschwitz simply as 'fever' and had been in the hospital for over a week. He got better just before an inspection by the SS doctor. If he'd taken a few days longer to get well, he'd have been sent to the Birkenau gas chambers.

Now that Papa was based in the Buna factories, he got to meet Alfred Wocher at last. He liked Alfred right away. 'He's all right,' Papa said. 'The man is anything but a Nazi.'

Papa's workshop changed suddenly that summer. Instead of upholstery, they were switched to making special curtains. The whole of Auschwitz was now in blackout mode, which meant that no lights could be shown at night. Lights could be seen by enemy bombers, so special thick black curtains had to be made for every window. Every officer's house, every factory, every office building had to have them. Fritz worked helping to install the curtains in the factories and offices. Papa's team was increased to twenty-four people, mostly Jewish women. Their sewing machines rattled and whirred all day long, stitching the black material.

There was no doubt now that Germany was losing the war. Allied planes were bombing German cities and factories to bits. On 6 June 1944, the long-awaited 'D-Day' happened, with British, American and Canadian troops landing on the beaches of German-occupied France. In Italy, too, German forces were slowly being beaten, and further east, vast Russian armies were pushing the Germans back. In his hideout, Adolf Hitler raged, insisting that he would turn the tables any day now and win the war. Everywhere, his armies fought furiously, determined to make the Allies pay with blood for every kilometre they advanced.

Two of Papa's workers, young Hungarian brothers called Jeno and Laczi, thought up a clever plan to get extra food for them and their friends, to top up the starvation rations the SS provided. Jeno and Laczi were tailors, and they thought the black curtain material would make excellent raincoats, which they could trade to the civilian workers in exchange for food. They had worked out that they could make the coats from spare bits of cloth so that their German bosses wouldn't notice it was being used up. They suggested the idea to Fritz, and Papa agreed to let them try.

Jeno and Laczi's coats were excellent. Two Polish women from the workshop next door smuggled the coats out and sold them to other workers. The price per coat was one kilo of bacon or half a bottle of alcohol (which could be swapped elsewhere for food).

The coats became so popular that even some of the German engineers and bosses wanted them. Soon Jeno and Laczi were making as many as six coats a day. The food for which they were traded was more precious than gold.

Fritz and his friends also received small gifts of food from Polish workers and German civilians. Many Germans working in the factories were disgusted by the way the SS behaved and by the destruction Hitler had brought upon Germany. They did what little they could to help the victims.

The circle of kindness was completed by British prisoners of war. There was a prison camp nearby full of captured British soldiers. These British prisoners of war were forced to work in the Buna factories. They were allowed to receive aid parcels from the International Red Cross, and they shared as much as they could. Fritz was very fond of their chocolate and English tea. He understood how precious these things were to the soldiers, and how generous they were to give them away.

It was wonderful to have these gifts, but being caught with them by the SS could earn you a whipping, or an even worse punishment, so Fritz and the others had to take great care smuggling the extra food back to the camp to share it with their friends.

Monowitz was so crowded with starving prisoners that it tore at Fritz's heart. He and his friends were doing everything they could, but it was just a drop in the ocean. It tormented Fritz that he couldn't help everyone. Thinking back to his first months in Buchenwald, he remembered the way men like Leopold Moses, Stefan Heymann and Robert Siewert had helped the young boys. He decided that if he couldn't help everyone, he would try to do the same.

There were two boys in his block. One was Walter Ansbacher, who was sixteen. He came from the German city of Augsburg. Walter's parents had been sent to the gas chambers as soon as they arrived. The same had happened to the parents of Artus Fischmann, who was only fourteen. Both boys had been transported there from one of the ghettos in Poland. Fritz took Walter and Artus under his wing, giving them whatever extra food he could get hold of.

A third boy was soon added to the little group. He was none other than Leo Meth, Fritz's old friend from the Karmeliter market. The last time Fritz had seen him was just after the Nazis had taken over Vienna, when Leo's parents took him away to France. They'd thought they would be safe there. But when France was conquered, they were eventually caught by the SS. And here Leo was now, all alone in this terrible place.

Hardship had changed Fritz and Leo, and they weren't the same boys they'd been in the old days. But they were still friends. Fritz shared with Leo the bread and bacon he'd earned from the coats scheme. He remembered how they'd shared the cakes the baker used to give them at the end of the day. They could never have dreamed back then that one day they would be here, in the worst place on earth, still sharing food.

Leo wasn't the only person from the old days to turn up in Auschwitz. Fritz briefly met his aunt Hilda, his cousin Richard's mother. She'd been in the Birkenau camp for a year before coming to Monowitz. Fritz remembered how sad Kurt had been when Richard, his best friend, had left for Belgium. The Nazis had conquered that country too, before Richard's family had a chance to get on a ship to New Zealand. Richard and his father were still safe, but his mum was seen as Jewish by the Nazis and they had taken her. The women in the camp were kept separate from the men, so there was nothing Fritz could do for her.

Papa also found an old friend from his childhood. In those days, Papa's mother – Fritz's grandmother – had worked for a Jewish family called Koplowitz. She'd been very fond of them. When their son, Georg, turned up in Monowitz, Papa took care of him. All the rest of Georg's family had been killed in Birkenau. Papa gave him his spare food and got Stefan to arrange a safe job for him in the hospital.

A new danger for the prisoners came when the first American bombs began falling on the Buna factories. The SS hid in underground bunkers, while the prisoners were left to find whatever shelter they could. Despite the danger, some of the prisoners were happy to see bombs smashing up the Nazi factories.

The resistance were disappointed by the air raid. They'd thought it might mean that the Allies would soon start parachuting soldiers in to set them free, but that didn't happen.

All the time they heard news of the Russian army getting closer and closer. They'd captured all of the Ostland and most of Poland and it wouldn't be long before they were at the very gates of Auschwitz. The great fear was that when the Russians got close, the SS would quickly murder all the Jewish prisoners and then race back to Germany to save themselves. That had already happened at another big concentration camp further east, at a place called Majdanek.

Fritz couldn't bear the thought of it happening here. He and Papa and their friends had survived through so much, it would be awful to die when they were so close to freedom. Fritz decided he would do something about it. If the SS started killing everyone, he wanted to be able to fight back.

CHAPTER TWENTY-ONE

A Desperate Plan

Fritz didn't tell anyone what he intended to do. Not even Stefan or Leo or Papa. One day at work, he went to Alfred Wocher and said quietly, 'I want you to get me a gun.'

'Get you what?' Alfred couldn't believe his ears.

'A gun. Can you do that for me?'

Alfred hesitated, but he didn't ask why Fritz wanted such a thing. He'd probably guessed. 'I don't know. I'll have to think about it. It's dangerous.'

'You've done so much for me, Alfred. This won't be any more dangerous than that.'

'This isn't just dangerous, Fritz, it's crazy!' Alfred put a hand on Fritz's shoulder. 'I've got a better idea. We should escape together, you and me. Listen, I've got a plan all worked out. I'll help you get out, then we'll make our way south to Austria. We can find the American army and be free.'

'I can't do that,' said Fritz. 'I'm not leaving my papa behind.'

'We'll take him with us,' said Alfred.

'He's too old to walk so far in winter. Besides, he'd never abandon his friends.' Fritz shook his head. 'It's impossible, Alfred. What I need is a gun. Can you get me one?'

Alfred was disappointed that Fritz wasn't interested in escaping. 'I'll try. But I'll need money.'

'OK.'

'And German money won't do. The way the war's going, it'll soon be worthless. It has to be American dollars.'

American dollars! Getting hold of any kind of money in Auschwitz was extremely difficult, but dollars would be just about impossible.

Fritz thought about it. By the time he got back to the camp that evening, he had a plan.

In fact, he had two plans. Alfred's talk of escaping had given him an idea. But that could wait for the time being. The money and the gun were more urgent.

First he went to the store building where the SS kept all the belongings stolen from the new prisoners. It was an eerie place, filled with racks of clothes, heaps of shoes and hats, and stacks of suitcases. Each case had a name and

address painted on it. The names flicked past Fritz's eyes –
a Gustav or a Paul, a Frieda, an Emmanuel, Otto, Chaim,
Helen, Mimi. And the surnames – Rauchmann, Klein,
Rebstock, Askiew, Rosenberg, Abraham, Herzog, Engel.
Each one had an address – Vienna, Berlin, Hamburg,
Amsterdam – or sometimes just a date of birth. The aisles
between the racks smelled of stale perfume, leather, wool,
sweat and dust.

Fritz knew a prisoner who worked in the store, an old
Buchenwalder called Gustav Taeuber. Fritz didn't like
him. He was a selfish man who seemed to have no feelings
for his fellow prisoners. Fritz knew that Taeuber often
found money and valuables that had been so carefully
hidden in the clothing that the SS had missed them.
Taeuber usually pocketed the cash for himself. Sometimes
he found American dollars.

He shook his head when Fritz asked him for some.
Taeuber knew Fritz was involved with the resistance, and
he was frightened of getting into trouble. Fritz begged
him, but it was no use.

Fritz left the store building and went to the main
shower block. This was his last hope. New prisoners were
always brought here after being stripped of their
belongings. Sometimes they managed to hide cash and
valuables in their hands or mouths, but it was almost
always discovered by the chief kapo when they came to
be showered and shaved.

The shower attendant was Fritz's friend David Plaut. (It was David who had helped reunite Fritz and Papa after Fritz's fake death.) Although the camp kapo took whatever was found on the prisoners in the shower block, Fritz suspected that David must manage to pocket a bit himself.

Fritz told David that he needed money to bribe the chief kapo to move some of his friends to easier work teams. David was a good friend. He went to his secret hiding place and came back with a small roll of American dollars. Fritz thanked him and put the money inside his jacket.

It was a terrible thing to do. Lying to David was bad enough, but Fritz felt sick at the thought of the poor souls whose belongings and money had been looted from them. Men and women like his mum and papa, dragged from their homes and families, robbed and tormented. Fritz was ashamed that he was taking advantage of that crime. This little roll of dollars in his pocket had once been someone's hope for the future. Auschwitz had made him like this. Auschwitz took good people and made them so that the best they could hope to do was survive and help the people closest to them.

The next day, Fritz showed Alfred the money. Alfred was astonished he'd managed to get it. He took the dollars and promised to see what he could do.

Days went by. Fritz waited anxiously, but each time

he met Alfred, he hadn't yet managed to get a gun. Then one morning he showed up at their meeting with a triumphant look on his face.

Checking that they were alone, Alfred reached under his jacket and brought out a pistol. It was a Luger, the kind that most German army officers carried. There was also a box of bullets to go with it.

Alfred quickly showed Fritz how the pistol worked – how to take out the magazine and load it with bullets, how to use the safety catch and make it ready to fire. Fritz handled the pistol nervously. He was so used to feeling like a helpless slave that the sense of deadly power in the palm of his hand was exciting.

Now came the challenge of smuggling it into the camp. Fritz found a quiet corner out of sight. Dropping his trousers, he tied the pistol to his thigh. The bullets went in his pockets.

That evening, he marched into the camp tingling with excitement. After roll call, he hurried to find Stefan.

'Come with me,' he said. 'I've got something to show you.'

Puzzled, Stefan followed Fritz to the hospital laundry room. Once they were alone, Fritz showed him the pistol and described how he'd got it.

Stefan was horrified. 'Are you crazy? Get rid of that thing! If you get caught with a gun it'll be the end of you.'

'I don't care. I'll fight them.'

'They won't just kill you, Fritz, the Gestapo will come after everyone you're close to! Me, your father, our friends. You're putting the whole resistance at risk. You have to get rid of it.'

Fritz was surprised and hurt by Stefan's reaction. 'You taught me to be like this,' he said. 'You always taught me that I had to fight for my life.'

Stefan couldn't answer that. Fritz explained his reasons. When the Russians got near, there would be a fierce battle, and anyone trapped in the middle of it might be killed. And the SS were likely to massacre the Jewish prisoners if they had to abandon the camps.

'We can all fight,' Fritz said. 'I'm sure I can get more guns if I have the money.'

Stefan thought about it. 'All right,' he said at last. 'I'll see what I can do. But the whole thing has to be organised properly. No more going it alone, Fritz.'

Stefan managed to scrape together two hundred dollars. Fritz took it to Alfred and asked him to get as many guns as he could.

Days went by, then more days, while Fritz waited anxiously. Then Alfred turned up one morning and led Fritz to a quiet place in the factory.

'Here,' he said, and from a hiding place he brought out another Luger pistol, plus two sub-machine guns. They were the type called an MP-40, used by German soldiers. There were boxes of bullets for all three guns.

Fritz planned how to smuggle them into the camp. It would take several trips. He got one of the big metal soup canisters that were used to bring the prisoners' lunch and built a hiding place in the bottom of it. The bullets went in there. Another resistance member would take the canister back to the camp. Fritz tied the pistol to his leg. Then he took one of the machine guns apart and tied the pieces to his body under his shirt. The other one would have to wait until the next day.

That evening he stood at roll call with bits of guns tied all over him, his stomach churning with fear. Because of the blackout, they didn't have the floodlights on any more. There was just moonlight, so no kapos or guards noticed Fritz's bulky, lumpy shape.

The moment roll call ended, Fritz hurried to the hospital laundry. A friend who worked there was waiting for him. Fritz quickly stripped off his uniform and untied the gun parts. His friend took them away to a hiding place he'd prepared. (Fritz wasn't told where the guns would be hidden. This was for security, in case he was caught and tortured.) The next day Fritz brought the rest of the parts there. Now all four guns and their boxes of bullets were safely inside the camp.

Fritz was thoroughly pleased with himself. If the SS tried to kill everyone, the resistance could now fight back.

On 18 December 1944, with Christmas approaching, the Americans bombed the factories again. Papa was in his workshop when it happened. He threw himself to the floor as the bombs thundered and boomed. The workshop windows were blown in, and the room was filled with smoke and broken glass.

Once the bombers had gone, Papa went looking for Fritz. Outside the workshop, the road and yards were strewn with rubble and dead prisoners. SS men were rushing about in the billowing smoke, yelling and trying to restore order. Some of the fences had been destroyed, and they were afraid that prisoners would escape. Papa knew that Fritz had prepared himself a kind of air-raid shelter in a corner between some buildings, so he ran to it.

Turning the corner, Papa found the shelter gone. A bomb had fallen right on it, leaving just a mound of broken rubble and twisted metal. Fritz must be somewhere beneath it, blown to pieces and crushed.

Papa was stunned. After all they'd survived, his beloved Fritz was gone – killed by the Americans!

He was about to turn back to his workshop, his heart breaking, when a familiar figure in a striped uniform came walking through the smoke. Papa couldn't believe his eyes.

'Fritz! My boy, my Fritz! You're alive!'

Papa hugged him and kissed his face, sobbing and saying his name over and over. Fritz was startled. He and his workmate had been fitting curtains in one of the factories when the air raid happened.

'What is it, Papa? What's going on?' His father didn't usually act like this.

Papa led him by the arm to the corner where the smoking rubble of his shelter was. 'It's a miracle,' he kept saying. Papa's faith in their good luck was stronger than ever. He felt even more sure that they would both live through this.

His spirits rose even higher the day after New Year, when Alfred Wocher returned from Vienna with letters and packages from Olly and their other friends. Soon the war would end and they would be free. They'd go home to Vienna. Maybe they'd be reunited with the rest of the family eventually.

Fritz wasn't quite so confident. But neither he nor Papa could guess just how wrong Papa was about the future. They had suffered abominably at the hands of the Nazis, but the worst was still to come.

The Russians were very close now. Their army was just the other side of Cracow, the nearest city. The Germans were fighting hard, but the Russians outnumbered them four to one. By the middle of January, people in Auschwitz could hear the thump of the big guns. The sound was like a great clock ticking away the hours to Germany's defeat.

Fritz tried to persuade Alfred to run away and save himself. When the Russians came and saw Auschwitz, they would be appalled. Any Germans they caught there would be punished horribly, even innocent ones like

Alfred. But he refused to go. 'I've never run away before. I'm not about to start now.'

A few days later, Alfred was called up into the German 'People's Army' – the *Volkssturm*. It was a desperate force made up of boys, old men and disabled people. Although Alfred hated the Nazis, he still loved Germany and wanted to defend its women and children against the Russian troops. Russia had suffered terribly in the war, and the soldiers were likely to take revenge on German civilians. Alfred said goodbye to Fritz and Papa. They all hoped they would meet again one day when this was over.

Fritz thought about the hidden guns. He might need them at any moment.

Aside from the guns, he also had a Plan B prepared. He knew that if the SS didn't try to kill everyone, they would probably evacuate them, taking them west into Germany. Fritz was prepared for that.

At the same time as he was smuggling the guns, Fritz had gone to see David at the shower block and had got some civilian clothes from him. Fritz's idea was that he and Papa could wear them under their uniforms. Then, if they got the chance to escape during the evacuation, they could strip off their uniforms and look like civilians. To complete their disguise, he and Papa had been dodging the weekly head-shaving. Because roll call was always in darkness now, nobody saw that under their caps their heads were no longer bald.

Fritz hid the civilian clothes in a tool shed in the camp and waited. What would it be – a gunfight or an escape?

For a short while, life went on just the same in Auschwitz. It was a bitterly cold winter, with thick snow and fog. There was a sense of doom among the SS, and they were drunk most of the time.

One day, not long after Alfred had left to join the fighting, an order came through from the commandant of Auschwitz. The SS was to begin evacuating all the prisoners who could walk. The sick and disabled were to be left behind. Any prisoners who resisted or tried to escape would be shot immediately.

The following day, Thursday, 18 January 1945, the Monowitz prisoners were kept standing all day on the roll-call square. The cold was bone-numbing. Fritz and Papa, knowing that the end was near, had put on the civilian outfits under their uniforms. The extra layers helped keep them a little warmer, but they were still freezing.

It was getting dark when the SS began ordering everyone into lines, ready to march. There were eight thousand prisoners altogether. The SS divided them into groups of several hundred, each with an SS officer and guards. The SS all had rifles, pistols and sub-machine guns poised and ready, with the safety catches off.

Fritz thought again about his guns. It would be impossible to get to them now.

At last the order was given and the ranks of prisoners began to move. They marched out of the square, five abreast, and along the camp street, past the blocks, the kitchens, the little empty building where the orchestra usually played. For the last time they walked out through the gate.

This place they were leaving had been a home of sorts. Some had been here for over two years. A few, like Fritz and his papa, had helped build it up from grassy fields. Their friends' blood had been spilled here. The pain and terror had been endless. But it was still a kind of home, however much they hated it.

As for where they were going, they had no idea. Somewhere out of reach of the Russians. All the sub-camps around Monowitz were being emptied, spilling out thirty-five thousand men and women and their guards on to the snow-covered roads leading west from Auschwitz.

CHAPTER TWENTY-TWO

The Death March

'Come on, get up!' Fritz hooked his arm under the older man's elbow. Papa helped lift him from the other side. An SS guard was prowling alongside the trudging column of prisoners, rifle at the ready, looking for anyone not keeping up.

'Up now!' said Papa.

The man struggled up and stumbled on through the icy snow. The SS guard carried on past and lashed out at another prisoner who was further back.

They'd only gone a little way beyond the town of Auschwitz and already the older, less healthy men were struggling to keep up. The younger and healthier ones like Fritz and Papa and their friends helped them to stay on their feet and keep moving. Anyone who lagged behind got hit by the guards.

After a few kilometres more, even Fritz and the others were starting to struggle. They didn't have the strength to help anyone any more. They just kept their eyes down, hugged their jackets tightly around them and forced their legs to move, one foot in front of the other, over and over. They tried to close their ears to the sound of gunshots coming from behind.

The SS had begun shooting anyone who couldn't walk. From time to time the bang of a rifle or the bark of a machine gun echoed through the night. An SS block chief was walking near Fritz. Fritz could sense how frightened the man was of the Russians, who were somewhere in the distance behind them, advancing like an incoming tide. He had a pistol in his hand, ready to shoot anything he didn't like the look of.

Dawn was starting to break when they reached a town. The guards wanted to rest, so they herded everyone into the yard of a brick factory. The prisoners found sheltered spots among the stacks of bricks, huddling together for warmth. Fritz and Papa made themselves stay awake. They guessed that anyone who fell asleep in this terrible cold might never wake up again.

Talking to some of their friends who'd been further back on the march, they learned that several prisoners had escaped. They'd simply run off into the darkness when the SS weren't looking.

Papa said, 'We should do that, Fritz – make a run for

it. I speak Polish, so we'd have no trouble finding our way. We could find the Polish resistance or just head for Vienna.'

That was what Fritz had planned for. But there was a problem. 'I don't speak Polish, Papa. What if we get separated? We should wait until we reach Germany. Then we'll both speak the language.'

'It's a long walk to Germany, Fritz. Look at us. Who knows if we'll ever reach it? If the walk doesn't kill us, the SS might put bullets in us before we get there.'

Their talk was cut short by guards yelling, 'On your feet! Move now! Get up and march!'

They went around kicking and shoving everyone. The prisoners who still had strength hauled themselves up on their feet. Some of the ones who'd fallen asleep had died.

On the surviving prisoners trudged. Behind them was a nightmare of trampled snow dotted with the bodies of the people too weakened by cold and hunger to make it any further. The trail of misery stretched all the way back to Auschwitz, where Birkenau and the other camps were still being evacuated. It became known as the Death March. All over German territory, death marches happened as the Allied armies closed in on the concentration camps.

It was daylight now, and Fritz and Papa had no chance of escaping without being seen. Eventually they reached the town of Gleiwitz, where there was an outlying sub-camp of Auschwitz that had already been abandoned. They were marched in and kept there for two days. They had nothing to eat, but at least they had shelter from the worst of the cold. Meanwhile, SS officers were trying to organise the next stage of the retreat.

For the Monowitz men, their future lay on a different path from most Auschwitz prisoners. While other poor souls walked on towards Germany, the Monowitzers were going by train.

The guards herded them out of the Gleiwitz camp and down the road to the rail depot. Their transports were waiting there – four long trains of goods wagons. These were not like the wagons they'd been in before. These were the open-top kind that normally carried coal or gravel.

Each person was given half a loaf of bread and a piece of sausage, which was meant to last the whole journey. If past journeys were anything to go by, it could take days. Every second wagon had a small hut built on the end of it, where the man who worked the brakes normally stood. SS guards with guns got into the brake huts – from there they could see across the tops of all the wagons.

'Get in! Quickly! Into your transports!' yelled the SS block chiefs.

There were no doors. Fritz and Papa pocketed their food and climbed up the side of the nearest wagon, struggled over the top and dropped down inside. Their shoes clumped loudly on the floor. Other men followed, the noise echoing less and less as the wagon filled up. There were over a hundred men per wagon, and the last few had to squeeze in among the others.

The guards shouted: 'Anyone who puts his head above the side will be shot!'

Steam and smoke belched out from the locomotive, making a thick fog in the cold air. Rumbling and clanking and shuddering, the train began to move. As it picked up speed, the wind came moaning over the sides of the wagons. The temperature was minus 20 degrees Celsius, so cold that your skin would freeze to bare metal if you touched it. The men's muscles began to seize up and it became difficult to move or speak.

The train headed south. The rumour was that they were going to Mauthausen concentration camp in Austria. Despite the guards' warning not to look out, Papa peeped over the side from time to time, trying to work out where they were.

Hour by hour the train rolled and groaned onward, wheels hissing, brakes squealing, wagons clanking, rumbling, making a hideous, never-ending music of suffering. There wasn't room to squat down. The men stood jammed together. Kilometre after kilometre, the cold ate away their strength. As night followed day, the weakest – the ones who had struggled to make it as far as the train – began to die.

The bodies were laid in the corner, where they soon froze solid. As they piled up, it made space for the survivors to sit down. The food ran out quickly, and there was no water. Papa and some of the others dangled a tin cup on a string over the side to scoop up snow. They sucked thirstily on it, munching the snow as if it were food.

It was truly desperate. They could sense the SS men getting more and more nervous, and fear was making them more savage than ever.

Even if they survived the journey, the prisoners were sure they would die in Mauthausen concentration camp. It had an evil reputation – almost as bad as Auschwitz. Fritz and Papa had no friends there. Papa wouldn't have his safe job any more, and Fritz hadn't seen any of their close friends since reaching Gleiwitz. They might not even be on the same train.

The only way to avoid it would be to escape. To do so, they'd have to climb over the side of the wagon and jump off without being seen by the guards. It would have to be at night, most likely while the train was moving. Fritz and Papa agreed to try once the train reached Austria.

Fritz looked at the gaunt faces around him, like dead men, but still breathing. The fourth day of the journey passed. Men who'd managed to make their food last nibbled on their final crusts. Fritz and Papa had none left.

'We'll have to go soon,' said Papa. 'Otherwise it'll be too late.'

He was right. They tested the guards' watchfulness that night. With help from some friends, they lifted one of the dead bodies. Raising it to the top of the sidewall, they pushed it over.

There was no reaction from the guard hut. No shouts, no burst of gunfire. They were probably too tired to bother keeping watch. Fritz and Papa agreed that as soon as they were in Austria they'd make their escape. Their companions in the wagon weren't coming; it was too dangerous, and they didn't fancy their chances.

The train crossed the Austrian border the next day. It stopped for a while, then got going again as darkness fell.

Fritz shook his father. 'Papa! Wake up! It's time to go.'

Papa woke up and tried to stand, but his body had grown too weak. 'I can't do it,' he said. 'I don't have the strength left.'

'You have to, Papa! We have to leave while we can. It can't be long until we get to Mauthausen.'

But Papa just couldn't get up. His voice was hoarse and faint: 'Fritz, you have to go without me.'

Fritz was appalled. He remembered Robert Siewert's words, long ago in Buchenwald – *If you want to go on living, you have to forget your father.*

'No, I won't leave you,' he said. It had been impossible

for Fritz back then, and it was impossible now. Papa begged him to go without him, but he wouldn't.

Dawn came. The slow-moving train steamed through countryside that was familiar to Fritz. Soon they were rolling through the outskirts of Vienna. It was torment to be so close to home and yet unable to see it. They passed within less than a kilometre of Island Street and the Karmeliter market. The wheels rumbled over the Danube Canal bridge, through the suburbs and back out into the countryside.

By afternoon, they were less than forty kilometres from Mauthausen. It had to be tonight or never. The train halted for a while, then carried on in darkness.

Papa squeezed Fritz's hand. 'Fritz, you have to go. I can't make it. I'm old, my strength is gone. Leave now – *please.*'

'No, Papa, I can't.'

'Please, Fritz, before it's too late. *Please.*'

Fritz couldn't resist the desperate pleading in Papa's eyes. Finally he gave way. It hurt him deeply to do it, and he knew the pain would never leave him. To tear himself away from his father was like cutting out a part of his own heart.

The train had reached its top speed. Fritz peeled off the loathsome striped uniform with its star badge and camp number. He flung off the striped cap.

Fritz hugged his beloved Papa one last time and kissed him on the forehead. 'Goodbye, Papa.'

One of the other men helped him climb up the slippery sidewall. At the top, the full force of the savage wind buffeted him – it was like being pummelled with blocks of ice. The train shuddered and thundered under him. The moon was bright tonight, but there was no sign of life from the guard hut.

Building up his courage, Fritz launched himself into the night.

He tumbled through the air. For a moment he lost all sense of left and right, up and down. The ground slammed into him, jarring his body, knocking the wind out of his lungs. He rolled and rolled through the deep snowdrift and came to rest. The wheels of the train clattered past his face.

Fritz didn't dare move until the last wagon had passed and the train was in the distance. He was alone in the bright moonlit snow, silent except for the fading *rat-a-clack* of the train.

He stood up and brushed off the snow – no bones broken – and looked back along the tracks. Vienna was that way. He started walking, following the gleaming rails towards his home.

Nearing the first town, Fritz decided to skirt round it. He slithered down the railway bank and set out across open fields. The snow was up to his hips. He ploughed through and was soon on a country road heading in the right direction.

He walked for several hours without meeting anyone. At last he came to a small town called Blindenmarkt. The train had passed through it the day before. There was a little station here where trains heading to Vienna stopped. Fritz was worn out and he had a few German coins in his pocket that he'd scavenged in Monowitz. He wondered if he should risk catching a train.

It was still dark and nobody was about. Fritz left the main road and walked to the station. It was shut, so he found an empty cattle wagon in a siding and climbed inside. It was too cold to sleep, but better than being out in the wind.

After a while, he saw lights come on in the station. Did he dare? Summoning his courage, he went and looked inside. It was quiet, with just a lone clerk behind the ticket window.

Fritz approached nervously and said as casually as he could, 'A ticket to Vienna, please. Third class.'

The clerk looked at him in surprise. 'You're early. There's no train for a while yet.'

'I'll wait.'

Did the clerk seem suspicious? Had it been a mistake to draw attention to himself? The clerk shrugged and took Fritz's money. Clutching his ticket in relief, Fritz went to sit in the waiting room.

After a few minutes, the clerk came in and lit the wood-burning stove. Fritz moved closer to it. It was the first warmth he'd felt since leaving Monowitz a week ago. It caressed his face and enfolded him in a wonderful hug, seeping into his aching bones. He was sleepy and began to drift off into a doze.

He was woken by the Vienna train puffing into the station and halting in a squeal of brakes and a rush of steam. He hurried on to the platform and got into one of the third-class carriages.

Closing the door behind him, he looked around and realised with a jolt that the carriage was filled with German soldiers. There wasn't a civilian in sight. They were Wehrmacht men – the German regular army, not SS. Even so, the sight of them sucked every bit of warmth out of Fritz's body.

He reminded himself that he wasn't wearing stripes any more, and in their eyes he was just a civilian. He kept calm, and the soldiers barely glanced at him. They were busy dozing or chatting or playing cards.

Fritz found a seat and sat down. His insides were boiling with anxiety, but he controlled his fear. He'd had a lot of practice. Listening to the soldiers chatting, he guessed they'd been at the front lines, fighting the Americans. They were going to Vienna on leave.

The train clatter-clacked for a couple of hours, stopping at a few stations. Nobody else got on, and Fritz was starting to relax. In just a few hours' time, he'd be in Vienna again! They reached St Poelten, the last big town before Vienna. The carriage door opened and two men in Wehrmacht uniforms got on. They both wore crescent-shaped steel plates below their collars – the badge of the military police. Fritz's optimism instantly disappeared.

The policemen came along the aisle, demanding to see the soldiers' passes. The men near Fritz got out their passes and ID cards and handed them over in one big pile. All Fritz had was his ticket, so he put that in with them. One of the policemen went through them quickly, glancing at each one and handing it back. Then he came to the solitary ticket. He frowned at it, then looked at Fritz.

'ID, please,' he said.

Fritz's heart pounded. What could he do? He made a show of searching through his pockets. 'I'm sorry, I've lost it.'

The policeman's frown of puzzlement turned into a frown of suspicion. 'All right. You'd better come with us.'

'Please, I need to get to Vienna,' he said. 'It's really important.'

'You're not going any further until you prove who you are,' they said. 'Don't you know there's a war on?'

Fritz knew better than to argue. He got up and followed the policemen off the train. They took him out of the station and down the street to a small army outpost, where they put him in a room. After a while, a sergeant came in.

'Why did you get on that train?' the sergeant asked. Fritz was surprised by his tone of voice – he wasn't angry or aggressive like the SS. But then, he didn't know that Fritz was Jewish.

'I need to get to Vienna,' said Fritz.

'Why did you choose that particular train? You must have known it was a front-line special, full of troops. There'd have been a regular train not long after.'

'I–I didn't know it would have soldiers on it. It was a mistake.'

The sergeant smiled. 'A young fellow in civvies with no papers decides to board a troop train "by mistake"? That's not normal behaviour, is it? What's your name, lad?'

Fritz hesitated. 'Kleinmann,' he said. 'Fritz Kleinmann.' He didn't see any point in lying – it was a perfectly ordinary German name. A lot of Kleinmanns were Jewish, but many were not.

'Where's your ID?'

'I must have lost it,' Fritz said, knowing what a feeble excuse it was.

'Home address?'

He quickly made one up. 'It's 24 Bismarck Street, Ettersburg.' Ettersburg was a little town near Buchenwald. Fritz had no idea if it had a Bismarck Street.

The sergeant wrote it down. 'Wait there,' he said, and left the room.

Fritz was left alone for a long time. Eventually the sergeant came back.

'We checked the address,' he said. 'It doesn't exist. Now, where do you really live?'

'I'm sorry,' said Fritz. 'My memory plays tricks on me.'

He gave a different address. The sergeant went away. A while later he came back.

'That was another false address. Try again.'

Fritz tried again. He didn't know what else to do. He was just desperately playing for time. It couldn't be long before they worked out that he was an escaped prisoner.

When the third address turned out to be false, the sergeant ran out of patience. He summoned two guards. 'Take Mr Kleinmann to the barracks,' he ordered them. 'The security section. They'll know how to make him talk.'

CHAPTER TWENTY-THREE

The End of the World

Fritz was driven across town to a bigger army base, where he was taken to a jail-like building with an office and cells. The soldiers presented him to the army officer in charge, along with a note from the sergeant.

The officer, a lieutenant called Schmidt, read the note and studied Fritz. 'Identify yourself,' he said. 'If you lie to me, you'll be locked up.'

There was nothing Fritz could do. He gave yet another address. It was checked and found to be false. Lieutenant Schmidt wasn't angry. He didn't shout or threaten Fritz with torture. He simply beckoned to his men and said, 'Put him in a cell. Perhaps he'll remember his real identity once he's spent a few hours locked up.'

The cell was quite big. There were three prisoners already in it, all soldiers. They looked curiously at Fritz as

he came in and the door clanged and locked behind him.
Fritz guessed they were in trouble for being drunk or
disobeying orders. He knew what soldiers could be like
from Papa's stories.

They asked Fritz who he was. He told them he was a
civilian who'd lost his papers. 'I'm waiting to be cleared,'
he said. That seemed to satisfy them.

The cell was nothing like any cell in a concentration camp. It was quite warm, there was a table and chairs, and a bed for each man. It even had a basin and toilet in the corner. It might be a cell, but it was the most comfortable place Fritz had been in for years. He sat on the spare bed. It had a mattress. Turning back the blanket, he found cotton sheets underneath. Amazing.

Dinner was brought to the cell. Fritz had scarcely eaten in over a week. It was hot and delicious, and he had to force himself not to make himself ill by gobbling it down too quickly.

At lights-out, he took off his jacket and eased his aching body into bed. Sheets! Comfort! No stench, nobody's knees or elbows poking into him. It was heavenly. He slept blissfully through the night.

Fritz didn't think it could get any better, but it did. In the morning, a guard brought breakfast. It was simple jail fare, but to Fritz it was so wonderful it made his head spin. There was hot coffee – real coffee, not the acorn stuff – bread, margarine, sausage, and plenty of it. While his cellmates chatted among themselves, Fritz ate with relish.

The pleasure couldn't last, of course. After a while he was taken to Lieutenant Schmidt again.

'You will now tell me who you really are,' Schmidt said.

Fritz just kept on repeating that he was a civilian worker, that he'd lost his ID and that he just needed to get to Vienna so that he could get it all sorted out.

As the questioning went on, Fritz realised that Lieutenant Schmidt suspected him of being a deserter from the army. It made perfect sense. Fritz was old enough now to be a soldier. In Lieutenant Schmidt's mind, Fritz had got on a troop train from force of habit. The idea that this respectable-looking young man could be an escaped Jew from Auschwitz never crossed the lieutenant's mind.

Fritz refused to answer any more questions, so he was put back in the cell. Schmidt obviously thought the cell was a punishment. How wrong he was. When lunch arrived, it was a rather nice stew and a piece of bread. Yes, Fritz thought, he could be quite happy here for a very long time.

And yet he knew he couldn't stay. Fritz had survived

for so long in the camps by always being aware of his situation, knowing where the dangers were. He understood that this army officer would sooner or later figure out the truth. If not, Fritz would be handed over to someone willing to torture him. The only way to avoid that was to do something drastic.

That evening, while his cellmates were busy talking and playing cards, Fritz quietly looked at their belongings and noticed a stick of shaving soap. Unlike regular soap, shaving soap is poisonous, which was just what he needed. He secretly bit off a piece and swallowed it.

By the next morning, Fritz was horribly ill – hot, sweating, and with terrible diarrhoea. He couldn't move from his bed. His cellmates called the guards.

He was carried out and taken to the base hospital. When the doctor examined him, Fritz had his wits about him just enough to keep his Auschwitz tattoo hidden.

'There's nothing seriously wrong with him,' the doctor said. 'Stomach cramps, a raised temperature. He's eaten something that didn't agree with him.'

Fritz was put in a side ward by himself and kept under guard. It was even better than the cell. A soft bed with crisp white sheets, friendly, motherly nurses bringing him tea and medicine. The doctor visited from time to time. After a day or so Fritz felt able to eat. He still had diarrhoea, but it was worth it to postpone the questioning.

He'd been in the hospital for over two weeks by

the time he was really well again. The effect of eating the soap had perhaps been made worse by the weak state he'd been in. Now he was well fed and feeling good.

Again Fritz was brought to Lieutenant Schmidt to be questioned.

The lieutenant's patience was wearing thin. 'It's time for this case to be closed. If you don't confess, I shall hand you over to the Gestapo.'

He obviously expected Fritz to be so terrified by that threat that he'd break down and confess. But Fritz didn't say a word.

Lieutenant Schmidt was seething with frustration. He couldn't understand why this seemingly ordinary young man seemed so relaxed when he should be quaking with fear. 'Take him back to his cell!' Schmidt shouted at the guards. He pointed a finger in Fritz's face. 'Two more days and then I'm done with you! You'll go to the Gestapo.'

Back in the cell, Fritz settled in for two more days of lovely comfort. But his pleasure was marred by the thought of being handed over to the Gestapo. They would find out who he really was. Fritz was a camp veteran though – he knew how to not think about it, to just keep his head down and eat as much as he could get his hands on.

When Fritz was brought back to the interrogation room, Lieutenant Schmidt was smiling. To Fritz's alarm, he said, 'I've guessed who you really are now. You're not an army deserter at all, are you?'

Fritz said nothing.

'I believe you're an enemy agent,' said the lieutenant. 'You've been parachuted into this country by the British. You have a mission – sabotage, maybe? Or gathering information? Only an agent would be able to resist questioning for as long as you have.'

Fritz was horrified. He'd heard that when spies were captured, they were shot.

'I'm not a spy, I swear,' he said.

'Don't lie. Sneaking about, mixing with German troops, resisting interrogation. Only a trained spy would do all that.'

Fritz kept on denying it, but Lieutenant Schmidt wouldn't listen.

'Take him back to his cell!'

Fritz was force-marched to the cell. Suddenly it didn't seem so pleasant. He tried to decide what to do. Confess that he was an escaped Jew? No, they'd send him back to the SS, and he'd be shot or gassed or hanged for escaping. But they'd do the same if they thought he was a spy, wouldn't they? Anyway, Lieutenant Schmidt was so pleased with himself for capturing an enemy spy that if Fritz had shown him his tattoo he probably wouldn't have believed it – he'd think it was just a spy trick.

The next day, Fritz was brought to Lieutenant Schmidt once more. This time, three soldiers were standing by.

'I've had enough of you,' Schmidt said. 'You're going to Mauthausen. Let the SS deal with you.'

A guard put handcuffs on Fritz's wrists. The cold steel clicked tight.

'If you try to escape,' said Schmidt, 'you will be shot immediately.'

The three soldiers marched him out of the base and back to the railway station. They kept their guns at the ready in case he tried to run away. They caught a train to Linz. At Linz they changed to a train to Mauthausen.

The town of Mauthausen was a pretty little place, nestling in a bend of the river Danube, beneath rolling green hills that were a patchwork of fields and woods. Fritz was marched through the streets with the soldiers' rifles aimed at his back. A winding road led up a steep valley to their destination.

When Fritz finally saw it, Mauthausen concentration camp didn't look like any camp he'd ever seen. It was built of stone, like a castle, with thick walls and gun positions and towers.

Somewhere inside that fortress were Papa and their friends. Or so Fritz hoped. Papa had been horribly weak and sick when they parted, nearly three weeks ago. But, deep down, Fritz felt sure that he'd survived. He had faith in Papa's strength. As awful as this place looked, Fritz was looking forward to being reunited with his father.

Beside the fortress, the ground sloped away for a few metres, then there was a sheer drop, like a vast, wide ravine lined with rocky cliffs. As Fritz was marched past it, he looked down and realised that it was a stone quarry. It was far bigger and deeper than the one at Buchenwald. The bottom was teeming like an ants' nest with prisoners working. It rang with the clinks and clangs of picks and chisels on stone. There were no rail tracks or wagons. On the far side was an enormous staircase cut into the rock. Up it, hundreds of prisoners were carrying blocks of stone on their backs. They called it the *Todesstiege*, which meant Stairway of Death. Just one slip and a man might fall with his stone, knocking down dozens of others like dominoes.

At the main gate of the fortress, the soldiers handed Fritz over to the SS guards. The sight of the little silver skulls on their collars was familiar and sickening.

Fritz expected to be questioned and beaten, but the SS didn't seem to know what to do with him. A sergeant took him in through the gate, which was flanked by massive towers bristling with machine guns and floodlights.

Inside, the camp was surprisingly small and filled with ordinary wooden barrack blocks. Fritz was left standing by the gate tower while the sergeant went inside.

A prisoner standing nearby came up to him. 'Who are you?' he asked. 'What're you here for?'

'My name's Fritz. I'm from Vienna.'

The man walked off. A moment later he came back with another red-triangle prisoner, who had the air of a kapo. He studied Fritz's clothes and face.

'I'm from Vienna too,' he said. 'Been in this place for

years. It's pretty bad, but the one thing you don't want to be in here is a Jew. Jews don't live long in here.' With that, he walked off.

The sergeant came out again. To Fritz's surprise he asked, 'Have you got an Auschwitz tattoo? There's been some transports in from up there. We're on the lookout for strays.'

'No, I haven't,' Fritz said. 'Look.' He rolled up his right sleeve. (The tattoo was on his left arm.)

The sergeant believed him. (After all, how would an Auschwitz prisoner have a full head of hair and civilian clothes?) He handed Fritz over to a kapo, who took him to the shower block. Inside, the Viennese prisoner appeared again. This time, out of sight of the SS, he introduced himself properly. His name was Josef Kohl, though everyone called him Pepi. He was involved in Mauthausen's resistance (Fritz learned later that Pepi was the resistance leader).

Pepi was smart, and he had guessed on sight that Fritz was a prisoner on the run. Fritz was so relieved, he told Pepi everything – or almost everything. He told him about Buchenwald and Auschwitz and how he'd escaped from the train and been captured again. But he didn't mention being Jewish. He claimed he'd been a political prisoner. Any hope of surviving here depended on nobody knowing that he was a Jew.

Once again, Fritz went through the ritual of being a

new prisoner. His clothes were taken away, he was showered and his head was shaved. As his hair was shorn away and he put on the striped uniform, he knew that he was back in the nightmare for good this time. There would be no escape.

In the Gestapo office, he was put on the register. The Gestapo clerk smirked at him. 'This is the price you pay for keeping your address secret.'

'Sorry?' said Fritz, puzzled.

The clerk pointed at a note on his desk from Lieutenant Schmidt. 'Only reason you're here.' Fritz opened his mouth to speak, but the clerk interrupted. 'Too late for that now, my lad.'

Fritz was in a horrible fix. If he confessed the whole truth, they would kill him. If he didn't, he felt sure they would torture him and shoot him as a spy. There was only one thing he could do – tell the same half-truth he'd told Pepi. He rolled up his sleeve and showed his tattoo.

'I jumped off the Auschwitz transport,' he said.

The clerk stared at him. 'I see. Grounds for imprisonment?'

'Political,' said Fritz. 'German Aryan.'

To Fritz's relief, the clerk didn't bat an eye. He wrote the information down on the register and gave Fritz his new prisoner number: 130039.

'What's your trade?'

Fritz hesitated. He guessed that they didn't need

builders here. 'Heating engineer,' he said. It was almost true; he'd worked on constructing heating plants. And he'd learned from Papa how to bluff his way in a trade. Whatever happened, he had to avoid being sent to work in that quarry.

The clerk noted it down and ordered a kapo to take him to his block.

The blocks were bursting with prisoners evacuated from Auschwitz, all gaunt and starving. Fritz was thankful for his few weeks' holiday in Lieutenant Schmidt's little jail. The good food and rest had made him stronger and healthier.

At the first opportunity, Fritz went looking for Papa and his friends. He asked around, but nobody seemed to know where they were. He talked to countless Auschwitz prisoners, but all of them were strangers, and none had ever heard of Gustav Kleinmann or any of their friends.

Fritz realised with a sinking heart that the train hadn't come here after all. If Papa was still alive, he'd gone somewhere else. Fritz couldn't even begin to guess where. He had no hope of ever finding him.

After a short stay in an overcrowded block, Fritz was sent to another camp nearby called Mauthausen-Gusen. Many of the prisoners there worked in secret aeroplane factories that had been set up in rocky tunnels dug underneath the hills. Fritz was put in a labour team in the underground factory where Nazi engineers were making parts for their super-advanced new jet fighters. Hitler believed he could still win the war with these miracle planes.

For Fritz, it felt like the end of the world. He had no Papa and no friends. Although he was surrounded by thousands of other prisoners, he felt totally alone. Now he knew how the Hungarian Jews arriving in Auschwitz must have felt.

Everyone was starving, and there were no scams or schemes that could get Fritz extra food. Dinner was a lump of bread not much bigger than Fritz's hand and a small bowl of watery turnip stew. And that was all you got for a whole day. The SS and the green-triangle kapos murdered prisoners at random in the tunnels. Anyone who became too weak to work was sent back to the main camp, where most of them died. Hundreds of these unfortunates were sent back every week – three thousand just in the month of March.

From time to time, a truckload of food was delivered to the camp by the Red Cross. It was meant for the prisoners, but the SS plundered most of it for themselves, then ruined whatever they couldn't carry away. They broke open tins of condensed milk and threw them to the prisoners, who had to scrabble and fight for them. The guards laughed at the sight.

All the time, more and more death marches kept arriving, bringing more prisoners on their last legs.

Fritz wasn't the same person he'd been when he jumped from the Auschwitz train. With the wretched diet and arduous work, the flesh was wasting away from his bones. By the end of April, he was a walking skeleton. His eyes were sunken in, his cheeks hollowed out, and his ribs stuck out from his sides like the bars of a cage. In one week or maybe two, he would have nothing left to give, and he would certainly die.

And yet, the spirit of his father lived in him. He still wouldn't give up all hope. Fritz could hear the sounds of war approaching – the faint thump of big guns in the distance. The Americans were coming.* If he could just stay alive for a few days longer, he might get through this.

But the SS had made other plans. Their chief, Heinrich Himmler, had sent out a message to all the concentration camps: 'No prisoner may fall alive into the hands of the enemy.'

One morning, as the American guns grew closer, the air-raid siren sounded in the Mauthausen-Gusen camp. The guards and kapos started herding the prisoners into the shelter of a disused tunnel near the camp.

The vast tunnel had three entrances. Most of the prisoners didn't notice that the two others had been blocked. Once everyone was in the tunnel, SS guards set

---

* Mauthausen was in the western half of German territory, where the Germans were fighting the Allied armies advancing from that direction.

up machine guns outside so that nobody could escape. The day before, the rock around the entrance had been secretly wired with explosives. On the commandant's order, the explosives would be detonated and thousands of prisoners would be trapped inside to die.

Fritz stood in the dank darkness of the tunnel with no idea of the fate in store. He listened to the echoes of twenty thousand people breathing the chilly air. Minutes passed, but there was no drone of approaching bombers, no thump and crash of bombs falling. The minutes turned into hours. Fritz struggled to stay upright, he was so weakened by hunger and exhaustion. If the air-raid warning was a false alarm, why weren't the SS letting everyone out?

Outside the tunnels, the SS pressed the button to detonate the explosives.

Nothing happened. They pressed it again. Still nothing. They checked their equipment, but couldn't find anything wrong. They blamed each other, blamed the commandant, blamed the engineer who'd put the explosives there, but they couldn't work out what was wrong.

At last, after six hours, the all-clear sounded and the prisoners were herded out of the tunnels and back to their blocks.

Later on, the prisoners learned what the SS had tried to do. It was said that a Polish prisoner who was an electrician had discovered the wires to the explosives and sabotaged them so they wouldn't work.

A few days went by with the usual routine of work and roll calls. Then suddenly everything stopped. Fritz was in a daze of hunger and weakness, but he sensed a mood among the SS. Fear. Tension. Anger. Just like the guards in Monowitz when the Russians were coming. But this time there wouldn't be a death march – there was hardly anything left of Hitler's empire to retreat into. North, south, east and west, armies of Americans, British, Poles, Indians, New Zealanders, Russians, Canadians and a host of other countries were squeezing the Germans into a smaller and smaller space. Mauthausen concentration camp was in one of the last tiny slivers of territory that Germany still held.

Then, one day, the SS vanished from the camp. All of them, just gone. The most fanatical ones were planning to fight the Americans in the mountains. But most had thrown away their uniforms and badges and gone into hiding.

The camp was now being managed by a mixture of Vienna police, German air force, and the Vienna fire brigade. Their job was just to hold the place together until the American army arrived.

Fritz felt utterly broken. If the routine of work had gone on one or two days longer, he would have died. He was scarcely clinging on to life, little more than skin wrapped round bones, and covered in bruises and sores. He had no friends here, only fellow sufferers, ghosts and skeletons. Fritz had once thought that Buchenwald was the worst a human being could suffer. Then he'd thought the same of Auschwitz. He couldn't have guessed, as he suffered in those camps, that there could be anything worse. For Fritz, Mauthausen was the ultimate horror: the pit of the world, the end of everything.

A couple of days after the SS had left, the first tanks drove into the Mauthausen-Gusen camp. They were olive green with the bright white star of the United States Army. Jeeps and trucks and American soldiers came with them.

The Americans were stunned by what they found. There were vast piles of dead bodies, and thousands of ghost-like people living among them. The whole place stank of unwashed people and rotting corpses.

Fritz felt relief when he saw the American uniforms and heard their strange English-speaking voices. But he didn't feel joy or happiness. He was too exhausted, his spirit too broken. He guessed he could go home now. But was there a home to go back to? There was no reason any more to hope that Papa was still alive. Everyone Fritz had loved must surely be dead now.

CHAPTER TWENTY-FOUR

They All Fought

It was just a regular Wednesday and Kurt was walking home from school. Life in America was completely normal to him now. He was at high school and he spoke English in a Massachusetts accent with just a hint of Vienna. He had lots of friends and was in the Boy Scouts. One day he hoped to make the rank of Eagle Scout. In a couple of months, he'd be going to Camp Avoda for his fifth summer. There'd be baseball and swimming and boating, as well as learning new things about Jewish culture and history.

He passed a newspaper stand. On the front of the *Boston Daily Globe* was a huge headline:

NAZIS SAY HITLER DEAD

WORLD HOPES IT'S TRUE

The war was almost finished. 'Let's all fight,' the posters for war bonds had said. Everyone had fought, in their own way. Even Kurt had fought. Selling bonds had helped to raise the money that paid for the tanks and planes and trucks and ships that had won the war.

And now they were saying Hitler was dead.

Kurt thought back to those anxious days in Vienna, when they all wondered if Hitler would come and what would happen to the Jewish people. The monster himself had come to Vienna, with his SS and his Gestapo and his soldiers, and it had been worse than any of them had imagined. Now the monster that Fritz had seen scowling from his limousine was dead, but his armies were still fighting over the last few kilometres of ground.

Somewhere in the midst of it all, Kurt's family were scattered, broken up and taken away to places Kurt knew nothing about. He'd kept in touch with Edith in England, but he had no idea if any of the others were even alive. Three and a half years had gone by since he'd heard anything from them.

The last Kurt knew, Fritz and Papa were in Buchenwald and Mum and Herta were living in Vienna. Kurt recalled Vienna so vividly, as it had been in the days before Hitler. Running in the Karmeliter market . . . Climbing the lamp posts . . . Playing ping pong with Fritz on Papa's workshop table (Papa liked to join in, then got cross with them for distracting him from his work) . . . Herta and her friends putting on fashion shows ... Fritz teaching him to play chess ... The two of them climbing round the apartment without touching the floor ... Setting off caps to confound the pigeon-catcher ... Helping Mum coat the cutlets for Wiener Schnitzel on Shabbos. Every moment was filled with joy and love and excitement. Kurt wondered if any of it would ever come back. He knew nothing of Auschwitz or transports to the Ostland or death marches.

He ran up the steps of 91 Rotch Street and in through the front door. Uncle Sam was waiting there, with aunts Sarah, Esther and Kate. There was a letter for Kurt, postmarked from London – news from Edith!

He tore it open and read it. Edith had received a message from the British government. It said that a Mr Gustav Kleinmann had been found among the survivors of a concentration camp at Bergen-Belsen in Germany.

Papa was alive!

Questions flooded into Kurt's mind. What about Fritz? Was he with Papa? Was he well? Would Kurt be going home to Vienna? The message just said that Papa was in something called Block 83, and that was all.

Kurt had never heard of Bergen-Belsen. It had been discovered a few weeks earlier by British soldiers. Of all the concentration camps discovered by the Allied armies, Bergen-Belsen was perhaps the one that horrified them the most. A lot of the SS death marches had ended up there, and unimaginable numbers of people had died of disease and starvation. What the British found was a nightmare beyond everything they had seen so far.

Right away, Uncle Sam got Kurt to write to the Red Cross to try and get a message to Papa. But the Red Cross said it was virtually impossible. The situation in Germany and all across Europe was chaos. Millions of people had been transported to camps and other far-flung places. They all had to be fed and registered and helped. The system was already breaking down, and people who had survived the camps were still at death's door. In Bergen-Belsen, where Papa had ended up, the British Army was struggling to cope with the number of sick and dying people.

When no reply came from Papa, Uncle Sam wrote to one of his friends in the government, asking for help. His friend replied that there was no way to make contact with people in the camps. Uncle Sam didn't say so to Kurt, but he couldn't imagine how anyone could survive for so long in a concentration camp unless God himself was helping them.

Summer came. Kurt went to Camp Avoda, and when the holiday was over, he began another term at high school. And still no news came. No news of Papa. No news of Fritz. Nothing from Mum or Herta. Were any of them alive?

CHAPTER TWENTY-FIVE

The Journey Back

Fritz opened his eyes. He was lying on his back, looking up at the canvas roof of a tent. For a moment, it was as if he was back in the Little Camp in Buchenwald, right at the very beginning. But the bed beneath him was soft and the smell in the air was clean, like soap and fresh sheets.

Then he remembered where he was. And he remembered that the nightmare was over.

When the soldiers had found Fritz in the remains of the Mauthausen-Gusen camp, he'd been nearly dead. His weight had fallen to 36 kilos.* For a twenty-one-year-old man, that was dangerously underweight. Right away the army medics took care of him. For the first time, Fritz

---

* About 79 pounds, or just over 5½ stone.

experienced kindness from people in uniforms. They gave him first aid and put him, along with other survivors, on a transport to the German city of Regensburg. The American army had set up a mobile hospital there.

And here he was. The day he arrived, the news broke that Germany had surrendered. Hitler was dead and the war was over. Fritz's journey had brought him a long, horrible way. It had begun on the day he was seized from his mother and thrown into the police van. But the journey wasn't finished yet, not until he returned to Vienna and found out what had happened to the people he loved.

The doctors gave him a diet of biscuits, milk pudding and a special concoction that was meant to help him put on weight. Soon he had gained 10 kilos.* He wasn't healthy yet, but he couldn't wait to get home. He asked the hospital staff to let him go, and they agreed. They gave him some civilian clothes and a transport ticket that would get him back to Vienna.

Summer was coming when Fritz reached the border between the American zone and the Russian zone. All of Germany and Austria was divided up between the Allies, who were running the two countries until proper governments were in place again. The border between the Americans and the Russians was near Mauthausen.

The Americans couldn't take him any further, so an

---

* 22 pounds or about 1½ stone

American officer arranged a place for him in a Red Cross van going to Vienna.

At last, on a Monday in late May, Fritz set foot on the pavements of his home city. The last time he'd been here was when he was forced on to the goods train bound for Buchenwald. There had been 1,048 Jewish men on that train. Fritz later found out that only twenty-six of them were still alive.

The war had damaged Vienna quite badly, though some districts were virtually unharmed by the American bombs and Russian shells. Other cities in Germany – such as Berlin – had been devastated.

It was evening when Fritz's footsteps finally brought him to the Karmeliter market. It was exactly as he remembered it. The stalls had been packed away and the cobblestones were swept clean. Everything was as it had been on those summer evenings when they kicked their rag football around and climbed the lamp posts and dodged the police. Fritz remembered the taste of cream cakes and pink wafers and the sound of kids laughing and chattering. The market was silent now. The Jewish kids he'd known were gone – either emigrated or dead or missing. Fritz's friend Leo Meth didn't return from Auschwitz, and Fritz would never discover what had happened to him.

Fritz's thoughts were shattered by a Russian voice shouting at him: 'What are you doing out?'

He turned to see two Russian military policemen. 'What?' he said.

'Don't you know there's a curfew? Nobody's allowed out after eight p.m. Go home quickly or you'll be arrested!'

Fritz hurried across Island Street. The front door of the old apartment building was locked for the night. He knocked on it and heard the familiar grumpy voice of Mrs Ziegler, the concierge.

'Who is it? What d'you want?'

'It's me, Fritz Kleinmann!'

'There are no Kleinmanns here! There are no Jews!'

'I used to live here. You know me.'

'No, I don't. Go away!' He heard her apartment door slam.

Fritz gave up. He tried to take shelter in an alley, but the Russian police found him again.

'Didn't I tell you nobody's allowed out?' one of them said.

'I tried going to my old home. The concierge won't let me in.'

'Where've you come from?'

Fritz rolled up his sleeve and showed his Auschwitz tattoo. The Russians knew what it meant. They'd seen the news films of their army comrades liberating the Auschwitz camps.

'Son, tell your concierge that if she doesn't let you in,

we'll make sure she gets sent to a prison camp herself – in Siberia!'

Siberia, a remote region in the east of Russia, was almost as terrifying a name as Auschwitz itself. Fritz went back and knocked on the door again. When Mrs Ziegler answered, he repeated what the Russian had said.

Grumbling and complaining, she opened the door. 'You can sleep on my floor tonight. But in the morning you're out, all right?'

Fritz had slept in more uncomfortable spots than Mrs Ziegler's floor. In the morning he ventured back out on to the street.

Word had spread around the district – 'The Kleinmann boy is back!' they said. A few people said it nastily, but others said it with amazement. Some people heard the news with joy. Olga and Karl and the others who had loaded Alfred Wocher up with gifts to take to Auschwitz came looking for Fritz and welcomed him.

Olga was overjoyed to see Fritz again. But she was also grief-stricken that his father wasn't with him. She invited him to come and stay in her apartment for the time being.

Fritz was looked after by his good friends, but they weren't rich and they could only do so much. After a couple of months, he was fit enough to take a job as a bricklayer. There was lots of rebuilding to be done in Vienna.

But it wasn't just buildings that needed to be rebuilt. Fritz had to make a new life for himself, with no family to share it with.

As day followed day and month followed month, Fritz longed to find out what had happened to everyone. Olga told him about the transports of Jewish people that had taken Mum and Herta and Aunt Jenni to the Ostland. Only a handful of the Jews on those transports had ever come back. These few survivors told horrific stories of thousands of people killed in the forests of the Ostland.

Fritz knew that Edith and Kurt were safe, but he hadn't heard anything from them for four years. He didn't know their addresses and they didn't know his. As for Papa, Fritz kept on hoping. But as the weeks passed and he thought back to his last sight of Papa, close to dying on that cursed train, his hope grew weak and small.

Fritz met a girl called Hedy Wurst. She wasn't Jewish, and she had lived in the city all through the Nazi era. Hedy was beautiful and full of joy and life, with a smile that could light up a room. Fritz fell in love with her and they started making plans to get married.

It should have been a happy time, but Fritz couldn't escape the ghosts of the camps that haunted his dreams. If only he had his papa again, he might find the strength to truly live.

It was the end of September, with the wedding less than two months away. Fritz was living alone for the time being, in an apartment in the same building as Olga. One day there was a knock at the door. Fritz opened it and there was Olga. With her was a gaunt figure of a man, smiling at Fritz – a warm smile, with kindness and delight in the gentle eyes. It was a smile Fritz had seen a thousand times.

Fritz found his voice. 'Papa?'

'Hello, Fritz, my boy. I'm home.'

'Papa!'

Fritz stood astonished as his papa threw his arms round him. Together they wept for joy. Beyond all hope, beyond all fear and suffering, Fritz could scarcely believe it was true. Their journey had ended right back where it began. They were home at last.

What Happened After

In the months following their return to Vienna, Fritz and his papa finally learned what had become of all the other members of their family. They heard about Edith and her husband and their two children in England (Papa was now a grandpapa!) and about how well Kurt was doing in America.

Fritz investigated what had happened to their friends and relatives who'd been taken by the Nazis. He made the shattering discovery that their fears about Mum and Herta were true. Along with thousands of other Jewish women, children and men from Vienna, they had been taken by train to the Ostland, where they were all murdered by the SS. Besides Mum and Herta, Aunt Jenni, Kurt's favourite aunt, who had the talking cat, was one of the victims.

Papa and Fritz talked about bringing Kurt back from America. But in the end, they accepted that he was settled and happy with the Barnets. And without Mum, they felt they didn't have much of a home to offer him. So they let him carry on growing up to be an American. Besides, Edith and her husband were planning to emigrate from England to the United States, so Kurt would soon have family of his own over there.

For Fritz and Papa, life began anew. On 20 November 1945, two months after Papa returned to Vienna, Fritz and Hedy were married. Fritz still hadn't fully recovered from his suffering in the camps, and in the wedding photos he looked thin and a bit unwell. Two years later, Hedy gave birth to a baby boy, who they named Peter.

In 1948, two big events happened for Papa. One was that he and dear Olga, who had so bravely helped him and Fritz to survive Auschwitz, got married. The other event was that Papa finally managed to start up his upholstery business again. It was bigger than it had been before the Nazis came, with a big sign over the doorway once again proclaiming:

GUSTAV KLEINMANN, MASTER UPHOLSTERER
Modern Furniture – All Repair Work Accepted

On the other side of the world, Kurt grew up and went to college to study to be a pharmacist. Shortly after, he was called up to serve in the United States Army. (For many years after the war, young men in Britain and America had to serve for a short period in the armed forces after leaving school or college.) Kurt was sent to serve in Germany, where the Allies were still helping to run things. In 1954, thirteen years after he'd left on the train with a leather wallet round his neck, all-American soldier Private Kurt Kleinmann arrived back in Vienna.

He visited Fritz and Papa. Although they were overjoyed to be together again, it was difficult to get along, because Kurt had almost completely forgotten how to speak German, and neither Fritz nor Papa spoke any English. But they did their best, and enjoyed being together again.

In the years that followed, Kurt got married to a young woman he had met while he was at college, named Dianne. They had three sons: Bill, Paul and Jim. By that time, Edith's children were growing up. Both families travelled often to Vienna to be with Fritz and Papa, and in 1966, Papa and Olga visited America. By that time Papa was a great-grandpapa, and Edith's little grandchildren sat on his knee, just as Kurt had done back in Vienna all those years ago when the Nazis first came.

Of the people Fritz and Papa had known during their nightmare years, most had died in Buchenwald or Auschwitz or Mauthausen or some other terrible Nazi camp. But some dear friends survived.

After being evacuated from Auschwitz, Stefan Heymann and Gustav Herzog had ended up back at Buchenwald, where they were reunited with Robert

Siewert and Fritz's old best friend Jakob Ihr ('Itschklerl'). All four of them were still alive when American troops liberated Buchenwald a few months later. So was Paul Heller, the doctor who had tried to care for Papa when he was deathly sick.

To Fritz's heartfelt joy, Alfred Wocher managed to survive the last battles for Germany in 1945, and returned to his wife in Vienna. He often visited Fritz and Papa. It made Fritz sad that Alfred didn't receive any honour or award for his kindness and courage in helping prisoners to survive Auschwitz. Fritz made sure that at least Alfred knew how grateful he and Papa were.

As for the people who had caused the nightmare, who had started the war and carried out the Holocaust, some of them were caught and held to account. Hitler shot himself during the last few days of the war. Many of his chief henchmen also died by suicide or were put on trial by the Allies and hanged for their crimes. But many war criminals got away with it. They went into hiding, changed their identities, and in some cases fled to other countries. Of these, a few were tracked down years later and put on trial. In 1963, both Fritz and Papa gave evidence at the trials of several Auschwitz guards and kapos.

Maximilian Grabner, who had tortured Fritz in Auschwitz, was captured by the Allies in 1945 and was hanged in Poland two years later.

But Fritz's suffering continued. The injuries that

Grabner inflicted on him never got completely better. As he began to grow old, Fritz suffered increasing pains in his back and joints which forced him to retire early from his job. And all those long hours of standing at roll calls in freezing weather had given him a fear of the cold that lasted the rest of his life.

Gustav Kleinmann – Fritz's beloved Papa – died, a very old man, in 1976. He had always tried to forget about the Holocaust and his own suffering in it. He just wanted to get on with life.

But Fritz had a different kind of personality. He couldn't forget, and didn't want to. He devoted the last part of his life to teaching people about the Holocaust, through interviews and lectures and writing and research.

He was helped in this by a document that had been left to him by his father. After they first got back to Vienna in 1945, Fritz discovered that Papa had kept a secret diary all the time they were in the camps, recording the things they saw and experienced. It was written in pencil in a tiny pocket notebook that Papa had kept hidden all that time. It was an incredibly dangerous thing to do, because any kind of private writing was against the camp rules. Fritz was shocked at Papa's daring.

The diary was important when Fritz began his work of telling the world about their experiences. He gave public talks to students who were visiting Auschwitz, which is now a museum and memorial to the Holocaust.

Fritz even visited Auschwitz in person later in life. In 1995, Fritz published a book in Austria, made from Papa's diary and Fritz's own writings. It was titled *Doch der Hund will nicht krepieren*, which means 'And Still the Dog Will Not Die'. The title comes from a line in a poem that Papa had written in his diary. It referred to the spirit of prisoners who refused to succumb to the SS, even when they were beaten down on to all fours like a dog.

Kurt also went on telling his story to people in America, just as he had done when he was a boy selling war bonds. In 1994, he travelled to eastern Europe and visited the place near Minsk in Belarus where his mother and his sister Herta were killed by the SS in 1942. There is a memorial at the site in the forest where thousands of Jewish people met their deaths.

Fritz died, aged 86, in 2009. He gave interviews about the Holocaust right up until his final year.

As the teller of this story, I'm sad that I never had a chance to meet Fritz. I first came across his writings and Papa's diary in 2013, when a friend of Fritz's asked me to get involved in an English translation of Fritz's book. Because of the way the diary was written, it was very difficult to understand, even translated into English. But I knew right away that there was an incredible, important story to be told. So I decided to try to write a new book about the whole family – Gustav, Tini, Edith, Herta, Fritz and Kurt – which would be easy for everyone to read.

Right away I started doing research, and in 2015, I first got to know Kurt, who was still alive and well in America, by then a very elderly man, and we became friends. Sadly, Edith had died only a few months earlier. But her son, Peter, told me all that he could about her. Meanwhile, Kurt kindly spent hours telling me all about his memories of Vienna, of his parents and his brother and sisters, about Hitler coming, and about crossing the ocean to America.

My book was written and published, and Kurt flew to England to help me tell people about it. I noticed that when children met him, they were amazed to learn that when he was their age, he'd travelled halfway round the world by himself to escape the Nazis and live with a new family in America.

That gave me the idea of writing another book, telling the story again, but this time specially written for younger readers. It became the book you've just been reading. I went back to my studies in order to write it, and I made new discoveries. So this book has lots of new knowledge that isn't in the grown-ups' version.

I hope that you've been as moved and amazed by Fritz and Kurt's story as I have. And I hope you've learned as much about the Holocaust as I learned while I was writing it.

It is vitally important to remember what happened in those terrible years, and to do whatever we can to make sure nothing like it ever occurs again. As with so much else in life, we have to begin with memories and knowledge of what happened in the past, with understanding, and with compassion for our fellow human beings – all of them, not just the ones who look like us or share our beliefs.

Jeremy Dronfield
Holocaust Memorial Day, 27 January 2022

Postscript

It saddens me deeply to have to write that Kurt Kleinmann died on 15 March 2022. He was 92 years old.

I spoke at his memorial, along with many of the friends and family members who loved him. I only knew Kurt for a very short period of his long life, but I was proud to count myself a friend, and honoured to be entrusted with telling his family's story.

Although he never had a chance to read this new book, Kurt knew it was being written. I talked to him about it several times in his last months, each time learning new details about his experiences, from Vienna to New Bedford. It made Kurt glad to know that his family's story would now have a chance to be read by children, and that it – along with the stories of all those affected by the Holocaust – would never be forgotten.

Timeline of Events

This timeline covers important events connected with the Holocaust and with the Second World War as it was experienced in Europe. It also includes some events from the story of Fritz and Kurt.

Key events are marked in **bold**.

1923

Fritz Kleinmann is born in Vienna on 20 June.

1930

Kurt Kleinmann is born in Vienna on 14 January.

1932

In Germany, the **Nazi Party** gains more votes than any of the other political parties in national elections, but not enough to win power.

1933

January	**Adolf Hitler is appointed Chancellor** (prime minister) of Germany in a deal among politicians who think they can control him.
March	Hitler seizes absolute power and sets up a Nazi dictatorship.

The **first concentration camp** for political prisoners (communists and other opponents of the Nazis) is set up outside the town of **Dachau**, in southern Germany.

April	The Nazi government begins making **laws against Jewish people**. Many Jews start emigrating to other countries.

1937

July	**Construction begins on Buchenwald** concentration camp, near the city of Weimar in central Germany. It is the third major camp, the first two being Dachau (founded 1933) and Sachsenhausen (1936).

Many other camps, mostly smaller, are set up all over Germany. The prisoners are mostly political. Laws against Jews become more and more severe, but they are not yet sent in large numbers to concentration camps.

1938

March   **Nazi Germany invades Austria** on 12 March and takes control.

September   Germany takes over part of Czechoslovakia. The governments of Great Britain, France and other countries agree to let Hitler keep the lands he's taken so far, but only if he promises not to try to seize any more.

November   *Kristallnacht,* **the Night of Broken Glass** (also called the 'November Pogrom') happens, 9–10 November. Across Germany and Austria, synagogues and Jewish homes and businesses are attacked by Nazi mobs. Thousands of Jewish men are arrested, including Fritz Kleinmann and his father, Gustav. Many are released (including Fritz and Papa), but thousands are sent to Dachau, Buchenwald and other camps.

December   The *Kindertransport* begins. The first 1,000 children leave Vienna for London. Altogether, 10,000 children emigrate to Britain from Nazi Germany, Austria, Poland and Czechoslovakia.

1939

January   Fritz's sister Edith leaves Vienna for England.

Throughout this period, Jewish people struggle to emigrate from Germany and Austria. Many of the men sent to the concentration camps after Kristallnacht are released in order for them to emigrate.

September **Nazi Germany invades Poland** on 1 September. Great Britain and France declare war on Germany two days later. **The Second World War begins**. Eventually, over 3 million Polish Jews will come under Nazi rule.

Following the invasion of Poland, the Nazis begin experiments using poison gas to kill prisoners. The gas chambers are made from converted trucks.

In Germany and Austria, thousands of **Polish-born Jewish men are arrested** and sent to concentration camps. Gustav Kleinmann, Fritz's father, is one of them. Fritz is taken too.

October **Fritz and Papa arrive in Buchenwald** concentration camp on 2 October.

November An assassination attempt is made against Hitler on 8 November. The SS take revenge on Jews in concentration camps.

1940

April   A **new concentration camp is created at Auschwitz,** in German-occupied Poland. At first it is used for Polish political prisoners, and later for a wide variety of persecuted people from Germany and Nazi-occupied countries.

May–June   On 10 May, **Germany begins the invasion of Belgium, the Netherlands and France,** quickly conquering all of them. The British Army is evacuated from France at Dunkirk. The Battle of Britain begins, in which the Royal Air Force defends Britain from German bombers. Britain is under threat of invasion by sea.

1941

February   **Kurt Kleinmann leaves Vienna** alone to travel to America. He arrives in New Bedford, Massachusetts, where he is taken care of by the Barnet family.

June   **Nazi Germany invades the Soviet Union** (Russia's communist empire, which includes Ukraine, Belarus and other lands) on 22 June. Millions more Jews who live there come under Nazi rule.

September   Auschwitz's first gas chamber is used to kill captured Russian soldiers. The evil reputation of Auschwitz begins to spread through the other concentration camps by prisoners who are transferred between them.

December   **Japan attacks the US Navy at Pearl Harbor** on 7 December. Four days later, Japan's ally **Germany declares war on the United States.**

Great Britain, the United States and the Soviet Union join together as **the Grand Alliance** (known more simply as the Allies). Their leaders, Prime Minister Winston Churchill, President Franklin D. Roosevelt and Joseph Stalin, become known as the 'Big Three'.

1942

January   With the war preventing Jews from emigrating, Nazi leaders secretly decide to start killing them. They call it '**the Final Solution to the Jewish Question**'. Auschwitz becomes one of the main centres, but most of the killing is carried out in Germany's conquered eastern territories.

June   In Vienna, a train carrying 900 Jewish women, children and men sets out, destined for a camp in the eastern lands conquered by Germany. **Tini and Herta Kleinmann (Fritz and Kurt's mother and sister) are among them.** Nobody on the transport is ever seen alive again.

July American bombers make their first air raids against targets held by Nazi German forces. The Americans bomb by day, and the British by night.

October Heinrich Himmler, head of the SS, orders that all Jews in concentration camps in Germany must be moved to the Auschwitz and Majdanek camps in occupied Poland. **Fritz and Papa are transferred from Buchenwald to Auschwitz,** along with 400 other Jewish prisoners. They arrive on 19 October.

November British and American forces land in North Africa to begin fighting the Germans there. These will be the first land battles between the American and German armies in the Second World War.

1943

May **Fritz's papa and sixteen other Jewish men are made 'Aryan' by the SS.**

Summer **Fritz becomes involved in the Auschwitz-Monowitz resistance.** He is found out by the

Gestapo and tortured. He narrowly avoids being killed.

The war has begun to go very badly for Germany. Its military forces in North Africa were defeated in May, and in July the Allies invade Italy. The German armies in Russia suffer defeats, and Soviet forces begin to advance.

About Nov. **Fritz makes friends with Alfred Wocher.**

December Alfred Wocher first visits Fritz's relatives in Vienna.

1944

May After the invasion of Hungary by Nazi Germany, large **transports of Hungarian Jews arrive in Auschwitz.**

June **D-Day.** On 6 June, Allied forces (mainly American, Canadian and British) invade northern France. Meanwhile, the Allied advance in Italy is progressing, and Rome is captured.

July **Russian troops, advancing into Poland, capture Majdanek,** the first death camp to be taken intact by the Allies (other camps in the east have been destroyed by the retreating SS). The Russians find gas chambers, crematoriums and bodies. The news is reported around the world, but has little impact, as the war dominates the headlines.

The SS begin air-raid defences at Auschwitz. **Fritz's papa is given the task of making blackout curtains.** Fritz works as a curtain fitter.

August   American planes, flying from a base in Italy, bomb the factories at Auschwitz for the first time.

Allied forces liberate Paris, the capital city of France. France is now a member of the Allies. Soviet forces continue recapturing lands in eastern Europe.

October   American troops take Aachen in western Germany, the first German city to be captured by the Allies.

December   The **Battle of the Bulge** breaks out when Hitler makes a last big attempt to beat the British and American forces in the west. He fails, and Germany goes into defensive mode, trying to stave off defeat. Hitler still believes he can win the war.

1945

January   The Soviet Union launches a **major attack against German defences in Poland.** Russian troops advance quickly, and are soon close to Auschwitz.

The SS begin evacuating the Auschwitz camps and trying to destroy the evidence of their crimes. The **Death March** begins as the SS retreat towards Germany, taking prisoners with them. **Fritz and Papa are put on a train to Mauthausen** concentration camp in Austria. They become separated and are sent to different camps, and neither of them knows if the other is still alive.

The main Auschwitz camps are liberated by Soviet troops on 27 January, a date that will later be commemorated as Holocaust Memorial Day. However, the Holocaust is far from over.

March Having been separated from his father, **Fritz arrives in Mauthausen** concentration camp in western Austria on 15 March.

April **American soldiers liberate Buchenwald** concentration camp on 11 April.

Russian forces capture Vienna on 13 April after a fierce battle. Two days later, **British soldiers liberate Bergen-Belsen** concentration camp in north-western Germany. It is filled with tens of thousands of dead and dying prisoners. **Gustav Kleinmann,** Fritz's Papa, is one of the survivors found there.

Adolf Hitler dies by suicide on 30 April, having accepted that his situation is hopeless. German forces continue fighting to defend the shrinking territory remaining between the Allies advancing from the west and south (mostly British, Canadian and American) and those coming from the east (Soviet).

May   **American soldiers capture Mauthausen** concentration camp in Austria on 5 May. Fritz Kleinmann is one of the surviving prisoners.

Germany surrenders on 8 May, which is named **Victory in Europe Day (VE Day).** Japan carries on fighting the Allies in Asia and the Pacific Ocean.

September   On 2 September, Japan surrenders and **the Second World War ends.**

* * *

Six million Jewish people were killed in the Holocaust, which in the Hebrew language is called the *Shoah,* meaning the Catastrophe.

At least 250,000, and perhaps as many as 1.5 million Romani and Sinti traveller people were killed by the Nazis. In the Romani language this is called the *Porrajmos*, which means Devouring, or the *Samudaripen*, which means Murder of All.

Other victims murdered by Nazi Germany included at least 3.3 million captured Soviet soldiers, about 1.9 million non-Jewish Polish civilians, as well as thousands of political and religious prisoners, gay and transgender people, and people with disabilities.

Altogether, through battles, bombing, mass killings, disease and starvation, the Second World War caused the deaths of approximately 60 million people – equivalent in number to the entire population of England and Wales. The majority of the dead were civilians.

Note for Parents, Guardians and Teachers

After my original book *The Boy Who Followed His Father into Auschwitz* was published in 2019, I received many messages from readers telling me that they would love their kids to be able to read it. Even more movingly, I have vivid memories of sitting next to Kurt at public events and seeing children gazing at him in wonder when their parents told them that when this elderly gentleman was their age, he had to leave his family behind and travel alone halfway round the world to escape from Nazis.

I wanted those children to be able to read the story of Kurt and his brother Fritz in a form they could relate to and understand, so I decided to make it available for them. Merely simplifying or abridging the original book wouldn't do – I wanted it to be an all-new re-telling of the story with young readers in mind. And I didn't just re-tell the story. I went back to the research, dug deeply and managed to make further discoveries, so that this book contains new information and a better understanding of certain key events than was possible in the original.

For example, in his memoir and various interviews, Fritz did not describe his time in the Prater soccer stadium. But when researching this new book, I came across a previously unknown interview Fritz gave near the end of his life in which he did just that, and in which he mentioned, heartbreakingly, his last sight of his mother.

Another example is the November Pogrom, or Kristallnacht. I always knew from Fritz's recollections that on Kristallnacht the Kleinmann family were identified as Jewish to the Nazis by their friends and neighbours. But surely, I thought, the Nazi authorities must have already known who all the Jews were by that time? I skated over that issue in the original book. Returning to the research, I came across a contemporary account of SA stormtroopers visiting building concierges during the early weeks of the occupation of Vienna and demanding lists of Jewish residents from them. So why didn't they have a record of Jews in the Kleinmanns' apartment building? At the same time, I revisited Fritz's account of his encounter with concierge Frau Ziegler and his portrayal of her obstinate, unhelpful character. Putting these two elements together, I realised that if the stormtroopers visited Im Werd 11 and were met by the formidable Frau Ziegler in one of her typical bad moods, that could explain why they failed to get a list of Jewish people in that building. I reconstructed the scene as it probably unfolded, based around what we know of the process and what we know of Frau Ziegler's personality.

Imaginative reconstruction of real-life scenes has been an important part of telling this story, in both versions. In some cases, such as the incident with Frau Ziegler and the stormtroopers, it's based on inferring from the scraps of evidence available. In other cases, there is rich material. For instance, the soccer scene in the market square that opens Chapter 1 is an imagined event, but every element in it is taken from the detailed recollections of Fritz and Kurt, put together to represent a typical evening of play during those last golden days of freedom. The rag ball, avoiding the police, Frau Capek and her stall, blind Herr Löwy, the boys chasing the fire engine horns, cakes from Anker's bakery – all these are real-life details. The slogans painted on the pavements and buildings are taken from contemporary reports of Vienna in the last days before the Anschluss. The passage in which the boys wonder about Hitler coming to Vienna is based on Kurt's recollection of that time. Throughout his life, Kurt always referred to it as the time 'before Hitler came' and the occupation as 'after Hitler came'. Trauma, it seems, locked his phrasing into that period, giving us a window into his perspective during those terrifying days.

Dialogue – a fundamental element of human

interaction – is essential in bringing scenes and stories to life. In my non-fiction books for adults, I follow certain rules about quoted speech. Dialogue is allowed as long as it meets any of the following conditions: 1. It has been taken directly from primary sources, where conversations are recorded word for word. 2. It can be reconstructed from primary sources, where conversations are recorded in paraphrased or summary form. 3. In rare instances where dialogue is strongly desirable but we don't have 1 or 2, it may be inferred from conversations that are known to have happened, and where the gist (or at least the outcome) is known. In this book, in order to help the story flow smoothly and be fully relatable and immersive for young readers, I have allowed a fourth rule: 4. Dialogue can be imagined based on known events and circumstances and knowledge of the personalities, feelings and beliefs of the individuals at the time. For example, some of the words said to Fritz by his father in the book are taken from Gustav's diary, and thus reflect what he was thinking at the time. Frau Ziegler's response to the stormtroopers is inferred from her character (as portrayed by Fritz), and is based on an event that must have occurred. By contrast, examples of fully sourced dialogue include Fritz's remarks about his grandfather when he is on the scaffolding and his various conversations with Stefan Heymann, Alfred Wocher, and Robert Siewert, all of which are either directly quoted or reconstructed from Fritz's recollections.

I've taken other, smaller measures to help make the story accessible for young readers. I've anglicised the names of some places in Vienna. 'Im Werd' becomes 'Island Street' (*Werd* is an obsolete German word meaning 'island' referring to the island between the river Danube and the Danube Canal), 'Leopoldsgasse' becomes 'Leopold Lane', 'Ausstellungsstrasse' becomes 'Exhibition Street', and so on. Similarly, I've used 'oe' and 'ae' instead of 'ö' and 'ä' in names. I've simplified a few minor details of camp life – such as referring to block seniors as block kapos. And in five instances where the names of significant minor characters are not available (either because Fritz did not record them or Kurt could not remember them), I've used pseudonyms. These are 'Oskar' (the civilian who befriended Fritz in Auschwitz), 'Hannes' (the boy who bullied Kurt in Vienna), 'the Neubergers' (the Orthodox neighbours in the apartment building, whose real name I've so far been unable to establish from street directories), 'Lieutenant Schmidt' (the officer who interrogated Fritz after his escape from the train), and 'James' (Kurt's school friend in New Bedford).

In a few instances I have omitted some supporting characters in order to avoid complicating the narrative. For posterity, I want to mention two of them here. When Fritz's friends Stefan Heymann and Gustav Herzog faked his death, two other conspirators are known to have helped. Sepp Luger, a prisoner functionary who worked in hospital administration, entered Fritz's death in the register (although it's not clear whether, as a clerk, he actually knew that Fritz was really alive). A friend of Fritz's, Jule Meixner, who worked in the hospital laundry, helped him to hide from the SS doctor's inspections. (Jule was also the friend who hid Fritz's guns for the resistance.)

Undoubtedly the toughest part of adapting the story for children has been dealing with the upsetting, terrible events narrated in the original book: judging what to omit, what to include and how to convey the horror in an age-appropriate way. While I have not attempted to ameliorate or minimise any aspect of the Holocaust, some particularly disturbing and harrowing scenes and incidents have been either left out or narrated with minimal detail.

For parents and teachers who would like to know more about the events, background and context of the Kleinmann family's story or about the Holocaust in general, the best starting place would be the original version of *The Boy Who Followed His Father into Auschwitz*, which includes full, detailed endnotes with source citations and a complete bibliography.

For additional information (including some that isn't found in my original book), I recommend downloading the free Guide for Parents, Guardians and Teachers. It contains detailed citations, a full bibliography, recommended reading, further historical information on key parts of the story, extra historical details that were left out of the book for reasons of space, and topics to inspire educational discussions with kids around the events of the book and the Holocaust generally. The PDF can be downloaded from https://www.jeremydronfield.com/fritz-kurt.html

Jeremy Dronfield

Fritz
Kleinmann

Kurt
Kleinman

The inspiring true story of a
father and son's fight to stay together
and survive the Holocaust

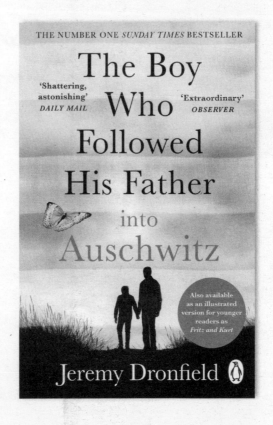

THE NUMBER ONE *SUNDAY TIMES* BESTSELLER

The Boy

'Shattering,
astonishing'
DAILY MAIL

Who

'Extraordinary'
OBSERVER

Followed

His Father

into

Auschwitz

Also available
as an illustrated
version for younger
readers as
Fritz and Kurt

Jeremy Dronfield

'Extraordinary' *Observer*

'Deeply moving and brimming with humanity' *Guardian*

NURTURING WRITERS SINCE 1935